THE STINGER MISSILE ABRUPTLY CHANGED COURSE

Seconds later the warhead rammed under the helicopter's turbine exhaust. Jack Grimaldi just had time to cut the fuel feed to the engine when it declutched from the damaged transmission and screamed on overrev as it self-destructed. "We're going down!"

The pilot frantically tried to establish autorotation with the plunging ship, but he was too low for the rotor blades to come back up to speed and lift. At the last possible second, he pulled full pitch to the blades with his collective to try to cushion the impact, but it barely slowed the fall.

The Huey hit a glancing blow against the ridge line and rolled onto its right side, the main rotor blades snapping off and flying away. The skids dug into the ground abruptly, stopping the ship and sending McCarter and Grimaldi slamming against their shoulder harnesses. The tail boom broke off and careened over the canopy while the shattered remains of the crew compartment slid toward the edge of the ridge....

Other titles available in this series:

STONY MAN II
STONY MAN III
STONY MAN IV
STONY MAN V
STONY MAN VI
STONY MAN VII
STONY MAN VIII
#9 STRIKEPOINT
#10 SECRET ARSENAL
#11 TARGET AMERICA
#12 BLIND EAGLE
#13 WARHEAD
#14 DEADLY AGENT
#15 BLOOD DEBT
#16 DEEP ALERT
#17 VORTEX

DON PENDLETON'S

MACK BOLAN®

STONY MAN™

STINGER

A GOLD EAGLE BOOK FROM

WORLDWIDE®

TORONTO • NEW YORK • LONDON
AMSTERDAM • PARIS • SYDNEY • HAMBURG
STOCKHOLM • ATHENS • TOKYO • MILAN
MADRID • WARSAW • BUDAPEST • AUCKLAND

First edition September 1995

ISBN 0-373-61902-2

Special thanks and acknowledgment to
Michael Kasner for his contribution to this work.

STINGER

Printed in U.S.A.

STINGER

CHAPTER ONE

Banda, India

A frenzied mob of young Hindu fundamentalists bearing sledgehammers, ropes and wrecking bars gathered at the end of a dusty street in the small Northern Indian town of Banda. The men wore saffron headbands inscribed with Lord Rama's holy name, and they chanted his name over and over.

At the other end of the street, a thin line of Indian provincial police stood in front of the entrance to a seven-hundred-year-old Muslim holy site. The mosque had been built by Islamic invaders in the twelfth century on the site of an earlier shrine to Rama, the Hindu god who exemplified virtue, duty and loyalty to humanity. The police had been ordered to prevent the impassioned mob from getting past them and sacking the shrine, but it was easy to see that their hearts weren't in it. Orders or not, their sympathies were with the mob. As devout Hindus, they had always resented the intrusion of the alien religion on what they saw as their sacred ground.

Across the street from the shrine, a CNN news team filmed both the approaching mob and the police whose orders were to stop that mob. The news team had received a tip that the mosque was going to be torn down much the same way as another mosque built over a shrine to Rama had been destroyed in 1992. Another Indian religious clash was in the offing, and CNN was on the scene to record the violence. But it wouldn't really be news, Northern India had long been a bloody battleground.

Four thousand years before, the chariot-driving Aryan warriors invaded the Indian subcontinent, and their wars of conquest began the recorded history of the region. Subsequent invaders, from Alexander the Great through the Muslims and down to the British, had all added their bit to the patchwork that was modern India. As a result, ethnic and sectarian violence had long been a part of the Indian cultural and historical tradition.

The violence was halted for a time after the British conquered the region and created their raj. In 1947, however, a Britain exhausted by World War II gave up its empire and created the modern states of India and Pakistan. The idea was sound, but the actuality of creating separate Muslim and Hindu states was critically flawed.

In the great partition of 1947 that followed the British withdrawal, millions lost their lives as Muslims and Hindus slaughtered one another in the name of their gods. Even after the creation of the separate states, the wars continued. Mostly they were border clashes, but in 1965 a short-lived but full-scale war broke out that the UN helped end. In 1971 war flared again in East Pakistan. The Indians won that one decisively and helped create the state of Bangladesh in the territory wrested from their Muslim enemies.

Though the peace between the two nations had more or less held since 1971, conflict between the Muslims and Hindu populations continued in India. Islamic fundamentalism in the Middle East had been exported to the Indian subcontinent, where it became particularly active in the northern provinces of India. In response, the Hindu majority in these areas grew more fundamentalistic, as well, and sectarian clashes became almost routine.

Now, with the name of Rama on their lips, the Hindu mob raced down the street and surged against the thin police line. With the CNN cameras focused on them, the cops had to appear to try to resist, as they had been ordered. After a few halfhearted blows with their rattan batons, though, the police line parted and the mob rushed past them.

Once inside the grounds of the mosque, the Hindus immediately went to work dismantling the ancient stone structure and carrying the pieces away. Those who had brought no tools pried the rocks apart with their bare hands and chanted prayers as their fingernails tore against the stone.

As evening fell, the mosque was no more. The ground where it had stood for more than seven hundred years was bare except for the inlaid mosaic floor, and even that was being torn up by torchlight. Under the mosaic were the remnants of the even more ancient shrine to Rama, and his worshipers were eager to expose the broken stones to the light of the coming dawn.

All around the compound joyful male voices raised in praise to Lord Rama could be heard. CNN sent the hymns to TV sets all around the world.

BY THE NEXT MORNING thousands of Hindus had gathered to celebrate at the newly cleared site. While they raised their voices in praise of Lord Rama, an Air India Airbus with 143 passengers on board was in-bound to a landing at the small airport outside of Banda.

Five miles from the runway, a flash of flame rose from the barren hills and streaked for the plane. Trailing dirty white smoke, the heat-seeking antiair-craft missile homed in on the jet's right inboard en-gine and detonated. The explosion sheared off the wing and slammed the Airbus nosefirst into the ground.

At first the wounded jetliner crumpled with the im-pact. The remaining wing tore off and slammed back against the fuselage, spraying it with JP-4 fuel from the ruptured tanks. In a flash the fuel ignited, engulf-ing the wreck in a boiling ball of flame. The explo-sion scattered the flaming wreckage a half mile wide.

On a hill below, a man lowered an empty Stinger launcher and looked out at the billowing column of dense black smoke rising in the distance.

"God is great!" he shouted in Arabic.

Taking the empty launcher with him, he hurried down the back side of the hill, where a Toyota four-wheel-drive pickup was waiting. Opening the passenger door, the gunner tossed the launcher under the seat and scrambled in. "It is done," he said.

The driver smiled. "It is God's will."

THE SMOKE HAD barely cleared over the crash site before an extremist Indian Muslim group claimed to have downed the airliner in retaliation for the destruction of the mosque. When the shattered wreckage of the passenger jet was examined by Indian air-force technicians, it was discovered that it had been destroyed by an American-made, shoulder-fired, heat-seeking Stinger antiaircraft missile.

This wasn't, however, the first time that a Stinger had been in the news as a terrorist weapon.

A few years earlier an attempt to use a Stinger to bring down an Italian airliner at Rome's Leonardo da Vinci Airport was foiled at the last possible moment. In 1993 Stingers were used in the breakaway Republic of Georgia to destroy three airliners. The body count there was 126 men, women and children. Early in 1994 a Stinger was responsible for downing an Italian-air-force humanitarian flight over Bosnia.

In April of 1994 the presidents of both Rwanda and Burundi were killed on their way home from peace talks in neighboring Tanzania when the plane carrying them was shot down by a Stinger. The tribal warfare that broke out after the assassinations claimed well over a half-million lives.

It was a bitter legacy for a weapon that had been designed to protect American troops from air attack.

During the Afghan-Soviet War of the 1980s, the CIA supplied hundreds of Stinger missiles to the Afghan Mujahedeen freedom fighters. This was done partly to field-test the missiles under combat conditions, but mostly it was to help even the odds for the poorly armed guerrillas battling the mighty Russian Bear.

In the rugged hills and valley battlefields of Afghanistan, the Stingers soon proved to rule the skies. They were so effective that Soviet close air support of their ground forces became a thing of the past. After the fall of the old Soviet Union, a Russian general of the Afghan army admitted that the Stingers had played a vital role in resolving the stalemate and the subsequent withdrawal of Soviet forces from the region. Without total control of the air, they'd had no hope of ever winning.

After the Russians left Afghanistan, however, there was no way to get the remaining unused missiles back under American control. Due to the lack of any kind of central authority among the Mujahedeen, there wasn't even any way to know which Afghan bands had Stingers and which didn't.

As was always the case in the Middle East, that which had a value could be bought and sold, and that maxim included American-made antiaircraft missiles. Hundreds of the deadly Stingers went on the international black market. Some were bought back by the CIA at several times their cost. Some were bought by the Russians, who wanted to copy them. Some were bought by terrorist groups such as the Italian Red Brigades and the PLO.

Most of them, however, had simply disappeared. Until now.

ON THE OTHER SIDE of the world, Modesto, California, seemed to have escaped the harsh urban realities of the 1990s. It still had the feel of a small town, and there were few signs in Modesto of the barbarism that had blighted so much of the Sunshine State. The buildings weren't defaced with spray-painted gang messages, trash didn't lie uncollected in the streets and the people didn't hole up in their homes at night to wait out the coming of the dawn.

One of the reasons why Modesto was still livable was that there were jobs in the town. One of the more prominent employers in the area was Century Microdyne, a manufacturer of long-life, high-capacity batteries that saw most of their use in computer applications. The company also produced a series of even more specialized batteries for various NASA and Defense Department applications.

Even with the relatively low crime rate in Modesto, the Century Microdyne facility was well guarded by both men and electronic devices. Industrial espionage had become big business, and Microdyne's CEO was taking no chances. The recent string of raids on Silicon Valley's microchip manufacturers had made security a major concern for all of California's high-tech companies.

In fact the Defense Department had given Microdyne the sole-provider contract for the CLA-219A battery because of the Modesto facility's security systems. The CLA-219A was a typically overpriced, high-tech, Pentagon-classified replacement part that had a limited application. Its only use was in the FIM-92A Stinger missile.

Microdyne didn't produce these specialized batteries in great quantities, but at the price they were being paid for each one, they didn't have to make many to turn a nice profit. And the Pentagon made a further quarterly payment to ensure that the company's assembly line for the CLA-219A batteries was maintained on standby to produce more on just a few days' notice.

The CLA-219A was a relatively minor item for Microdyne, but a government contract did a lot for a company's bottom line at the end of the year.

AT THE MAIN GATE to the Century Microdyne facility, the night guard stepped out of his shack to sign the Roach Coach food wagon into the compound for the midnight lunch break.

"Where's Willie Boy?" the guard asked when he didn't see the driver who usually had the night-shift run.

"He called in sick." The new driver grinned. "My bet is that he's been fighting with his old lady again and got his head smoked."

The guard glanced down at his watch as he filled out the logbook. "And you're a little early."

The driver shrugged. "I'm not used to this route and I didn't want to be late."

"Willie always drops off a pineapple Danish on his way out," the guard informed the new driver.

"No problem. I've got your Danish covered."

Satisfied that his handout would be forthcoming, the guard finished logging the truck into the compound and turned to release the electric lock on the gate.

No sooner was his back turned than the driver's hand appeared in his open window, holding a small, mat black automatic pistol fitted with a long cylinder on the end of the muzzle. The weapon spit softly three times, the reports muffled by the silencer until they sounded no louder than a baby coughing.

The three 6.35 mm soft-nose slugs drilled through the back of the guard's skull and mushroomed in his brain. He stumbled, fell forward and was dead before he hit facefirst on the pavement.

Stepping down from his truck, the driver dragged the guard's body into the shack and sat it in the chair behind the security console. After quickly examining the layout, he reached past the corpse and flipped several switches, opening the front gate and turning off the alarms along the perimeter fence.

Getting back in the cab of his truck, the driver hit the clutch, dropped the shift lever into first and slowly drove over to the break area by the side door of the battery assembly hall. When he brought the vehicle to a halt, six men in black combat suits and face hoods poured out from the hidden door in the rear of the truck. They carried 9 mm Uzi submachine guns with silencers threaded onto the ends of the barrels.

Once through the side door, one of the raiders ran down the central hall to the security station in the building's main foyer while the others continued on to the assembly hall. The dozen workers on the assembly line looked up in surprise when the black-clad gunners swept into the room. They didn't even have time to panic before the muzzles of the silenced Uzis started blazing flame.

When the last worker was dead, the raiders pulled soft nylon bags from their belts and started to fill them with the boxed batteries that had just been manufactured. When the nylon bags were full, the intruders were joined by the comrade who had gone to silence the men at the central security station. They quickly evacuated the building, climbed back into their hidden compartment in the truck and closed the door behind them for the ride back out of the plant.

Less than eight minutes had passed since the death of the guard at the main gate.

CHAPTER TWO

Stony Man Farm, Virginia

Barbara Price reached her hand up under her long honey blond hair and rubbed the back of her neck. Leaning back in her comfortable swivel chair, she stretched her long, denim-clad legs out in front of her and pointed the toes of her cowboy boots.

She closed her blue eyes, cleared her mind for a moment and rested. Being the mission controller for the nation's premier clandestine-operations organization had its moments. Lately, though, it seemed that she was spending more and more of her time looking after the routine day-to-day operations of Stony Man Farm than she did controlling missions for the Farm's action teams.

Running the installation, however, was not a nickel-and-dime matter. Situated in the Shenandoah Valley only eighty miles from Washington, D.C., the Farm was carved into the foothills of the Blue Ridge Mountains. Named after Stony Man Mountain, one of the highest peaks in the area, this farm didn't look much different from the other small farms in the fertile Shenandoah Valley.

In the center of the grounds was a three-story main farmhouse, flanked by two outbuildings, with a tractor barn in the back. On the surface, it looked like a legitimate agricultural enterprise complete with farmhands in blue jeans and cowboy boots, and the well-used machinery necessary for making a living from the land. The area closest to the house was planted in row crops, while apple and peach orchards formed a wall around the outer perimeter.

But this was more than just another working farm in the picturesque Shenandoah Valley. Along with the agricultural enterprise, the Stony Man Farm also served as the operational base for the most covert arm of the United States government, the Sensitive Operations Group. As the command center for the elite antiterrorist and antiorganized-crime operations, the innocent-looking buildings concealed the equipment and personnel needed to track data, gather intelligence and make war on the nation's most elusive enemies, both foreign and domestic.

Such a facility needed more protection than merely the passive camouflage of looking like a working farm, and Stony Man had it in spades. Video cameras, motion and heat detectors and emergency spotlights were hidden in the trees and fences of the outer perimeter. Even the rusty barbed wire surrounding the property was loaded with sensors. But the Farm's security was not left solely to the wonders of modern technology. For real security there was nothing like well-trained, armed men.

The men who saw to the Farm's day-to-day operations were more than your run-of-the-mill agricultural workers. Though they were clandestinely armed during the day, at night they traded their work-worn blue jeans and faded shirts for combat blacksuits, camouflage cosmetics, night-vision goggles and high-tech firepower. They patrolled the grounds during the hours of darkness, adding their trained eyes to the mechanical and electronic security systems.

All these people and equipment had to be fed and maintained, though, and that was what ate up so much of Price's time. She had a sizable staff to help her with these chores, but the boss always had to keep track of what was being done in her name. Sometimes she wished that she could find a replacement and demote herself to the communications center. That way she could keep track of the missions without having to run the facility, as well.

Hearing a discreet cough from the open door of her office, Price opened her eyes and spun in her chair to see the Farm's armorer and weaponsmith standing in the doorway. John "Cowboy" Kissinger didn't look as if he was having a particularly good day.

"What's the scowl in honor of?" she asked.

"I'm having trouble getting some weapons parts we really need," he said simply.

Price frowned. Getting supplies of any kind wasn't a problem they usually had to deal with at the Farm. Stony Man's requisition code had the same priority as the White House's. Kissinger also had personal contacts with almost every weapons manufacturer in the Western World and was a first-class scrounger. If he said that he couldn't get something, it was serious.

"What seems to be the problem?"

"It's the Stingers."

"What's wrong with them?"

"I was doing the quarterly maintenance checks on them and wanted to replace the batteries. Over half of the missiles we have in stock are reaching their battery change-by dates, and we need new ones."

Stony Man Farm might have looked bucolic to the passing visitor, but it was really a wolf in sheep's clothing—a timber wolf with big sharp teeth and a bad attitude. Along with enough small arms to outfit a battalion, the security force also had antitank missiles, as well as a full air-defense system. As last-ditch, rooftop antiaircraft weapons, Kissinger had two dozen FIM-92A Stinger missiles in the inventory. If they were good enough to be used in that mode for the White House, they were good enough for Stony Man Farm.

Kissinger's main job was to see to the personal weapons of the Farm's action teams. But when he wasn't working on small arms, his job was to make sure that this impressive arsenal was fully operational at all times day and night. If the Farm came under attack, there would be no excuses for it not being prepared to withstand anything less than an armored-battalion assault.

"Anyway..." Kissinger concluded his long explanation by holding out a federal supply-requisition form. "I keep getting Not Available in Inventory comments with my returned requisitions."

Price took the form. "I'll have Aaron check it out for you and see what's going on."

"Have him put a rush on it. We can't afford to have those missiles non-ops."

Price totally agreed with the armorer. Once a month or so, a plane strayed too close to the Farm and the air-defense system had to be activated. So far they hadn't faced a threat from the air, but the open skies were still the Farm's most vulnerable perimeter.

"I'll go see him about it right now."

"Thanks."

AARON KURTZMAN'S U-shaped computer console dominated the room with its crowded banks of monitors competing for space in the racks. The workstations for the other staff members were a little better organized, but no less crowded.

Kurtzman was deep into his computer files when Price walked up behind him. A line of numbers scrolled down the left side of his monitor, while the right side displayed three windows, each one filled with a computer-generated color graphic depicting nothing she had ever seen before. His fingers stilled when he detected her presence and he turned in his wheelchair to look up at her, but he didn't speak.

"Cowboy wanted me to ask you to look into something for him," she said. "He's run into a problem with the Stingers and he can't seem to—"

"No can do. I haven't got time for it. Give it to—" Kurtzman looked around the room to see who didn't look particularly busy at the moment "—Akira."

Price didn't react to Kurtzman's abrupt manner. She didn't recognize the data that was slowly scrolling down his monitor, but whatever it was, it had his entire attention. Rather than interrupt his train of thought, she would take the problem to Akira Tokaido, as he had so curtly suggested.

That was the main problem with working with someone like Aaron Kurtzman—to say that he could get lost in his work was a serious understatement. The up side was that time after time he delivered the goods when no one else could have even understood the problem. He could pull obscure data out of its cyberspace hiding places and make instinctive connections where no one else could even see a relationship. He was a true genius.

She walked over to Tokaido's workstation to brief him on Kissinger's problem. The junior member of Kurtzman's cybernetic team was leaning back in his chair with his feet propped up on a metal wastepaper basket. Earphones were wrapped around his head, and he was tapping one foot to the sounds blasting his brain. He recovered his feet when he saw Price approach and lifted the earphone of his headset off one side of his head.

"Kissinger needs you to run a systemwide check for him on these items," she said as she handed him the canceled federal requisition form. "He keeps getting a 'not available in inventory' message, but they have to be available somewhere and we need them instantly."

Tokaido took the forms. "I'll get right on it and sort it out for him."

"Great. He's waiting for the parts, so when you find them, put a Stony Man priority-shipment code on them."

"Can do."

On the way out of the lab Price stopped by Huntington Wethers's workstation and saw that the tall, dignified black scholar was scrolling through news-agency reports from all over the world. "What's new and hot in the world today, Hunt?" she asked.

"Not much," Wethers answered. "The Muslims and Hindus are going at it again in the Northern Indian provinces. There's been the destruction of another Muslim holy site and a suspected shootdown of a commercial airliner with almost two hundred Hindus on the manifest."

Price frowned. Shooting down an airliner was a serious incident, and not only because of the loss of life involved. Any terrorist group powerful enough and willing to take out an airliner could be a danger to the balance of power in a very shaky world situation.

The end of the cold war and the breakup of the Soviet Union hadn't brought the long-awaited peace the liberals had dreamed about for so long. If anything, it had made the world an even more dangerous place to live now that the Russians were out of the game of policing their part of the globe. The complete and utter failure of the United Nations to control ethnic violence in Yugoslavia and the breakaway ex-Soviet republics had only proved once again that the international body was impotent and not to be feared.

That lesson, combined with a United States government that didn't want to get too heavily involved in international affairs unless the nation's vital interests were directly involved, had created an atmosphere of anarchy in much of the world. Ethnic and religious groups seeking greater power and influence for their particular points of view felt that they were free to do anything they wanted because there were no Big Brothers looking over their shoulders and waiting to slap their hands anymore.

A resurgence of the Hindu-Muslim conflict in India could have serious repercussions on more than just the Indian subcontinent. Iranian-influenced Islamic fundamentalists had gained a strong foothold in Pakistani politics, and having Iran working behind the scenes was always dangerous. If they were putting pressure on the Northern Indian provinces, things could reach critical mass very quickly.

"Get me a printout on that incident," Price said, "and anything else you think relates to it. Go back a couple of months."

"I'm working on that right now," Wethers replied, "and focusing in on Islamic fundamentalist activities in the entire region—Afghanistan, Pakistan and Northern India."

"Good idea," she said. "Keep me informed."

BACK IN HER OFFICE, Price tried to return to the state of mind she had been in before Kissinger interrupted her, but she failed. Wethers's information had set her to thinking in an operational mode. Since a resurgence of religious violence in India was the last thing anyone needed right now, it was quite likely to happen. That seemed to be the way these things always went. Trouble never came when there were enough time and resources ready at hand to contain it.

And, thinking of resources, she clicked into the computer readout on Able Team's current mission. Stony Man's domestic action team had been loaned to the Defense Department to look into a series of break-ins at factories supplying classified parts for the Pentagon. They were in California and were scheduled to wrap it up before much longer.

The readout wasn't very helpful, however. According to the latest report, the team was still on a stakeout and had extended the mission until it was concluded.

She clicked over to Phoenix Force's status report. They were still on stand down. But at least they were ready for action if something popped up.

The phone on her desk rang and she picked it up. "Price."

"Barb, I need Able to look into something for me," Hal Brognola stated.

CHAPTER THREE

Palo Alto, California

Carl "Ironman" Lyons was angry. He'd spent entirely too much time on this mission, and so far he had very little to show for it. If there was anything that irritated the ex-LAPD cop, it was wasting his time. He wanted to be out there rocking and rolling, not cooped up doing what he thought of as a night watchman's job.

His partner, however, was in his element and didn't mind the slow passing of the hours they were spending on surveillance. Hermann "Gadgets" Schwarz had an entire bank of electronic snooper gear to monitor, and if there was anything that turned him on, it was electronic gadgetry.

The third member of Able Team, however, was siding with Lyons this time. Rosario Blancanales was at his best when he was working one-on-one with living, breathing people, not sensors and electrons. The smooth-talking operative wasn't called the Politician for nothing. And so far this mission was short on face-to-face contact. There had been nothing for him to do except take his turn keeping an eye on Schwarz's monitoring devices, and like Lyons, he was getting bored.

"Are you ever going to get something we can move on, Gadgets?" Blancanales asked.

Schwarz lifted the earphone from his left ear. "What'd you say?" His eyes never left the video screen showing the inside of the empty warehouse they had been monitoring for the past two days.

"I asked when you are going to have enough for us to move on."

"Wait!"

Blancanales looked at the screen but didn't see anything other than the warehouse they had been watching for far too long. If their Intel was correct, the break-in should have happened by now. If it wasn't going to happen, though, and it looked that way to him, he was ready to move on to the next assignment. This wasn't the sort of mission Able Team was usually given, and he'd be damned glad to be done with it.

In the past few months several raids on high-tech facilities supplying parts for the Defense Department had sent the Pentagon into panic mode. Since there was a possibility that government employees were involved, Able Team had been called in to handle the investigation and stakeout.

"What's happening?"

"I just got an IR spike and a low-frequency buzz. I think it's going down."

"Would you mind putting that in English for the rest of us morons?"

"Here we go!" Schwarz's voice rose. "Lights, camera and action, guys. We're rolling."

The video screen showed five men in black combat suits entering through the side door of the warehouse. One of the five was carrying an electronic device the size of a big boom box complete with earphones and a small keyboard.

"That's how they buggered the security systems," Schwarz said. "That thing's got to be some kind of portable jammer. But that means someone on the inside gave them the specs for the system."

Looking at the screen over Schwarz's shoulder, Lyons pulled the .357 Colt Python wheel gun from his shoulder rig and automatically checked the loads. Blancanales reached over for his 12-gauge Atchisson automatic assault shotgun and cracked the bolt to make sure that he had one up the spout.

"Do you have it?" Lyons reholstered his Colt. One of the parts of this mission that irritated him the most was being required to tape the break-in for possible later prosecution. That was the sort of nickel-and-dime stuff undercover cops did, not Able Team.

Schwarz grinned. "Its on tape and no grand jury can ignore it. We've got 'em cold."

"About time," Lyons said. "Now turn that damned thing off.

"I don't want to have the rest of this on tape," he explained when Schwarz looked up at him with a questioning expression. "You can always testify that you had a 'technical malfunction.'"

Schwarz's fingers flew over his central keyboard. "One made-to-order major malfunction of our state-of-the-art surveillance equipment coming up."

The screen started fuzzing up and after a few seconds went blank.

"Let's hit it!" Lyons growled.

INSIDE THE DIMLY LIT warehouse, the five men had fanned out and were checking the stock numbers of the boxes in their neat rows on the metal shelves. When they located what they were looking for, they started stuffing the small foam containers into nylon sport bags.

Able Team quickly infiltrated the building by their preselected routes. Lyons was on the mezzanine by the entrance, with the other two down on the main floor, Blancanales to his right and Schwarz on his left. Since there were no doors at the far end of the warehouse, the raiders would have to come past them to get out. Since that wasn't likely to happen without a fight, Lyons had exactly what he wanted.

He pulled a flash-bang grenade from his assault harness and pulled the pin. "Flash bang," he whispered to his teammates over the com link.

"Roger," Schwarz called back.

"Got it," Blancanales radioed.

Lyons pitched the grenade as far as he could into the middle of the floor and closed his eyes. The grenade detonated with a loud explosion and a flash of eye-searing light. Anyone looking at it would be blinded for several seconds.

"This is the police," Lyons called out over the miniloudspeaker built into the commo set on his assault harness. "Put your weapons down and come out with your hands in the air. If you surrender, you will not be hurt."

Lyons's call for rationality was answered by a burst of subgun fire. He ducked back, but when the barrel of a subgun appeared from behind one of the shelves, the Able Team leader drew down on it and fired. The .357 round punched through the cardboard boxes and the electronic components they contained as if they weren't even there. A scream of pain told him that he had scored. One down.

Numbers two and three went to Blancanales. A pair of the intruders charged his position by the side door that led to the parking lot. The assault shotgun in his hands roared twice. The two shots meant that the two bodies got hammered to the concrete by the 12-gauge buckshot loads.

Schwarz pulled a flash-bang grenade from his harness, thumbed off the safety catch and pulled the pin. After sending a warning, he tossed the grenade and shut his eyes. After the detonation, he sprinted across to the first row of shelves. A stunned raider recovered fast enough to send a long burst after him, but the shots went wide.

Reaching cover, Schwarz grabbed a box with his free hand and tossed it against the second row of shelves. The gunner fell for the old trick and turned to fire at the noise. Schwarz spotted him when he moved and loosed a burst of 5.56 mm rounds from his CAR-15.

The man spun from the impact of the high-velocity slugs and went down hard. The subgun dropped from his hands and clattered on the concrete.

The last raider broke out from his cover in panic, the subgun in his hands blazing 9 mm fire as he dashed for the main door under Lyons's perch. The big ex-cop thumbed back the hammer of his Python, took a wide stance and brought the pistol down in a two-handed grip. When the sights aligned over the gunner's heart, he touched it off.

The heavy slug drilled the intruder through the chest and lifted him off of the ground. When he slammed down on the concrete floor, he was dead.

When the shot echoed away, there was a short silence, which was broken by a moan from one of the downed raiders. "Check him out," Lyons radioed to the two men on the main floor.

Holding his CAR-15 at the ready, Schwarz cautiously approached the wounded man, who was writhing in pain on the concrete, then kicked the fallen subgun away from his hand. The hardman had taken a couple of Blancanales's buckshots in the thigh and another one in the side, but he looked as if he would recover. Leaning over, Schwarz patted him down for additional hardware, but he came up clean.

Blancanales joined him, carrying a sport bag full of electronic parts individually packaged in small foam containers. "Here it is," he said, handing over the bag. "What in the hell were they after that was worth dying for?"

Schwarz opened one of the containers and pulled out the electronic component nestled inside. "They're microinterval switches," he explained, "and they're worth several thousand dollars apiece."

"But what do they do?"

"They control things that need to happen at precise thousandth-of-a-second intervals. Things like the rapid sequential explosions of the specially shaped plastic-explosive charges that are used to initiate an implosion-type nuclear detonation."

"Oh."

He put the device back into its container and dropped it into the bag with the rest. "We just put some third-world nation's nuclear-weapons program back a couple of months until they can find another source for these damned things."

In the distance, he could hear the wailing of sirens. The local cops were on the way. "I think we're out of here."

"'Bout time."

AS ALWAYS, Lyons was the one who handled the local police authorities. And as usual he ran into the problem of having to explain why most of the intruders were dead. Usually all he needed to do was to flash the federal identification that went with his cover for the mission and he had no further trouble. The Palo Alto police lieutenant had glanced at it and immediately understood the situation. He had also received a call from the Justice Department ordering him to go along with whatever went down and not allow anything to get in the way of the operation.

This time, however, a woman civilian representative of the town's Citizens Police Oversight Committee was at the scene, and she had obviously never run into anyone like the Able Team leader before. "You will have to remain in town, of course," she said smugly, "until we can convene a shooting board."

"A what?" Lyons couldn't believe what he was hearing.

"A shooting board," she explained. "The Citizens Committee will have to determine if this was a 'righteous' shooting. And, since there are so many dead—" her voice was strained and she shuddered "—we will have to have an individual ruling on each death. You and your men will have a chance to testify, of course, but we will have our own independent experts who will examine the scene to determine if a crime was committed here."

This was the part of his job that Lyons hated most, dealing with civilians who didn't have the slightest idea of the realities of the world they lived in. Blancanales usually handled the civilians who wandered into one of their operations, but the Politician was busy, so Lyons was stuck with it this time.

"Lady," he said, "you and your 'committee' can do any damned thing you like. However, if you think that me and my team are going to sit on our asses while you and your fellow citizens make your decision about how I handled this operation, you have another think coming. You have absolutely no authority over me and my men. We're out of here as soon as this mess is cleaned up."

"But this incident occurred in our town," she replied, her voice carrying the force of her indignation, "and we are the Citizens Police Oversight Committee. We have the right to look into this matter. Callous police brutality is a very serious concern in this community."

"Lady, to start with, I am not a cop. Second, I don't work for the voters of this town. And thirdly, even if I had wasted those assholes in your living room, it still wouldn't be any of your business. I suggest that you go home and watch 'America's Most Wanted' if you want to do something useful. Maybe there's a fugitive from justice hiding in your committee."

"You can't say that to me," the woman said, her voice shrill. "The people of this town elected me to this position so I could investigate incidents of police brutality and I intend to carry out their..."

She fell silent when Lyons abruptly turned and walked off.

Turning to the cop standing beside her, she snapped, "I want those men arrested. They can't do this to me."

"Ms. Stein," the Palo Alto police lieutenant said patiently. While Lyons and his team didn't work for this woman, he did. And if he wanted to keep his job, he had to calm her. "I think it would be best if you just dropped it this time. I don't have the authority to hold these men for anything."

"But," she sputtered, "who are those men and why did they kill those people?"

"Even if I knew," the cop said carefully, "I couldn't tell you."

Ms. Stein looked at the cop as if he had two heads. "What do you mean, you couldn't tell me? I am the chairperson of the Citizens Police Oversight Comm..."

She stopped talking again when she saw that the lieutenant was following Lyons across the parking lot and she was speaking to empty air.

SCHWARZ HAD A GRIM LOOK on his face when Lyons joined him. "Now what?" the big ex-cop growled. "I want to finish up and get the hell out of here."

"I just got a call from the Farm."

"And?"

"There's been another high-tech-company break-in, but this time the raiders killed everyone in the plant."

"Where?"

"Modesto."

Lyons shook his head in disgust. Modesto was much too nice a place for something like that to happen. In L.A., sure, it happened all the time. Maybe even in East Palo Alto, but not in Modesto. "What does it look like?"

"The locals are still checking it out, but it looks like a planned hit, not a bungled break-in. Most of the employees were finished with a shot in the head execution-style."

"What's our connection?"

"The company's got a classified Defense Department contract for something," he replied. "Barbara said that Hal wants us to look into it."

"He would."

Lyons glanced at his watch, then looked around the parking lot for Blancanales. "Tell Pol we're ready to go. I want to get a shower and a good night's rest before we move on to Modesto."

Schwarz saw his buddy standing by a patrol car talking to a good-looking female officer. "It looks like he's getting a recommendation for a place to sleep tonight."

"Tell him to get a move on it."

Schwarz grinned. "I think he's doing that already."

CHAPTER FOUR

Modesto, California

Able Team was at Century Microdyne in Modesto first thing the next morning. Carl Lyons wanted to interview the company's owner before they talked to the local police about the killings. The cops would have their own take on the incident, and he wanted to get as much raw information as possible before he considered their conclusions.

Bill Harris, Microdyne's owner and CEO, had been told that they were coming and he met them at the front door to the office building. He didn't look much like a hard-charging, young high-tech entrepreneur that morning. The shock of having more than a dozen of his employees killed showed plainly on his unshaved face. Unlike many of California's Silicon Valley whiz kids, Harris cherished his workers and treated them more like friends than employees. Some of the people who had died had been with him from the very beginning of his company, and he would miss them.

Harris said little as he led the visitors to his office, and his hands shook as he poured coffee for them.

"First off," Lyons said after identifying himself and the team as Defense Department investigators looking into the break-in, "what was taken during the robbery?"

"Batteries," Harris replied as if the word were an obscenity.

"All they took was batteries?" Lyons asked. "No cash? No equipment? They didn't try to hit the company safe or anything like that?"

"No." Harris shook his head slowly. "All they took was the damned CLA-219A batteries we were doing on a rush order for the Defense Department."

Schwarz's and Blancanales's eyes met across the conference table. This wasn't like the other high-tech break-ins they had been investigating. In the others, the raiders had simply looted everything of value in sight. And they hadn't killed anyone. Had the looters at the warehouse in Palo Alto surrendered, they wouldn't have been killed, either.

"What are those particular batteries used for?" Schwarz asked.

"It's a classified application."

Lyons silently flipped open his wallet, took out a card and handed it over to the man. Harris read both sides of the card and handed it back.

"They are used to power the FIM-92A Stinger missile."

"How many were taken?"

"All we had in stock, enough to power at least 150 missiles."

"How many people were working that night?" Blancanales changed the subject.

"Five on the security staff and the nine people in the assembly room."

"According to the local police, your people were killed about midnight?"

Harris nodded. "That's right. Old George Billings, the guard on the main gate, logged in the snack truck for the night shift at 11:48."

"What's the story on that snack truck?"

"It was found abandoned at the edge of town. The police said that it had been wiped clean of prints."

"Wasn't there something about the driver?" Blancanales prompted him.

"Yes. The regular driver was found dead by the side of the road. He had been shot in the head, too."

"Can you show us where this took place?" Lyons asked.

"Certainly, gentlemen." Harris stood. "Follow me."

LYONS TOOK THE WHEEL of their rental car as they drove out of the Microdyne compound and headed for the town's police headquarters. "That was a professional hit and sure as hell wasn't an Asian gang rip-off this time."

Most of the high-tech-company break-ins over the past couple of years had been traced to California's Asian gangs. They were selling stolen microchips and chip-making equipment to shady computer manufacturers in the Far East. Other thefts had been tied to bootleg nuclear- or chemical-weapons programs in places such as North Korea and Iraq. None of them, however, had carried the same tag as the Microdyne job.

"Do you think there's a tie-in with that bunch of goons we fired up in Palo Alto?" Blancanales asked.

Lyons thought for a moment. "I doubt it. I don't know what Stinger missiles and nuclear-weapons development have to do with each other."

"That was cold," Schwarz said, shaking his head, "not some guys who were surprised in the middle of a job and panicked. It was planned to happen that way."

"That's what it looks like to me," Lyons agreed. "But unless the cops have something to follow, all we can do is file the report and move on."

"And wait until we hear something in the news about Stingers," Schwarz added.

"That's what they pay Kurtzman the big bucks for."

CIA AGENTS DICK JONES and Jack Hagerty sat in a high mountain camp of Afghan tribesmen, on a mission to buy back several Stinger missiles reported to be in their possession. The headmen of several Mujahedeen bands were in the tent, including one man with light brown, almost golden eyes, who hadn't dropped the veil from his lower face to talk to them. That man was leading the argument against selling the missiles back to the Americans at the offered price.

"These bastards are going to double-cross us," Hagerty quietly muttered under his breath in Spanish. "I can smell it coming."

Both of the agents had operated extensively in Latin America and they used Spanish as a convenient way to keep their conversations private during negotiations.

"Just keep a lid on it, hombre," his partner replied softly in the same language. "We've still got something cooking here. We just have to give it a little more time."

"I am very sorry," Jones told the Afghan with the golden eyes in English, the language of the deal they were working, "but I am only authorized to offer $75,000 American for each of the missiles."

Hagerty shook his head. "That's more money than any two of these guys will ever see in two lifetimes. What's holding them up?"

"CIA pigs!" The Afghan who wouldn't drop his veil in the presence of the two infidels spit in the dust at the feet of the Americans. "You are trying to cheat us again. Any fool knows that the Stingers are worth much more than that."

"I don't see it as cheating," Jones said smoothly. "It is a good price my government is offering, and it is more than twice what we paid to buy them from the manufacturer. And remember, the Stingers came to the Afghan freedom fighters as a gift from the American people in the first place."

"God gave those missiles to us," the Afghan shot back, his eyes boring holes in Jones's head. "God alone."

The CIA agent still didn't understand why he and his partner had been sent to Afghanistan on this Stinger buy-back mission. They were Latin American specialists and had never operated in the Middle East before, which put them at a definite disadvantage. But the ops center had given him the orders, and he was trying his best to carry them out. He had always thought of himself as being good with people. Somehow, though, he wasn't making it this time. He didn't have any knowledge of the local cultural references, to say nothing of the language problem, and he could tell that he was blowing the deal big-time.

Nonetheless, he had to keep at it. Recovering the missing missiles was a top national priority. The Rwanda shootdown and the more recent Indian airliner incident had made it even more important to bring the Stingers back under American control. He and his partner weren't the only two out-of-country field agents who had been flown into Pakistan in the past week to try to work the Muji camps.

"Dick!" Hagerty whispered in English. "There's a crowd of them gathering outside the tent, and they're all packing weapons."

"These guys always carry weapons, Jack," Jones answered in Spanish. "Just hold it together, man. We'll be out of here before too much longer."

"I just want to get out of here alive."

The golden-eyed Afghan turned back to his comrades. "And I know that you really did not come here to buy Stingers."

"What do you mean?" Jones asked. "Of course we want to buy Stingers."

"You have admitted to being CIA spies," the Afghan said as he turned back to him. "And we know that the CIA is cooperating with the Russians now."

Jones frowned. He didn't have any idea where the conversation was heading. With the cold war over, of course the Russian and American governments were cooperating on many fronts. Regardless of what Congress wanted, however, the CIA wasn't getting too friendly. Not after recently discovering a highly placed Russian mole in the Langley headquarters.

The Afghan again turned to his audience. "These men did not come here to buy the missiles, but to gather information on us for the Russians. We know that the Russians still want to return and impose their will upon us. Now that the Yankees have made their peace with the Russians, they come here with stories about wanting to buy Stingers, but they are spies!"

"That's crazy!" Jones sputtered. "We freely told you who we are and exactly what we are trying to do. We wouldn't have done that if we were spies."

"But you are spies, and you will pay for it."

The golden-eyed Afghan shouted in his own language, and four men rushed into the tent.

"I told you," Hagerty muttered as he was abruptly jerked to his feet by two Afghans.

Jones tried to keep his cool as he was marched out the door. He and Hagerty had both been in tight spots before and had made their way out. It could be that holding them hostage was a tactic to up the price. If that's what was going down, they could expect to spend a few uncomfortable weeks until someone got his act together and ransomed them.

"Oh, Jesus!" Jones muttered when he saw four more men with veils covering their lower faces and AKs in their hands standing at the edge of the camp. He didn't have to be an Afghan cultural expert to know what was going to happen next. He knew a firing squad when he saw one.

Now that it had come to this, Hagerty had nothing to say. He had never really thought that he would live long enough to draw his CIA pension, but he had never thought that it would happen this way. He had seen men die in front of firing squads before, and he had always vowed that if it ever happened to him, he wouldn't whine and grovel.

He had read somewhere that the Japanese thought that how a man died was more important than how he had lived. And if that was good enough for the Japanese, it was sure as hell good enough for an American. He would show these bastards how a real man, an American, died. If his old Marine gunnery sergeant was looking down on him, he wanted the old bastard to be proud of him.

Shaking off the arms that held him once he had been marched to the edge of the camp, he straightened his back and stood at attention. Looking his executioners in the eyes, he raised his right hand and shot them the finger.

Jones stood at his side, his face white, but his hands were steady. "Jack," he said with a slight catch in his voice, "I'm sorry, man."

"So am I, old buddy." Hagarty eyed the AKs aimed at them. "So am I."

The golden-eyed Afghan barked a command, and the AKs blazed fire. A storm of 7.62 mm slugs tore through the two Americans.

Hagarty was dead before he hit the ground. Jones, though fatally wounded, tried to get to his knees. A single shot rang out, and a bloody hole appeared in his forehead. He twitched once and lay still.

The Afghan leader walked forward, drew the curved dagger from his belt and leaned over the bodies of the two CIA agents. With a single slash of the razor-sharp blade, he slit the throats of the two corpses. Straightening, he whipped the dagger to the side, slinging the blood off the blade.

"God is great!" he cried, raising the still-bloody blade high.

The men of the firing squad raised their AK-47s high over their heads and fired into the air on full automatic. "God is great! God is great!"

ONE OF THE OLDER AFGHANS stepped back from the crowd and made his way to where his horse was tied. He had fought against the Russians back in the days when the Americans had supplied his band of Mujahedeen with the arms and ammunition to kill their enemies. He had made friends with many of the Americans and, for infidels, he had always found them to be honorable men. This killing was a disgraceful way to repay them for the help they had given when it had been needed the most.

But then, the man in the veil was Iranian, and all the Afghan had ever seen come out of Iran was disgrace. The self-proclaimed ayatollahs weren't God's appointed messengers on earth. They were merely men who hungered after power for themselves, not for God. As far as he was concerned, they were the Great Satans, not the Americans.

But he hadn't lived to enjoy his long years by letting everyone know what he thought. Now that the Russians were gone, his country was in greater turmoil than it had ever been under the Red Bear's boots. The groups fighting to establish an Islamic republic in Afghanistan were financed by Iran, and the money was fueling the factional fighting. This violence had killed more of his people than the Russians ever had. And to less effect. If it kept up, it wouldn't be long before his nation ceased to exist. God would see to that.

The two CIA agents had been invited into the camp as guests, and the Koran said that the guest was sacred. These killings would certainly bring heavenly retribution. He just hoped that God's wrath would fall on those who had been responsible for the crime, not on those who had merely watched and done nothing, as he had.

He and his small band didn't have any of the Stinger missiles. But after this, if they ever came across any of them, he would turn them over to the Americans without payment. What had been given to his people as a gift had been turned into a curse. Nothing good could come of them now.

CHAPTER FIVE

Portland, Oregon

Mack Bolan was closing in on the trail of a dead man. At least the man would be dead as soon as he caught up with him. Everywhere the man went, he left a trail of corpses behind him. El Hakim was an assassin, a hit man for Hamas, the radical Palestinian terrorist organization that was working to end the peace that had been established between the Arabs and the Israelis.

Now that the U.S.-brokered peace plan had finally been implemented in Gaza and the West Bank, radical groups on both sides were pulling out all the stops to torpedo the process. For every man, Israeli or Palestinian, who wanted peace, it seemed that there were two who didn't want the conflict to end. Not only was a sea of blood being shed in both Israel and the newly created Palestinian zones, the fighting had now spread to everywhere in the world Jews and Palestinians lived. And that meant to the United States of America, as well.

El Hakim had come to the States to silence the voices of moderation among the sizable American Arab population. If presented with the opportunity to kill a Zionist, he would take the time to do that, as well, but his primary targets had all been prominent

Palestinian Americans who backed the hope of peace with Israel in their homeland.

Bolan felt good now that he saw the chase coming to an end. He had no patience with terrorists. Much of his long career had been spent ending the careers of terrorists, and he would be especially satisfied when this one was put down. Killing those whose only crime was to work for peace was particularly repugnant to Bolan. El Hakim would soon join the long list of men whose last view before becoming bloody corpses had been the Executioner's cold blue eyes staring at them over the blazing muzzle of a gun.

Thus far, though, the warrior had remained one step behind El Hakim. He had tracked the Hamas killer by the bodies of men, women and children he had left behind. Now, though, he had made the leap across the gap and should be ahead of him for once.

In the process of tracking him down, Bolan had compiled a thick file on the assassin and how he operated. Equally important was the file he had compiled on the people who had made it possible for El Hakim to operate in the United States. After he took care of the assassin, the warrior intended to pay a brief visit to several of the men who had been instrumental in supporting and financing the terrorist's activities. They, too, would have to learn that terrorism wouldn't be tolerated in the United States.

One of the reasons he had such a difficult time tracking this particular killer was that most of his hits had been cleverly disguised to look like accidents or routine crimes, not political assassinations. Burglaries, fatal muggings, hit-and-runs and even a boating accident had been his methods of choice. The more traditional car bombings and .22-caliber bullets in the back of the head would have alarmed the authorities and brought attention to his activities.

In fact, had it not been for a tip Bolan received from an agent of the Mossad, the Israeli secret service, he wouldn't have even known that this particular foreign killer was on the loose in the United States.

JERED DOV, the Mossad agent, had contacted him through a mutual friend and asked if he was interested in information about a Hamas hit man who was operating in the United States. That was like asking a hungry baby if he wanted his mother's milk. Hamas was the most radical of the Palestinian terrorist groups and was responsible for thousands of needless deaths among both the Israeli and Palestinian peoples, to say nothing of Europeans and Americans.

The meeting took place in a public park in Atlanta, a spot chosen by Bolan. The Israeli agent allowed himself to be patted down for both hardware and wires before he briefly outlined El Hakim's activities.

"Why haven't you passed on this information to the FBI or the CIA?" Bolan asked when he was done.

Dov shrugged. "There are those in my organization who do not think that your government has our best interests at heart at the moment. And to put it simply, we are not certain that your official agencies would be able to put their hands on this man."

"They did a pretty good job of tracking down the World Trade Center bombers."

"That was good work," Dov agreed. "But that job was not carried out by Hamas. They were amateurs, trained amateurs to be sure, but they were not professionals like this man. Plus, we have information that El Hakim made certain connections when he was working in Lebanon that the Trade Center bombers didn't have."

"What do you mean?"

"We believe that he was a CIA stringer when they were trying to track down the Marine-barracks bombers in Beirut. We think that he was brought inside the Company then and is still in contact with the pro-Arabic faction."

This was something straight out of a paperback thriller—a CIA renegade cabal utilizing terrorists for their own ends. But Bolan knew that it was a long-held belief in Israeli government circles that there was a pro-Arab as well as a pro-Israeli faction within the American CIA. It had been, of course, officially denied several times. But regardless of official pronouncements, the Mossad was not convinced.

"So you're saying that this guy still has active CIA connections?"

"We know so," Dov stated flatly.

That was a strong statement about a situation as nebulous as an unofficial relationship that might have existed in Lebanon more than a decade earlier. But then, it was almost common knowledge that the Mossad also had their agents inside the CIA, and if they did, they would know about any shadow ties to terrorists. The idea of foreign agents working in America's most secret government agency wasn't all that farfetched. The Russians had done it for years and had got away with it many times. Aldrich Ames, the latest mole to be uncovered, hadn't been the first to be planted in the Company, nor would he be the last. And if the Russians could do it, the Mossad sure as hell could, too.

"Why are you telling me this instead of taking care of it yourselves?"

Dov met his eyes squarely. "Your interest in terrorists is well-known in my organization."

That was an understatement if Bolan had ever heard one. He had worked with the Mossad on more than one occasion.

"And," Dov continued, "with the political situation in both our countries the way it is right now, we cannot risk having one of our men caught working in the States. But you do not have this problem. It was felt that if you were notified of El Hakim's activities, you would take care of him."

"As a favor for the Mossad?"

Dov shook his head. "No. We know better than to expect anything like that. We thought that you would want to do it for yourself."

Bolan smiled thinly. The Mossad knew him well. He had always been leery of doing quid pro quo "favors" for anyone, even the American government. You never knew when they would come back to haunt you. But he had always welcomed information on potential terrorist targets no matter where the information came from.

"Thank your people for me," he said. "I don't promise that I'll take action, but I'll promise to study the information carefully."

"That is all we hoped for."

Back in his hotel room, Bolan went over the data Dov had provided and quickly saw that El Hakim was in fact killing influential moderate Palestinian Americans as the agent had claimed. He decided to undertake the mission.

UNDERTAKING THE MISSION had led him to Portland, Oregon. At first glance Portland seemed to be a very unlikely place for a Hamas terrorist to go in search of a victim. The Rose City, as it was known to its inhabitants, was a small but thriving city in northern Oregon at the juncture of the Willamette and Columbia rivers.

In recent years Portland had been the promised land for people burned out on East Coast big-city life and the rabid insanity of Southern California. In the eighties it had been the most common destination for U-Haul trailers and trucks rented in Southern California. These new Oregonians brought with them an ultraliberal, activist mind-set that quickly transformed the sleepy little town. As a result the Portland of the nineties exhibited some fairly bizarre behavior for a city of its modest size.

For instance, Portland was one of the few towns in the nation where a near majority of the city council members had voted against having a Gulf War veterans homecoming parade. Other local politicians had openly supported the Communist Sandinistas, and still did even after they had been voted out of power in Nicaragua.

Every time a Republican President visited Portland, the riot police had to be called out to contain the rock- and egg-throwing protestors. In fact, President Bush's security team had nicknamed Portland Little Beirut and brought extra personnel whenever he visited.

This liberalism allowed drug dealing to become a growth industry in Portland in the eighties, when the city's first female chief of police disbanded the narcotics unit. Almost immediately the Bloods and Crips moved north with their crack-and-coke concessions. And once in place, the drug problem had only grown even after the chief had been canned. Even so, civic groups in Portland regularly tried to stop the U.S. Immigration Service from deporting illegal immigrants who had been arrested for openly dealing drugs in the downtown business district.

For a sleepy little Northwest town, Portland had a bizarre side to it that one didn't normally find north of San Francisco.

But it also had a good side. Portland was a favorite with groups trying to place refugee families in the United States. Anytime there was trouble in the world, refugees from the fighting ended up in Portland, Oregon. In the process, the city had acquired a fairly large Palestinian population. Many of these immigrants were pro-PLO, as frequent public demonstrations proved. But in the last few years several groups of moderate Palestinians had moved there, as well. One of them, a Dr. Ezadeen Amal, published an Arabic-English Palestinian newspaper and ran an Internet computer forum dedicated to promoting peace and ending the violence in the Middle East.

Most Portlanders had no idea who the doctor was and knew nothing of his activities. It wasn't that he kept a particularly low profile, it was more that he wasn't radical enough for Portland to take notice of him. He was a voice of moderation, and trendy Portlanders weren't into moderation. But the fact that El Hakim was moving against him was proof that his ideas had a wide following outside of his new hometown. He encouraged new thinking on the old problems, and if there was anything that Hamas and the other radical Palestinian groups couldn't tolerate, it was the free exchange of ideas. If their people started thinking for themselves, they would quickly lose the power they had come to enjoy.

And the endless war in the Middle East had always been about power rather than being about religion or the redress of past injustices. Seekers of personal power always found their road smoother if they could hang a religious tag on their quest. Religion, any religion, was always ready to give murder a good name.

DR. AMAL HAD BEEN STUNNED to find Mack Bolan waiting for him in the study of his modest West Hills home. The warrior stood and kept his hands open in front of him when the doctor walked in. "My name is Mike Belasko," he said, "and I have an important message for you."

Amal was cool and kept his head. He didn't even try to go for the .38-caliber revolver he kept in his desk drawer. If the man had meant to harm him, he would be dead by now.

"Please have a seat, Mr. Belasko," he said as he sat behind his desk.

Bolan quickly briefed him on El Hakim and his Hamas-sponsored mission in the United States.

"So that's what happened to Ali and his family," Amal said softly, referring to a Palestinian refugee friend who had died in a boating "accident" in Michigan.

"And," Bolan concluded, "I have reason to believe that you are next on his hit list."

"It is the newspaper, isn't it?" Amal asked.

"And the Internet forum. You're too convincing for your own good."

"You are with the government, then," the Palestinian said. "May I see your identification, please?"

"I'm not with the government. I received this information from an Israeli source, and when I followed up on it, I found it to be true."

"If you are not with the government, then why are you here?"

"I intend to make sure that El Hakim is put out of business permanently."

"I see," Amal stated. And he did.

Having spent most of his life in the Middle East, he knew the realities of politics, particularly the politics of terrorism. If this Hamas assassin was after him, he would have to be stopped. But as he knew only too well, Western governments, the American government most of all, had proved to be almost powerless to stop terrorist attacks. He had heard, however, of nongovernment operatives who had proved to be very effective when official agencies had not. Apparently he now had one of these shadow agents sitting in his den.

"What do you want me to do?"

"Is there someone you can send your wife and children to visit? Preferably somewhere out of state. It would help me to have them safely out of the way."

Amal shook his head. "I won't send them into hiding," he said flatly. "They have been with me throughout all of this so far, and they will stand by me this time."

"It's going to make it more difficult for me to protect you," Bolan stated bluntly. "If he gets his hands on one of them, he can use them as a hostage."

"I'm smarter than that. I know what Hamas does to their hostages. Plus, if they are not here, it will tip this man off that I have been warned about him. I am well-known as a strong family man."

Bolan had to admit that Amal had a good point. "Okay," he said, standing. "I'll plan around them. Can you show me the layout of your house?"

"Follow me."

CHAPTER SIX

Los Angeles, California

Instead of calling the men of Able Team back to the Farm after they'd wrapped up the mission, Barbara Price had ordered them to try to develop leads from the bodies and the one survivor. Working with the California authorities, the FBI, Immigration and Kurtzman's computer banks, they soon hit pay dirt.

Of the four hardmen killed in the warehouse shoot-out, two had been Iranians and two had been Afghans. That in itself wasn't surprising. The radical Afghans and the Iranians had been working together closely since the fall of Kabul to the radicals. What was interesting was that all four men had entered the country on Pakistani business visas, further proof that the Iranians were branching out into their neighboring nations. Beyond that, there was little they could get from the corpses, but their captive had proved to be a gold mine.

Once the wounded man's medical condition had been stabilized, he was transported to a government medical facility and put through chemical interrogation. Under the drugs, he claimed to know nothing at all about the hit at Century Microdyne. He did, however, have a wealth of information about the aborted plot to steal the microsequencers. Some of the nuclear-bomb initiators had been destined for Iran, some for North Korea and some for Pakistan. Best of all, however, was that he knew about a second group of high-tech raiders who were smuggling restricted electronic and microtool supplies out of the country.

The operation was being fronted out of a high-priced Middle Eastern art gallery in Beverly Hills and Barbara Price gave Able Team orders to move on it immediately.

THE GOLDEN PALM GALLERY catered to a well-heeled clientele that wanted a touch of the "authentic" Middle East in their home decor. For the right price, the gallery could supply anything from illustrated Persian manuscripts to Egyptian mummy cases. No matter when or where an artifact had been made, the gallery would also gladly give the buyer a signed Certificate of Authenticity to make him or her feel better about the exorbitant price that had been paid. The fact that few of the items sold, or the certificates that went with them, would stand up under an art historian's scrutiny didn't bother most of the buyers. The Golden Palm Gallery was on Rodeo Drive, and that was all that mattered in Los Angeles.

"Are you sure that this is the right place, Ironman?" Hermann Schwarz asked when he pulled their rented limo to the curb in front of the gallery. "This looks like a yuppie palace, not the headquarters for a terrorist smuggling operation."

"What better place to have it?" Lyons replied. "Yuppies don't know anything about terrorists."

The man who met them at the door was wearing a thousand-dollar Italian suit and had a practiced look of disdain on his classic Middle Eastern features. When he let his eyes travel down to Schwarz's worn jeans and cowboy boots, he almost sniffed. He let his dark eyes slide right past Lyons's colorful attire before settling on Rosario Blancanales's tasteful imported sport suit and Gucci loafers.

"How may I be of assistance, sir?"

"Steven told me that you might be able to help me find something I've been looking for." Blancanales's voice had exactly the right casual tone to imply he had more money than common sense.

"Steven?"

"Spielberg."

"Of course." The man blinked. "And what would that be, sir?"

"I'm redoing the foyer," Blancanales replied, waving his hands to vaguely indicate a large area, "and I'm thinking of doing something Egyptian this time. You know, something massive like Cecil B. deMille. Maybe a facade with a lot of carving and a pillar or two. I always did like *The Ten Commandments.*"

The salesman's eyes almost glittered. "I am sure we can accommodate you, sir. Allow me to show you pictures of a fine piece we currently happen to have in our warehouse."

While Blancanales kept the salesman occupied, Lyons and Schwarz quickly cased the place. While they looked at the artwork and artifacts in the tasteful displays, they carefully noted all of the gallery's security systems.

"That should do nicely," Blancanales said, tapping the color photograph of a gaudy, gilt and brightly painted entryway that looked like it was straight out of the movie *Cleopatra*.

"We can have that piece cleaned and ready for you to look at the day after tomorrow," the salesman said after consulting his leather-bound appointment calender.

"I think I can make it that day," he said. "And where did you say your warehouse was?"

After copying the address, he called to his "driver" and "assistant" and left.

"Do you really think that it's going to be this easy?" Schwarz asked when they were back in the limo.

"Why not?" Blancanales replied. "I fit the profile of a would-be social climber with more money than taste, and that's exactly who they cater to."

"But why would they run a smuggling operation out of their legitimate warehouse?"

"Why not?"

"It had better be where they're holding the goodies," Schwarz said, "because that gallery's wired with everything except lasers. They have both motion and heat sensors, as well as tremblers on all the windows. We'd never get in there without having half the police in the county down on our ass."

After he dropped Blancanales and Lyons at their motel, Schwarz went to return the limo to the agency.

When he got back to the motel, he found his partners suiting up and getting ready for war.

THE UPSCALE GALLERY'S warehouse didn't look different than any of the others in the run-down industrial district south of Marina Del Rey. Even in the dark of night it was shabby and dusty and had no fewer potholes in the cracked pavement in front of it. The only real difference they could see was that it was well lit.

The team parked their four-wheel-drive in an unlit spot two buildings down and stepped out.

"Someday I'm going to walk into a warehouse without packing a gun," Schwarz said as he settled his assault harness over his shoulders, "and I'll get to leave without blowing the damned place up."

"Dream on," Blancanales said with a grin. "Not as long as you run around with the Ironman and me."

"Maybe that's the problem," he replied thoughtfully. "I was always told that I needed a wider circle of friends."

"Cut the crap," Lyons growled as he settled his .357 Colt Python in his shoulder holster. "We've got work to do."

The Able Team leader's plan was the picture of simplicity, which was the way he preferred to operate. He wasn't about to waste his valuable time putting the place under surveillance to prove his informant's report. As far as he was concerned, any information he recovered from a chemical interrogation was gospel and he could act on it without further confirmation.

This would be a simple break-and-enter job. Once they got inside they would simply tear the place apart until they found what they were looking for. Then they would back out, call in the Feds and let them deal with what was left. All told, it shouldn't take more than an hour or so at the outside.

While the front of the building was well lit, the back side was dark, and they quickly went up the wall and in through an unsecured second-story window. Once they were inside they made a quick tour of the ground floor to familiarize themselves with the layout.

"I really think you should have let me scope out this place first, Ironman," Schwarz said when he saw the security-system panel on the wall by the main door. "This place is wired three ways from Sunday."

"Quit bitching. We're in, aren't we, and we didn't trip anything off."

Schwarz reached out and hit a switch on the front of the panel. "I think that killed the silent alarm."

"What silent alarm?" Lyons frowned.

"The silent alarm you activated when you came through the window."

"Where does it go?"

He opened the front of the panel and peered at the maze of wires. "There's no way for me to tell. It's wired into the phone lines. But my bet is that it's not plugged into the local cop shop. Not with what they've got going on in here."

Schwarz flicked the selector switch on his CAR-15 to the full-auto position. "It's time for the old 'prepare to repel boarders' routine again."

"How long do we have, Gadgets?" Lyons asked.

"How the hell do I know?" His eyes flicked back to the control box. "They didn't put a response-time sticker on this thing."

"We'd better quit screwing around, then, and find some cover."

DR. AMAL'S HOUSE was built back in a wooded area on a hillside, a typical residence location for West Hills, Portland. It was scenic, quiet and rustic, but it was a defender's nightmare. With the trees surrounding the house on three sides, the only cleared areas were the driveway and the small lawn in front of the house.

"He's going to be able to get in close without our seeing him," Bolan stated, explaining the tactical problem to the doctor. "And once he's inside the grounds, the shrubbery gives him good cover all the way up to the house."

"So, what do we do?"

"From the way he's been operating so far, my guess is that he will go for a burglary scenario again. The kind where your neighbors or work associates come looking for you a couple of days after the fact and find that your house has been ransacked and that you and your family are dead. The way your house is situated makes it a natural. He can be in and out of here with no one ever seeing him."

Amal shuddered. Along with Portland's vaunted liberalism, it also had one of the highest crime rates on the West Coast. Break-in murders were almost common fare on the local six-o'clock news. The news anchors always called one of these crimes a "burglary gone wrong," as if there were a right way to commit a burglary in Portland.

"There are two ways that he'll try to pull this off," Bolan went on. "The first way is to break in when the house is empty and then pick you off one by one when you come home. The other way is to wait until night and do it while you're asleep. Either way you won't have a chance once he's in the house."

"How long do you think we have before he comes?"

That was the big problem Bolan had to work around. He had no idea when El Hakim would appear or even if he would. Based on his past actions, the assassin spent only six or eight days between hits. He moved into an area, reconned the target for a couple of days, made the hit and then moved on to the next name on his list.

"I don't think we have very long," Bolan said. "Considering the date of his last probable hit, he should be arriving in Portland today if he isn't here already. But since I don't know how far ahead of him I am, we have to start getting ready for him now."

"What can I do to help?" Amal asked.

"The first thing I want you to do is to call a home-security company and have an alarm installed tomorrow."

Bolan raised his hand to caution the doctor. "It will be completely useless against him, of course. But after he disables it, he might get a little overconfident because you aren't supposed to know that he even exists.

"Then," he continued, "I want you to get cellular phones and beepers for yourself and your family. Good communications is the key to making this thing work. Get one for me while you're at it, but get it in your name, too."

Bolan reached into his back pocket, pulled out his wallet and peeled off five one-hundred-dollar bills. "Here," he said, "this will help with the expenses."

"I cannot take the money," Amal stated, shaking his head. "Not from someone who is defending me and my family."

"Consider it a loan, then."

"What are you going to do after we've done all this?"

"I'm going to become your houseguest while you and your family go about your normal routines."

"My home is yours," Amal said, bowing his head.

CONSIDERING the circumstances, the members of Dr. Amal's family didn't go into a complete panic when they came home and Bolan briefed them on the threat they were facing. They had lived most of their lives in a land where violent death was a commonplace event. And that death didn't always come from the enemy. During the *intifada* resistance in Gaza and the West Bank, more Palestinians had been killed by their own people than had been killed by the Israelis.

"I would feel better, Mrs. Amal," Bolan said over coffee after dinner, "if you and the children went out of town until this is over."

"No. I understand your concern, but one way or the other, we will stay together. We have already gone through too much to allow the destroyers to break up our family."

Since he had gotten a no from both of the Amals, Bolan dropped that subject. "Since that's the case," he said, glancing at his watch, "I think that you had all better get some sleep. You'll be busy tomorrow. Your husband and I will keep watch tonight."

"I'll stand the first watch," Amal volunteered. "I have a pistol in my desk."

"I'll sleep on the couch," Bolan said, "so I'm close if you need me."

CHAPTER SEVEN

On the Indian Subcontinent

The ashes of the cremated bodies from the Air India crash at Banda were barely cool before a second Airbus full of Hindus fell to a Stinger missile. The airline promptly canceled all its flights to the northern states until the crisis could be brought under control.

In the Indian parliament the leader of the Hindu-fundamentalist Bharatiya Janata Party demanded that the government avenge these outrages by taking immediate action against what he called the Pakistani-sponsored Islamic groups in India. The leader of the more moderate Gandhi Socialist Party cautioned against taking any action against anyone until more information was available about who was actually responsible for these crimes. After much heated debate, his suggestion carried the vote that day.

The next morning the Socialist leader was found assassinated in his modest home. The bodies of his wife and children were found in their beds, as well. While never proved, the consensus was that the deaths had been ordered by the fundamentalist party.

Later that day anti-American riots broke out in several Northern Indian towns and cities. Even though the President of the United States had made a strong statement condemning this new outbreak of sectarian terrorism, whenever there was a problem in the world, it was still fashionable to blame America. At the head of each of the riots were men carrying the banners of the BJP extremists.

A few days later a Pakistani Boeing 757 in the landing pattern for Lahore airport in Pakistan was hit by a Stinger missile. Again more than one hundred men, women and children lost their lives in the fiery crash that followed.

Even though a Hindu radical group immediately claimed credit for the attack and said that it had been done in retaliation for the downing of the Indian airliners, anti-American riots broke out almost instantly throughout Pakistan. The missiles had been made in the United States, and the Great Satan of Islamic fundamentalism was seen as being responsible for the deaths.

The fact that the Stingers hadn't been under American control for more than a decade wasn't discussed. A nation in mourning needed a place to focus its anger and rage. That rage boiled over when an American tourist was caught a block away from the embassy in Islamabad and was beaten to death by a rioting mob. His female companion barely escaped with her life when a shopkeeper offered her refuge.

The next day the American State Department issued an urgent tourist advisory for both Pakistan and Northern India.

ALONG THE TENSE India-Pakistan border, Indian airforce Flight Lieutenant Ram Laloo led his flight of three MiG-21bis jet fighters on a routine patrol of the high mountain area. Since the downing of the two airliners, the patrols had been stepped up, and the Russian-built fighters were carrying full ordnance loads on board. They had orders to fire to protect Indian airspace.

Laloo was flying the mission with a heavy heart. His favorite uncle had been on board the first Air India Airbus with his entire family when it went down, and he had just returned to his squadron after attending the funerals. Though the Indian military tried to stay out of partisan politics as much as possible, Laloo was a devout Hindu and closely followed the line of the fundamentalist BJP.

When Laloo's air-to-air radar showed that a flight of two Pakistani Chinese-built MiG-19 fighters was approaching the invisible border, his heart raced. He instantly banished his sorrow and replaced it with resolve to extract his private vengeance against those he saw as being responsible for his family's loss.

Reaching out to his fire-control panel, his gloved fingers activated the targeting radar and selected the AIM-9L Sidewinder air-to-air missiles mounted on his underwing pylons. He wasn't an adept aerial gunner with the MiG's 23 mm cannons in his belly pack, but the heat-seeking missiles would more than make up for that small deficiency.

"Thunderbolt Flight," he radioed to his two wingmen, "this is Thunderbolt Lead. We are going to check out those two bandits on approach."

"Two, roger. Three, roger," the other two flyers responded. They were both fresh out of flight school and new to the border-patrol flights. They didn't see the Pakistani fighters as a threat, but they were more than willing to follow their more experienced flight leader.

Laloo continued flying parallel to the border until the Pakistani MiGs made a turn and headed back toward their base. Once their tail pipes were exposed, he hit the afterburner on his fighter. The MiG-21 rocketed forward under fifteen hundred pounds of thrust from the screaming Tumansky R-11 turbine and went supersonic almost instantly.

Within seconds the Pakistani MiGs were in range for the Sidewinders, and the red diamond pip in Laloo's gunsight was on the trailing fighter. When he had a lock-on tone in his earphones, he fired his first missile.

The Sidewinder tracked after the MiG-19 as if it were tied to it with an unbreakable string that was being swiftly reeled in. It disappeared up the jet fighter's tail pipe and caused an explosion that tore off the entire aft fuselage and tail section of the stricken plane.

Seeing his wingman explode in midair, the second MiG-19 pilot headed for the deck and tried to make a run for it. But now that Laloo had made his first kill, his blood was up and he wasn't about to let him go.

Staying in afterburn, he chased after the MiG-19 as it fled. The Pakistani obviously wasn't much of a fighter pilot. Instead of trying to fight for his life, he headed away from the border straight and level as fast as he could go.

When Laloo closed in, he saw that the MiG-19 was a two-seat trainer version and smiled. The two men on board meant more blood for Lord Rama, and his family.

When he had a lock-on tone again, Laloo triggered a second Sidewinder missile. As had happened the first time, the missile homed in on the fleeing MiG at better than Mach 2 and headed straight up its tail pipe.

At the last possible moment the Pakistani pilot finally whipped his fighter around. But even though the missile missed the hot tail pipe, the radar-proximity fuse detonated as the missile sped past, and the explosion tore off the right wing. The MiG instantly flipped over and spun to the ground below.

Flight Lieutenant Laloo smiled even wider as he banked his MiG-21 away from the two columns of smoke rising from the desert floor. Those were three Muslim bastards who wouldn't kill any more innocent civilians. If they wanted to fight, let them come up and duel in the sky like men.

THE NEXT DAY the Pakistani representative to the United Nations stood up to speak in the General Assembly. In a voice shaking with anger, he demanded an international investigation into the aerial clash on his country's border with India, which had cost the lives of three Pakistani pilots. He denounced the criminal action and demanded that the Indian pilots be charged with crimes against humanity. He further claimed that the victims' MiG fighters hadn't been armed and had been flying a peaceful training mission.

After the Pakistani's impassioned speech, the Indian delegate stood up to denounce what he saw as an unwarranted attack on his nation. The Pakistani fighters, he said, had penetrated Indian airspace, and the victorious Indian pilots would be rewarded for defending their country against the armed aerial intruders.

The Pakistani stood again without being recognized by the chair and shouted that the Indian delegate was a filthy liar. The Indian yelled back and rushed the Pakistani's place in the chamber. In an instant the two men were at each other's throats.

Only the intervention of the security men in the chamber prevented the two delegates from beating each other half to death. As he was escorted from the room, the Pakistani delegate shouted that his country would have vengeance for this insult. The Indian delegate shouted much the same threat before he, too, was taken out.

BARBARA PRICE WASN'T surprised to get a call from Hal Brognola telling her to expect a visit. In the wake of the anti-American riots in both India and Pakistan, and the fistfight in the UN council, she had known it would only be a matter of time before the

President directed Stony Man Farm to get involved in this newest crisis.

This time, though, it looked as if they were a little ahead of the game. Hunt Wethers had been working up a background file on the situation for a couple of days and was doing impressive work as always. No matter what the President wanted them to do, they should be able to get right on it.

For a change Hal Brognola didn't look as if he had been dragged through a knothole backward when he invited Price and Kurtzman to join him and walked into the War Room at the Farm that afternoon. The Justice Department official looked well rested and almost dapper.

One look at the big Fed told Price that whatever this crisis was, they were getting in on it early, as she had hoped. As the mission—whatever it would entail—wore on, Brognola would take on a more and more worn and frazzled appearance. But as she well knew, getting an early start on the problem could be either good or bad news.

It would be good news if there was enough time for her to carefully plan this mission, rather than throwing the action teams into the caldron to sink or swim as fate decided. It would be bad news if the situation were so serious that they were being called in before anyone knew that the crisis even existed.

Brognola took his usual place at the head of the table and opened his locked briefcase. Reaching in, he took out a folder with a broad red Top Secret classification stripe running diagonally across the cover and laid it on the table in front of him.

"The topic today is Stinger antiaircraft missiles and their contribution to the current tension between India and Pakistan. You both are aware that we supplied hundreds of these missiles to the Mujahedeen guerrillas in the Afghanistan War to help level the playing field against the Russians.

"And you also know the CIA has been trying to buy these missiles back from the Afghans for years now, but with little success. Even though we've been offering tens of thousands of dollars apiece for them, they're worth much more than that to terrorist organizations, and they've been outbidding us at every turn.

"These latest incidents in India and Pakistan have the President and his security advisers worried. The Man feels that if this isn't resolved quickly, Northern India and Pakistan will become a battleground. And both the CIA and DIA think that it will be a nuclear battleground this time around. We know that the Indians have nuclear weapons in their arsenals, and they are ready to use them. The Pakistani government claims that while they have the capability to manufacture nukes, they haven't assembled any yet. There is sufficient reason, however, not to believe that claim.

"The President thinks the key to keeping a tight lid on this thing is to prevent any more airliners from being shot down by American-made missiles in *anyone's* hands. This is where you and your teams come in."

Price grimaced at that news. The anti-American sentiment in both nations meant that there would be little or no government cooperation for the mission. The teams would have to operate in a totally covert mode without any open support or backup from the American military.

"As you can appreciate," Brognola continued, "with the current world situation the way it is, the President is also very leery of involving U.S. forces for this mission. And he can't hand this one over to the UN. He needs action now, not in a year or so, after it has been talked to death. We have to get those damned things rounded up before the lid blows off of the Indian subcontinent."

He leveled his eyes at Barbara Price. "The bottom line is that the Man wants the Stony Man teams to get into the Stinger-repossession business ASAP. But if they can't be recovered, he wants them destroyed in place. How soon can you get Phoenix Force assembled for a mission briefing?"

Price didn't have to consult her notebook for that answer. Phoenix Force was on stand down and was available on short notice. "Give me a day."

Brognola nodded. "And what's Striker doing right now? How close is he to terminating that Hamas hit man?"

Again Price knew the answer without having to call up the latest information. Mack Bolan had checked in yesterday evening and had given her an update. "Last night he said that he thought he'd be finished in a day or two."

"Good. We need him to work on this one, too, if he's available."

Brognola glanced at his watch. "That's it for now. I've got to get back to Wonderland. Let me know when Phoenix Force arrives. I'll come back down to give them the word.

"Until then—" he turned to Aaron Kurtzman "—start pulling your data together. You're cleared to pull anything you need from the NSA, DIA and CIA files on this one and won't have to use your back door."

Kurtzman smiled. One of his favorite amusements was hacking his way through the latest CIA security systems every time they were changed. His Stony Man priority let him see almost anything he wanted to, but it was far more fun to play with the security systems. "I'm already on it."

"I figured as much."

CHAPTER EIGHT

Los Angeles, California

Able Team was in position in the warehouse and ready to rock and roll long before the opposition showed up to answer the intruder alarm. Schwarz, with his CAR-15, stood on the walkway of the mezzanine floor, where he would have a good field of fire over the ground floor. Blancanales and his 12-gauge blaster were situated along the rear wall to cover the entire front of the building. Lyons had picked a dark corner opposite the main door, where he could cover the ground floor in a cross fire. Now came the hard part, the waiting.

"It's been over half an hour, Gadgets," Lyons growled in a half whisper. "Where the hell are those people?"

"Just keep it in your pants, Ironman," Schwarz replied. "Like I said, they didn't put a response-time sticker on the control panel. If they're who we think they are, they'll be here. If they're not, maybe we'll get a visit from the local security company. But someone will come, believe me. This is L.A."

Lyons was about to give it up when he heard the sound of a car screeching to a stop in front of the warehouse. When he heard four doors open and shut, he knew that their party had arrived in force.

Six men entered through the main door by the loading dock, pausing inside to let their eyes adjust to the darkness. The smirking salesman from the Golden Palm Gallery appeared to be the man in charge. The other five gunmen looked like typical L.A. thugs, but their hardware was dead serious—full-auto Uzis equipped with silencers.

The gunmen spread out along the wall by the main door while the salesman walked toward the office to turn on the inside lights. Gadgets had pulled the fuses, so they didn't have to worry about lights snapping on and ruining their night vision, but now it was time to go to work.

This was the part Lyons hated, telling the bad guys to throw their weapons down and to come out with their hands up like good law-abiding citizens. It looked good in the cop movies, but as far as he was concerned it was a total waste of time and always cost him the element of surprise. He would have rather simply started taking out anyone who showed up with a weapon in his hand. Like it or not, though, he knew that he had to go through with it.

"This is the police!" he shouted. "Throw down your guns and lay on the—"

One of the gunmen spun, the muzzle of his Uzi looking for the voice, and Lyons didn't hesitate. The hammer of his Colt Python was already cocked back for a smooth, single-action first shot, and he stroked the trigger. The bellow of the .357 as it rocked back in his hand was the signal for everyone to open fire.

For a few seconds the only sound in the warehouse was the roar of Able Team's unsilenced weapons. Blancanales's 12-gauge bellowed as it sent its .36 caliber buckshot loads into the gunmen diving for cover. The first two blasts connected and slammed a thug back against the wall, dropping him next to Lyons's victim.

Even though Able Team had had the drop on them, the gunmen reacted like pros. Their salesman leader took cover behind the corner of the office cubicle and immediately brought his subgun into play. Since the Uzi was silenced, Lyons only knew that he was being fired upon when he heard the 9 mm slugs tearing into the wall beside him.

Spinning, he caught the muzzle-flashes of the Uzi and triggered two snap shots in that direction before diving out of the line of fire. Neither one of his rounds connected, and another silenced burst sent chips from the concrete floor beside him.

Up on the mezzanine, Schwarz leaned over the walkway one-handed and dumped a half magazine from his CAR-15 into the plywood wall of the office cubicle. The high-velocity 5.56 mm rounds punched through the ply as if it were paper and found the salesman crouched on the other side.

He staggered out into the open, obviously wounded, but he still had the Uzi hanging at his side. Lyons dropped him with a head shot.

Of the five gunmen by the main door, Lyons had taken out one with his initial shot, and Blancanales had tagged another with his shotgun. But the last three were still in the game, and they were working as a team. Two of them sent a hail of 9 mm bullets at Lyons and Blancanales while the third gunner dashed across the open floor, snapping short bursts from his Uzi.

Schwarz ignored the running man and concentrated his fire on the other two gunmen. Since they were behind a stack of crates, his teammates couldn't get to them. But he could. The CAR-15 chattered at its full eight-hundred-rounds-per-minute cyclic rate, flame blazing from the muzzle brake, as he dumped a full 30-round magazine at the enemy.

The running gunman whirled to bring his Uzi to bear on Schwarz and presented a target to Blancanales. His big 12-gauge roared, and more than half the buckshot load caught the gunner dead center. He went over as though he had been hit with a club and skidded to a halt on the concrete.

Seeing their partner fall, the remaining two gunmen rushed for the door, their silenced weapons blazing. All three Able Team commandos came out from their cover and zeroed in on them. It was over in a split second and the last two gunmen joined their comrades on the floor.

When a quick check showed that all six gunners were dead, Lyons holstered his Python. "Get the lights on, Gadgets," he said. "As long as we're here, we might as well finish checking this place out. I don't think we're going to be interrupted again."

"I'll bring the truck around to the back so we can get out of here if someone heard the shooting."

"Go ahead," the ex-LAPD cop replied. "But like you said, this is L.A. Someone's always shooting around here."

BOLAN RELIEVED Amal after letting the doctor stand guard for only two hours. The warrior was restless, and the short nap on the couch had been all he needed to be back at a hundred percent.

"I'll take the watch for the rest of the night," he told Amal. "It's almost midnight, and I need you to be well rested in the morning so you can take care of the things we talked about."

"Are you sure? You flew in today and you have not had much rest."

"Go ahead and get your sleep," Bolan said. "I'm used to doing this."

Once he was alone, the Executioner prowled the ground floor of the house to refamiliarize himself with the layout in the dark. He had been given a complete tour of the house after explaining his presence to the doctor, but he knew that any building looked different when it was pitch-black.

As he toured, he stopped by each window and, being careful to keep his face far enough away not to be seen, studied the grounds outside from each location. He saw nothing out of the ordinary, but he knew that

El Hakim was already in Portland. He could feel it as surely as if the assassin had sent him a postcard.

After he had familiarized himself with the darkened house, Bolan decided to go outside and recon the grounds. Letting himself out by the back door, he slipped into the wooded area between Amal's house and the grounds of the next residence, a hundred yards farther down the road.

He acquainted himself with his immediate surroundings, then started surveying the area on foot, looking for the most likely approach route for the assassin to take. Since El Hakim had no idea that Amal had been warned of his coming, more than likely he would take the easiest way to the house, the one that would get him under cover and out of sight from passersby the fastest.

When Bolan saw a flash of dim light from the doctor's study, he frowned. If the doctor was looking for something in his den, he would have turned on the overhead light, not used a flashlight. Suddenly he realized that he had left the family unguarded and the assassin had come in behind him from the other side of the house.

Unleathering his Desert Eagle, Bolan sprinted for the house and hoped that he could get back fast enough. It would only take a few seconds for El Hakim to make the hit and be gone.

SCHWARZ HAD BEEN going through the boxes and crates stacked around the floor and shelves for more than a half hour when he spotted a bin full of used packing materials. When the logo printed on a wad of padding caught his eye and looked familiar, he went over to investigate it.

"Ironman!" he shouted when he saw that the logo he had recognized was that of Century Microdyne. "I think these are the goons who knocked over that battery factory in Modesto. I've found some of the company's packing material in a trash can."

"Hal will be glad to hear that," Blancanales said, looking around. "Now if we can find where in the hell they put those damned batteries, we can wrap this up and go home."

An hour later a complete search had failed to turn up the Stinger batteries and Lyons realized that it wasn't over by a long shot. While they had taken out the gang that had massacred the Century Microdyne workers, they had been too late to recover the stolen batteries. He had wanted to keep this simple, but the discovery of the Microdyne packing material ended all chance of that happening. Now he would have to go through the circus of dealing with all the agencies who were looking into the Modesto massacre.

When Lyons was finally doing his thing with the state, city and federal agencies, Schwarz went out to the four-wheel-drive rig and got on the horn to Barbara Price at Stony Man Farm to report the completion of their mission. Since all of the gunmen were dead this time, he hoped she wouldn't order them on another follow-up assignment. As it was, she let them off the hook and said that Brognola wanted to debrief them at the Farm as soon as possible.

BY THE TIME Bolan got close to the house, the light in Amal's den was on, and he saw that his fears had been realized. As he crouched on the lawn outside the window to the den, he saw that El Hakim had got past him, had woken the entire family and had herded them into the room. The daughter was clutching her mother, her face pressed against her hip. Amal looked stunned, but his son kept glancing around as if he was looking for the man who had said that he would protect him. Bolan willed him to calm down and not give him away. As if the boy had read his mind, he turned back to his father.

The warrior had a clear shot from outside the window, but he knew better than to try to shoot El Hakim through the double-paned window glass. It always worked when they did it that way in the movies, but it wasn't the way things worked in real life. The glass might deflect the bullet and prevent him from making the first-round kill he had to in order to save the Amals.

In a hostage situation such as this, the first round had to be good. So, like it or not, he had to go inside the house to take out the assassin.

Pulling back from the window, Bolan jogged around the corner of the house to the back door. Slipping through the unlocked door, he flattened himself against the wall, his Desert Eagle near his right ear in a two-handed stance.

He could hear voices from the den but couldn't make out who was talking or what was being said. More than likely El Hakim was lecturing Amal and his family on the error of their ways that had brought them to their present circumstances. Bolan had noticed that Palestinian terrorists often liked to raise the emotional ante before they made their kills.

It might be good terrorist psychology to talk their victims to death, but it was giving the warrior the time he needed to move into position. He just hoped that Amal had sense enough to keep the hit man talking as long as he possibly could.

The rubber-soled boots made no noise as he slipped down the carpeted hallway toward the den. Now that he was closer, he heard that El Hakim and Amal were speaking Arabic. Mrs. Amal's voice could be heard interjecting every now and then, but most of the conversation was a one-sided tirade from the terrorist.

In his black combat suit, Bolan was all but invisible in the darkened hallway as he inched toward the open door. When he had a clear shot at El Hakim, he stopped.

There was a final shouted exchange, and the assassin turned away to bring his silenced pistol around to bear on Mrs. Amal. Bolan stepped into the light of the open door.

As if sensing the Executioner's presence, El Hakim whirled. But he was too late.

Bolan tripped the trigger of the Desert Eagle, and the .44-caliber slug took El Hakim high in the chest right above his heart and slammed him backward.

For an instant the assassin's eyes went wide with shock as he met the cold blue eyes of his assailant.

"Who are you?" he gasped before the loss of blood shut off his brain.

Mrs. Amal and the children immediately rushed for the doctor and sobbed as they clung to him. He held them to him and murmured soothingly in Arabic. Bolan backed away to let the family have its privacy. Dropping into the chair behind Amal's desk, he reached for the phone.

"Who are you calling?" the doctor asked. "The police?"

"No," Bolan replied, shaking his head. "I'm calling the cleanup crew. You don't want to get involved with the police over this. In the morning all this will be gone." He motioned toward the corpse and the blood seeping into the carpet. "You'll be able to get on with your lives as if it had never happened."

"How do I thank you?" Amal asked sincerely. "I don't even know how to begin."

"Just keep on doing what you've been doing, Doctor. Keep on working for peace in the Middle East and that will be payment enough."

"It seems so little in return for my life and the lives of my family."

"Peace is never something 'little,'" the Executioner said. "It's the most valuable thing in the world and one of the rarest. That is why your work is so valuable."

Amal's eyes went back to El Hakim. "But why don't they want peace?"

"I think you'll have to ask someone else. El Hakim won't be answering any more questions in this life."

CHAPTER NINE

Eastern Pakistan

The hulking sandstone fortress was perched on a jagged outcropping a hundred yards above the barren hills surrounding it. The stone structure told of days long past when men went to war with swords and horses, not with armored vehicles and laser-guided missiles. The brightly colored flag flying from the fortress's main gate announced that the fort was not abandoned, but was still occupied. A closer look revealed that the casemates that had once housed muzzle-loading bronze cannons were now filled with wire-guided antitank missile launchers and heavy machine guns.

The troops on sentry duty atop the battlements wore colorful traditional turbans, but their desert-camouflage battle dress and weapons were as modern as money could buy. So was everything else inside the fort.

Shielded from casual eyes by the massive walls, the interior of the fort wouldn't have looked out of place in many Middle Eastern towns. Tall date palm trees and a cooling fountain in the corner of the courtyard were fed by the spring under the fortress's outcropping. The rooms built onto the insides of the walls were cooled by air conditioners and shielded from the glare of the desert sun by reflective glass in all the windows.

The massive fortress had once been home to hundreds of men and women. Now it was the home of one man, plus his servants and employees, and he used it as his business office. The owner, Ali Noor, considered himself to be a businessman, a dealer in commodities. If someone was willing to pay for something, and if there was a good profit in the deal for him, Noor would provide that item.

He had started his empire by dealing in drugs, always a good commodity in the Middle East. Once he had established himself in that shadowy arena, he branched out into dealing in girls, another commodity that always had a solid market in his part of the world. Then he discovered his real calling, and while he had been fairly well-off before, he soon became quite wealthy—wealthy enough, in fact, to buy the abandoned fortress and convert it into a secure headquarters for running his far-flung financial empire. In his line of work a man needed to be secure.

He had found his ticket to wealth two years earlier when he had been across the border in Afghanistan making arrangements to buy the year's opium-poppy crop from the mountain tribesmen. While in one of their camps he happened upon a cache of U.S.-supplied weapons left over from the CIA's support of the Mujahedeen in their war against the Russians. He bought the weapons along with the poppy resin and immediately turned a handsome profit on both commodities. What surprised him was that he made much more money from the weapons than he did from the opium.

From that humble beginning, he had swiftly expanded that part of his business. Now that the Russians were no longer giving weapons away to anyone who was willing to take them, there was an even greater need for someone to broker arms to the emerging factions all over Africa, the Middle East and the ex-Soviet Asian republics.

There was no shortage of international arms dealers trying to work that particular market, but most of them were from the West. Since many of the peoples who were in the market for weapons were Muslims, as was Noor himself, he had an instant in with them that the traditional Western arms dealers would never have.

Also, he didn't demand payment in hard currencies for his goods as did the Western dealers. Revolutionary groups and provisional governments were always short of hard currency, and Noor would take drugs, girls, raw gold, precious stones or anything of value in trade for his weapons. This also gave him an advantage over the Westerners, whose governments didn't consider opium or underage girls to be legitimate currency. Even more important, Noor's drug-smuggler contacts gave him an established network of deliverymen who were experienced with crossing national borders without drawing attention from the border guards and customs authorities.

The arms business had been very good to Ali Noor, and he expected that it would only get better. Peace in his part of the world was less likely now than it had been at any time in the past fifty years, and he expected to do well from the turmoil.

AS NOOR SAT at his desk one morning, putting together an arms deal, the door to his private office slammed open. He looked up to see a tall, golden-eyed Iranian storm into the room, accompanied by a half-dozen cold-eyed fighters in well-worn, dusty battle dress.

"You are Ali Noor," the Iranian stated as he walked up to the startled man. "A follower of the Prophet and a dealer of drugs, whores and weapons."

"I am Noor, yes," the dealer said humbly. "How may I be of service to you?"

"It is not me who demands your service," the Iranian said sharply. "But God."

Noor froze. Only the fanatic followers of Iran's ayatollahs dared to speak for God in that manner. And anything they wanted of him had to be bad news. Nonetheless, he bowed his head, less in submission to the will of God than to the AKs in the hands of the Iranian's bodyguards. He was wise enough to know that if he tried to run they would cut him down.

"What does God, blessed be his holy name, require of me?"

"I am Major Inman Fuad," the Iranian introduced himself, "and I bring a message for you from the leaders of the Islamic Party. You have been a disgrace to your faith all of your miserable life, but a merciful God has granted you a chance to redeem yourself in his eyes."

Noor was careful to keep the sarcasm out of his voice. "And what is it that I must do to receive this grace?"

"God is displeased with the way that his people have been treated in this part of the world. But as long as they are poor and weak, they cannot regain the rightful place here that he intended them to have. You are going to help his holy rule become established again in Pakistan and Northern India. To do that, though, a war must start, and the Hindus must be provoked into starting it."

Noor knew what those provocations would be—Indians killed by Muslims—and he shuddered. He considered himself to be a good follower of the Prophet, but he wasn't a fanatic. He had no particular dislike of the Hindus. In fact, he dealt in his commodities with many of them. Along with some of the better poppy resin, a large percentage of his best girls came from impoverished rural villages in Northern India.

His Indian agents bought delicate, sloe-eyed girls from their farmer parents and passed them on to Noor, who trained them and then sent them on to his customers around the Persian Gulf and Africa. Now that China was opening up again, he had recently sent a shipment of older Indian girls to Shanghai, where they had fetched a very good price from newly wealthy Chinese merchants seeking exotic concubines.

Even though he wanted no part of this mad scheme to start a war, he knew only too well that this was a deal he couldn't turn down. The Iranian ayatollahs who were apparently behind this madness considered anyone who was not on their side to be their enemy. Were he to refuse to do exactly as he was told, the Iranian major's cold-eyed killers with their sparkling-clean weapons would make short work of him on the spot.

"I hear and obey," Noor said, bowing again.

"You are much wiser than I was led to believe." Fuad didn't even try to keep the contempt from his voice.

In his years of promoting his party's strict policies, the Iranian had been required to work with many people he wouldn't otherwise have associated with. But this fat pimp and drug runner who didn't even know his father was the lowest of the low. Nonetheless, he had connections that no one else in Pakistan and India had. But once his usefulness had come to an end, his foulness would be cleansed from God's new lands, as would the foulness of so many others. God required purity in his domains.

"And just how am I, a mere dealer in drugs, women and guns, supposed to bring these great events to pass?"

"You are not," Fuad replied. "Your job will be to use your contacts and agents to buy every last Stinger antiaircraft missile you can find, regardless of the cost. The missiles will be brought here, where they will be checked over before I issue them to be used."

Noor wasn't pleased to hear that he had to get into the Stinger business just to keep his head on his shoulders. For all the commodities he dealt in, he had never touched the American-made missiles. He knew better than to get involved with them, as they were too high profile. The Intelligence services of several nations were in the Stinger-purchasing business, and he didn't want to bring that kind of attention to himself and his enterprises. The weapons he sold were nothing that anyone cared about.

"I will get started on that right away," Noor said.

"Good." Fuad smiled for the first time. "You understand your position."

The deal included Noor's having to turn his fortress and all of its facilities, including his staff, over to Fuad. Until further notice the Iranian would be his second-in-command and chief security adviser. In return the Iranian would move in three dozen crack Islamic Guard troops and enough heavy weaponry to defend the fortress against anything short of a battalion-size assault.

When Noor protested that the additional troops and weaponry might draw unwanted attention to his affairs, Fuad reassured him that it wouldn't. "There will be no government interference," he promised. "Key people in the Pakistan defense ministry are with us, and they have control of the army in this province. There will be no interference in my—I mean your—activities."

If that was the case, Noor had no option but to do exactly what he was told. Letting the army know of his uninvited guests, as he had planned, would only bring more trouble down on his own head.

AS SOON AS THE IRANIANS were established in Noor's fortress, Major Fuad became a silent partner in his business. With the AK-toting guards backing him up, the Iranian oversaw every deal he put together. When Noor's men went out to make a deal, one of the Iranians went with them. Fuad himself accompanied the team that went to the meeting in Afghanistan where two CIA men had been invited. Their deaths shocked Noor and drove home the fact that his position was particularly dangerous. The CIA had a long memory, and now he was sure to be on their list.

The only good part of the partnership was that beyond providing room and board for the Iranians, Noor wasn't required to share his profits with the ayatollahs in Tehran. Their profits on the deal would come when the war they were working toward devastated Pakistan and Northern India and new Islamic "republics" could be born out of the rubble.

Spreading their version of Islam didn't seem like much of a profit to Noor, but then, religion wasn't a commodity he traded in. He had found that while there was always some demand for it, it was far too volatile a commodity, and a man couldn't count on repeat business. With guns, drugs and girls, however, the customers always came back for more.

The only real down side was that at night the Iranians helped themselves to the girls Noor had in training. When he protested that he needed to keep the virgins intact so they would bring higher prices, Fuad told him that his Islamic warriors needed to use the girls so that their fighting spirits wouldn't be impaired by sluggish seed.

There was nothing the arms dealer could reply to that.

IT TOOK NOOR almost a month to get the first of the Stingers into the fortress, far longer than Major Fuad liked. As soon as Noor had put out a call for the missiles, he had unintentionally created a feeding frenzy in the Afghan Mujahedeen bands. The price quickly went up and no discounts were given for buying in quantity. Eventually the missiles were purchased, and it was only when the first of them arrived at his stronghold that a problem showed up.

The Iranians had provided a French-educated electronic technician to service the weapons and check them over before they were sent out. He soon discovered that most of the missiles weren't fully functional. The compact, high-voltage batteries that powered the Stinger's guidance and tracking systems were long past their service life and had lost their efficiency. Without the guidance systems working properly, the missiles were almost useless.

Unlike the simpler heat-seeking missiles that just locked on to the greatest heat source in the sky and followed it, the Stinger also had an additional ultraviolet spectra guidance feature. This system prevented the missile from being decoyed by an aircraft dropping flares that were hotter than the plane's engine exhausts.

What this feature did was to search the sky along the line of sight of the IR-seeking head and determine if a large body such as an aircraft was blocking the ultraviolet radiation of the sun. If there was, the system told the IR-seeking head to lock on and fire. If, however, there was no body blocking out a part of the sky, it told the missile-guidance system to ignore that heat source and keep looking for another target.

This additional feature was what made the Stinger more deadly than other shoulder-fired antiaircraft missiles, such as the Russian-designed Strella and the British Blowpipe. It couldn't be decoyed by flares or the sun. It was also, however, a feature that made the Stingers much more dependent upon their having fresh batteries to power the systems.

Until the technician examined the newly purchased Stinger missiles and ran the maintenance tests on them, no one had even given a thought to the age of the batteries. Of the eighteen missiles that had been procured, only four were new enough that their batteries still held a full charge. Because of the design of the tracking housing, only the original shaped batteries could be used, and the only source for them was in the United States of America.

Even though the Iranian major promised that a new supply of batteries would be secured as soon as possible, Noor was no longer convinced that the Iranian's plan was foolproof. And if it wasn't, maybe there was a way he could get free of this unholy alliance that had been forced on him. He carefully started preparing a plan to abandon his holdings in Pakistan and transfer everything he could to his Moroccan office.

Meanwhile, the major had decided to issue the four serviceable missiles and at least get started, rather than wait for the batteries before putting his plan into action. Of the Stingers that were sent out, three had been fired, resulting in the two downed Indian planes and the one Pakistani airliner crash. The fourth missile was being held in reserve in case another incident was needed to keep the crisis from dying down before the new batteries could be secured.

WHILE HE WAITED for the batteries to arrive from the United States, Noor continued to buy up all the Stingers he could get his hands on. The problem was that the well was running dry. Though the Afghan tribesmen lived a primitive life, even for their part of the world, they weren't without their sources of information about the world outside their barren hills and valleys. It wasn't as fast as CNN, but it was just as effective.

When the Afghan leaders learned that the missiles were being used to kill women and children, many of them took their Stingers off the market. And for all his wealth, Noor wasn't able to get them to part with them.

Major Fuad wasn't happy that Noor was having difficulties. But, as the arms dealer pointed out, the Mujahedeen had minds of their own.

CHAPTER TEN

Shenandoah Valley

Yakov Katzenelenbogen rode through the Blue Ridge Mountains with Rafael Encizo in Calvin James's Land Rover. The black ex-SEAL had first come across these British four-wheel-drive vehicles during an operation with Phoenix Force and had come to appreciate their old-fashioned, rugged dependability. Any modern four-wheel-drive rig rode better and was more practical than a Land Rover, but no other had the character of the old British vehicle.

"I wonder what hellhole Hal's sending us into this time," James asked rhetorically.

Even though he was the youngest member of Phoenix Force, he had learned long ago that it didn't pay to try to second-guess the mission before he received the briefing. Nonetheless, he still couldn't resist wanting to know where and how he would be putting his life on the line again.

"Whatever it is," Katzenelenbogen grumbled, "you can be sure that it will be something that someone else should have taken care of months ago. And had they done it back then, it could have been taken care of with half the trouble."

The Phoenix Force leader's long years of fighting terrorists and other destroyers of civilization had given him a rather jaundiced outlook on life, particularly when it came to the politicians and governments who failed to do the things that were necessary to ensure that their people could live in peace and security. Of the many battles he had fought, most of them could have been easily prevented had the governments involved simply done what needed to be done in order to take care of the problem before it got out of hand.

But if they had been handled that way, there would have been no need for the specialized talents that had been brought together under his command.

The men of Phoenix Force were the best operatives that the Western world had to offer. Each man had the standard experience and specialized talents that one would expect to find in members of elite antiterrorist units. But each had something else as well—a dedication that went far beyond the mere call of duty.

DAVID MCCARTER AND Gary Manning were plugged into the intercom with Jack Grimaldi as the Bell Jet Ranger chopper flew low over the Blue Ridge Mountains north of the Farm. They weren't traveling with their Phoenix Force teammates because they had been mountain climbing in Manning's native Canada when they received Barbara Price's message. Grimaldi had flown north, picked them off a mountaintop and was now flying them back to the Farm.

"Stony Base," Grimaldi called on the skip-frequency scrambler used to secure all communications with the Farm. "This is the Flyboy. I'm inbound with my beeper on and requesting clearance to land."

"Roger, Flyboy," came the answer as soon as his message cleared through the voiceprint analysis. "We've had you on the scope for the past fifteen mikes. Conditions are green, SOP in effect. You are clear to land."

The last part of the message told him that the Farm wasn't under an alert and that he could set the chopper down without being tracked by the antiaircraft defenses and blown out of the sky if he made a wrong move.

"Roger," he sent back. "We're on the way in."

The dirt landing strip that cut through the farm looked like any well-to-do farmer's strip. But like everything else at Stony Man, appearances were deceiving. Under the dirt, grass and camouflage was a concrete runway long enough to land jet fighters. When Grimaldi set the aircraft down on the helicopter landing pad, he cut the fuel to the turbines, sat back and grinned. "Home sweet home."

Even though the Farm was not under an alert, a Jeep full of blacksuits met the chopper. As soon as the pilot and the Phoenix Warriors stepped out, they quickly went over the machine to ensure that it was not carrying any unwanted packages. Particularly explosive or tracer beacon packages. When the chopper was declared to be clean, it was towed over to the fuel tanks to be serviced.

Another Jeep had pulled up to transport the passengers and pilot to the farmhouse. Moments later, Grimaldi, Manning and McCarter were in the basement War Room. Mack Bolan ended his quiet conversation with Katzenelenbogen and nodded to them.

The other two Phoenix Force warriors, Rafael Encizo and Calvin James, were laboring over the tray of sandwich fixings and pastries that had been laid out on the table by the coffee service. Grimaldi immediately joined them. Flying down from Canada had given him an appetite. McCarter and Manning followed him.

Barbara Price walked into the room and went immediately to Bolan and Katzenelenbogen. "Hal's on the ground."

"Good," Katz replied. "Now we can get this show on the road."

She smiled. "In the air, you mean."

"Where are we going?" Bolan asked.

"You know the drill," she answered. "You have to wait for him to tell you."

"How about a hint?" He grinned.

"You won't need your arctic mittens."

"Damn, I just got them out of the cleaners."

EVEN THOUGH IT HAD BEEN only a few days since she had last seen him, Barbara Price noticed that Hal Brognola didn't look as dapper when he walked into the War Room. Apparently the crisis was heating up and his feet were being held to the fire to produce some tangible results.

Brognola nodded to each of the men as he walked to the end of the table and took his seat. "Okay," he said around the well-chewed cigar clamped in one side of his mouth. "The subject today is Afghan war surplus Stinger missiles in the hands of the bad guys in Pakistan and India.

"Most of you know this story already, but bear with me because I'm going to go through the whole thing. This twisted story has taken a few new twists lately that you might not be aware of.

"In the aftermath of the Soviet pullout from Afghanistan in 1989, some genius in the upper levels of the CIA realized that it would probably be a good idea to try to get the Stingers they had given the freedom fighters back under American control. They could see that having all those missiles in the hands of people who were seriously talking about creating another Iranian-style Islamic republic was an invitation to disaster. Unfortunately, though, the CIA's Stinger buy-back program has failed miserably.

"When it was first set up, they were authorized to offer sixty-eight thousand dollars per missile. They picked up a few at that price, but damned few. The offer was then raised to seventy-five thousand, but with terrorists and nationalists offering up to a quarter million each, it still didn't work as planned. Too many of them were appearing on the open market."

He stopped to take a red-striped folder from his open briefcase. "Even so, in the past couple of years we have been able to head off buys from the Medellín cartel, Iran, the IRA and various factions in what's left of Yugoslavia. As with any black-market commodity, though, for every buy we blocked, God only knows how many went through without our knowing anything about it.

"Everyone here knows that the Rwanda situation was kicked off when the plane carrying its head of state was shot down by a Stinger. A few months earlier a Stinger in Bosnian Serb hands took out an Italian transport ferrying humanitarian aid into Sarajevo. Then there have been the more recent airliner shootdowns in India and Pakistan.

"Primarily as a result of these last two incidents, the President ordered the CIA to step up its efforts to get the missiles back under American control. A couple of days ago two CIA agents on a buy-back mission in the Afghan border country were murdered and their bodies thrown across the Pakistan border with their throats slit. The word from the Mujis has it that an Iranian was responsible."

Brognola's eyes swept the conference table slowly. "The Man now wants all the stops pulled out. He wants these things either destroyed or back under our control, particularly the ones in the Indian-Pakistani area. And he wants it done before they're used to start a nuclear war on the Indian subcontinent.

"Even if you succeed, though, it won't mean that the religious strife in Northern India is going to end. The war between the Muslims and Hindus has been going on for over six hundred years, and not even you guys can put an end to a history of hatred like that. What you can do, though, is bring the level of combat back down to what it was before the Stingers were dealt into the game and buy us a little more time to try to get them to back down.

"The President is working hard to reduce the number of countries who have the bomb, and is concentrating on India and Pakistan. He's pressing Pakistan to dismantle its weapons program at the same time that he is trying to talk India into signing the nonproliferation treaty. But he can't make any headway, though, if they're rattling nuclear warheads at each other, like they are at the moment.

"The Pakistanis claim that they haven't assembled any weapons yet. However, it's believed that they have manufactured the components and the delivery systems for a dozen weapons. All they need are a few hours to put them together and they, too, can become a full-fledged player in the mushroom-cloud game. And as we all know, India has almost fifty nuclear weapons ready and waiting to be launched."

"So where do we come in?" Manning asked.

"Well, the bottom line is that we have to get this situation under control as fast as we can. And the key to doing that is to take the Stingers out of action before they can be used in any more provocative incidents. The President wants you in Pakistan as soon as possible. From there, he wants you to go to the source, Afghanistan, and do what has to be done to take them completely out of the picture."

David McCarter leaned back in his chair. "The Man doesn't happen to have an address for the nearest Stingers 'R' Us outlet, does he?"

"If he did," Brognola replied, "he wouldn't have sent me down here to jack my jaws at you people."

"But why only the Stingers?" James asked. "They're not the only shoulder-fired antiaircraft missiles out there. The Russians have given away hundreds of their Strellas, and the Brits have handed their Blowpipes out like peanuts. What's the big deal?"

"The big deal is that the Stingers were manufactured in America. Anytime one of them causes a loss of life, the United States gets blamed for it. And when we are considered to be the source of the problem, it makes it difficult for the President to bring the power of his office to bear on the warring factions to try to get them to back down from Armageddon."

Brognola turned to Hunt Wethers, who had been invited to the session. "If there are no more questions, Hunt will follow me with the results of his research into the threat level we are facing."

The tall, distinguished black man had been a professor of advanced cybernetics at Berkeley before Kurtzman invited him to join the Stony Man team. His years behind the lectern hadn't left him as he stood and walked to the podium. He looked and sounded like a college professor.

"I've been working on determining the danger level of this latest outbreak of religious violence in Northern India. We don't have a Richter scale for this sort of thing, but by running through news articles and the editorials in both Pakistani and Indian magazines and newspapers for the past month, we can get a pretty good feel for public sentiment."

He paused and flipped open the folder in front of him. "The way I see it, India and Pakistan are closer to going to war now than at any time since the shooting ended in their last war in 1971. In fact, the common man on the street in both nations will probably express even more interest in going to war than he would have back then. The difference, of course, is due to the recent rise in Islamic fundamentalism in Pakistan and the corresponding rebirth of Hindu religious extremists.

"Gentlemen, you will be going into a caldron that might boil over at any moment. It's always difficult to mathematically predict the behavior of humans, but I think that it's safe to say that one more serious incident on either side will be enough to set it off. Because of that, you cannot use a cover story that connects you to the United States in any way. The Islamic factions in both countries hate us, and the Indian population feels that we haven't treated them as if a worthy ally."

He looked over at Manning and grinned. "Your mission cover will be that of a Canadian oil-company survey team. Everyone likes the Canadians. They spend almost as much money as Americans, they drink more and are less likely to complain about the food and the sanitation. Also, they are more likely to go to someplace like Pakistan simply because they haven't been there before. Any Americans in Pakistan right now are likely to be involved with the drug trade, and you don't need the local police authorities following you around waiting for you to make a buy."

When Wethers returned to his seat, Brognola stood again. "Striker," he said, turning to Bolan, "I'd like you to go in first as the advance party."

The warrior nodded and turned to Kurtzman. "Do you have any specific targets for us?"

"Not yet," he said. "The CIA worked the last firm lead we had, and they lost the two operatives they put on it. I'm running through everything we have, and I'm even getting information from the Russians to try to develop something. But right now I can't point you to anyone or anything specific."

Like it or not, and he sure as hell didn't, Bolan had to accept that. If the Bear couldn't dig up anything specific, no one could. That meant that they would have to start cold.

He turned back to Brognola. "What kind of support can we count on from the U.S. military?"

"Absolutely nothing," Brognola replied. "The situation is so critical that even the appearance of American intervention in either nation might set it off. You'll be completely on your own."

Bolan nodded and glanced at Katzenelenbogen. The Israeli warrior's face was expressionless. This wouldn't be the first time, nor would it be the last, that Phoenix Force would be laying it on the line with nothing between themselves and annihilation except their wits and skills in the always chancy game of international intrigue.

Brognola shut his briefcase. "Barbara has your mission packets. You'll be leaving tomorrow morning. Good luck, gentlemen, and find those Stingers."

CHAPTER ELEVEN

Stony Man Farm

Mack Bolan had just finished unpacking his travel bag and was laying out his shaving gear when a sharp rap on the door made him turn.

"Come."

Aaron Kurtzman, nicknamed "the Bear," rolled his wheelchair into the room and braked to a stop. The burly computer genius looked grim. "I think you're heading into a real shitstorm this time, Mack."

"What do you know that wasn't mentioned in the briefing?"

"Like I said, I don't have anything specific," he admitted. "But Hunt's not the only one who can feel the tension building over there. It's been a long time, over twenty years, since the Indians and Pakistanis last went at it and they're like the Arabs and Israelis. They need a war every now and then so they'll always have a new generation of martyrs to mourn, and they won't be able to forget their differences. It's been too long since blood was last shed to slake that particular perverse thirst."

Bolan smiled at his old friend. "You're worrying, Aaron. How unlike you."

The big man spun his wheelchair to face out the third-story window of the farmhouse. The verdant greens of the Blue Ridge Mountains usually calmed him, but not this time. Instead of peaceful forests, all he could see was enemies hiding in ambush behind the trees.

"It's the fundamentalists on both sides who worry me. The Islamic radicals are as brutal as any barbarians who have ever lived on the planet, and the Hindu extremists are not a hell of a lot better. Both factions are praying for a war to break out so they can drown each other in blood again."

He shook his head. "And this is one of the few times that I believe in the power of prayer. Only when prayer is given in the face of evil does it work. The rest of the time, God usually has his call-waiting switched on."

"Don't tell me that you've taken up the arcane art of theology? You're going to look good in a handwoven monk's robe and tonsure, but I'm not too sure that you're going to do well chanting praises to God."

Kurtzman let a wry smile cross his face as he spun to face his friend again. "In this case, theology is actually a good source of information for that part of the world. I listen to those who are claiming to speak for Lord Rama and then I listen to those claiming to speak for God, and all I hear are cries for war and death to the unbeliever, whomever he might be. All it tells me is that it's going to get a lot worse over there before it gets any better.

"Then," he added, "there's the Afghan connection you're going to have to deal with. We keep getting reports that the Stingers are finally coming out of Afghanistan, and if you want to cut the supply off at the source like the Man wants, you're going to have to go there to do it."

"What's new with the Afghan situation?"

"Where do you want me to start?" Kurtzman shook his head. "That place is much worse off now than it was even during the darkest days of the Soviet war. At least back then the tribal factions spent some of their time killing Russians instead of slaughtering each other. Now that Ivan has finally gone home, they get to concentrate full-time on butchering each other. And I must say that they've been doing a very good job of it. More people have been killed since the Russians left than were killed during the war.

"Plus, the radical Islamic fundamentalist elements are in almost complete control of the country now. The Iranian-backed Islamic Party is the biggest, best armed and most radical of a very mixed bag of fundamentalist political groups. It looks like they're finally on the verge of taking over the entire country. There's virtually no civilian government operating there now, no legitimate economy to speak of and no civil law at all. It's an outlaw nation and their only source of income comes from growing poppy for heroin, gun smuggling and running the Middle East's biggest concentration of terrorist training camps. We have identified over twenty camps between Kabul and the Khyber Pass, and they're all under the control of the Islamic Party. The numbers of men they are training staggers the mind."

Bolan knew most of this already, but he let his friend continue without interruption. He knew that Kurtzman often did his best thinking while he was talking, and the Executioner wanted the benefit of his thinking on this explosive situation.

"Since the Afghans were the first Muslim people to defeat a Western army since the sixteenth century, they have revolutionary credentials that no other Islamic nation has, not even Iran. Recruits from all over the Middle East and Europe are flocking to them for training, and they are being well trained and well equipped at what is being called in the media the 'Jihad University.'

"The biggest threat is not that they are merely training terrorists. The problem is that they're exporting the bastards after they have been trained and armed. It's kind of like the Afghans are running a worldwide employment service for terrorism and Islamic *jihad.*"

"Aren't the Afghans behind the Islamic-fundamentalist uprisings in Egypt and Algeria?" Bolan prompted him.

Kurtzman nodded. "They've also been sending men into Bosnia, the ex-Soviet Muslim republics, Azerbaijan and even into the Muslim areas of China. Not even Khaddafi or the PLO has exported as many terrorists as they have, and there's no end to it in sight."

"Do you think the Afghans are behind the Indian and Pakistani problem?" Bolan asked.

Kurtzman nodded. "Even though the airline shootdowns were claimed by home-grown fanatics, there's a good possibility that they were at least armed, if not trained, as well, by the Afghan Islamic Party people. Also, the deaths of those two CIA agents in an Afghan camp points out the strength of the radical element. Usually when the Mujahedeen leaders offer to talk to someone, they guarantee safety until the meeting is over. Those two men were murdered in violation of the traditional Afghan rules of hospitality."

"I thought Hal said that an Iranian was responsible."

"An Iranian of the Islamic Party, yes. But what that shows is that the fundamentalists are strong enough to overturn the old ways in the name of *jihad.*"

Kurtzman shook his head. "Anyway, I'll pull together a briefing folder with some names and profiles from the good old days that you should look over before you move out. I'm including a laundry list of the principal bad actors, as well as a few men that you might be able to call upon for help. You'll have to step carefully, but you might be able to work up a lead from some of the names."

He glanced down at his watch. "And, speaking of that, I need to get going on it again. I'll have it done in a couple of hours."

"I'll see you then."

As soon as Kurtzman wheeled his way out, Bolan lay down on the bed for a short nap before dinner. The Bear's prophecy of doom and gloom didn't bother him. If the situation weren't critical, the President wouldn't have called them in to take care of it. As the old saying went, "The difficult we do immediately, the impossible takes a little longer." This time, though, there might not be that "little longer" that so often turned the tide in their favor. There was never enough time when nuclear weapons were in the equation.

Nonetheless, as they always did, they would try and they would do their best. Beyond that, it was up to the gods Kurtzman had been talking about.

IN NOOR'S FORTRESS in eastern Pakistan, Major Inman Fuad read the message that had just come in over Noor's fax machine. Even though it was situated in a remote location, one of the advantages of operating out of the arms dealer's headquarters was that he had all the modern business conveniences, such as satellite communications links and fax machines.

According to the message from the Islamic Party agents in the United States, the Stinger batteries were finally on their way from Mexico City with an air shipment of electronic parts manifested for Singapore. Once they arrived there, they would be separated from the rest of the shipment and sent on to Islamabad, where they would be picked up by Fuad's agents. Within days of their arriving at Noor's fortress, the final phase of the plan could finally be put into operation.

The Islamic Party's plan was actually simple, if killing unsuspecting civilians by the hundreds could be called simple. This time the deadly missiles would be smuggled deep into India and would be targeted at some of the nation's largest airports. Though the missiles had a range of several miles, the plan was to shoot down the airliners right before they touched down at an airport or right after they had taken off. This would cause the flaming wreckage to slam down into densely populated areas and cause an even greater loss of life. After each crash a spokesman for one of the Indian Muslim radical groups would claim responsibility for the tragedy.

It wouldn't take many of those incidents before the Indian people would force their government to put a stop to the radicals, and the resulting action would have to be military in nature. Nothing else would be acceptable to a Hindu population that was mourning their dead in the hundreds.

As had happened in both 1965 and 1971, Pakistan's relatively small army wouldn't be able to withstand the Indian military juggernaut. Bhutto's government would immediately collapse and the radicals in the military would take over the country. At that point Pakistan would unleash its nuclear arsenal. Though the government didn't have the number of warheads that India had, it had a better delivery system and its first targets would be the Indian missile-launch sites. Once those were neutralized, the three warheads targeted at New Delhi, Bombay and Calcutta would be detonated.

Several years earlier the United States had moved to keep the Pakistanis from obtaining delivery systems for their nuclear warheads, but that wouldn't matter now. A secret, elite group of Pakistani air-force pilots, known as the Eagles of Jihad, had been formed to deliver the warheads. These aerial Islamic warriors would deliver the nukes with their F-16 fighter jets in suicide missions. Their small fighters, flying close to the ground at supersonic speeds, would be almost impossible to detect and successfully intercept.

But even if they achieved complete surprise with their initial attacks, it wasn't expected that Pakistan would escape completely unscathed from the Indian counterstrike. It was expected that at least Islamabad, and possibly Lahore, would be destroyed by Indian nuclear weapons. Tens of thousands of Pakistanis would die, but that would be a small price to pay to liberate the Muslim peoples of Pakistan and Northern India. Out of the rubble of the greatest holy war of all time would be born bright new Islamic states as the Muslims of the region took back their sacred heritage.

It was a bold plan, but it was one that had no chance of failure. The Great Satan, the United States, wouldn't dare to become involved in a situation where its forces might be exposed to nuclear weapons. The Americans were a decadent people, and they were cowards, as had been proved most recently in Somalia. If a ragtag army of a few hundred men armed with castoffs could rout several thousand well-armed American Marines and Rangers, the Yankees wouldn't even try to come in on the side of the Indians.

The United Nations would also be powerless to block the will of the Muslim people of Pakistan and Northern India. Their so-called International Peacekeepers were even greater cowards than the Americans. Their pale blue helmets made good targets in Bosnia, Croatia, Lebanon and a dozen other places. If they dared to come to Pakistan, they would become helpless targets again. The time had finally come for the Islamic Party to lead the Muslim world to greatness again, and nothing would be allowed to stand in the way.

The fax message also mentioned that the Islamic Party's L.A. operation had been raided by the police the day after the batteries had been sent south, and that there had been no survivors. Fuad had expected something like that to happen sooner or later and put no importance to it.

It was the will of God.

The L.A. operation had served its purpose, and now that the Stinger batteries were on the way, it would have been shut down, anyway.

CHAPTER TWELVE

Peshawar, Pakistan

It was late morning when Mack Bolan walked through the crowded marketplace in the center of Peshawar, Pakistan. It had taken him two days to get from Washington, D.C., to Islamabad, and several hours more on a commuter flight to get to the border town. Yakov Katzenelenbogen and the rest of Phoenix Force were still in the air and were due in later that day, but now that he was on the ground, the Executioner wanted to start putting his feelers out. After checking into the hotel and reserving rooms for the rest of the team, he decided to hit the bricks.

The stakes were as high as they could be this time, and so was his sense of urgency about the mission. If they failed to locate and neutralize the Stingers the terrorists were using to kill airliners, Northern India and Pakistan would become a battleground again. This time, though, it would be a nuclear battleground with the resultant devastation and horrendous loss of life.

But even with this urgency, there was precious little information for Bolan to work with. All he could do was to try to develop Kurtzman's idea that the Afghan Islamic Party was somehow involved. And the first thing he needed to do to work that angle was to try to activate one of his old contacts from the Russian-Afghan war days and see if the man could give him a lead. Or at least point him in the right direction.

The man he wanted to see first was a former Afghan freedom fighter who, like so many of his countrymen, now lived in exile in Peshawar. He had once been the leader of one of the CIA's more reliable guerrilla groups during the war, but he had fallen out with the radical leaders who took over after the Russians fled, and he had been forced to flee himself. Kurtzman said that he had been reported to be running a small tea shop off Peshawar's main bazaar as recently as six months ago. It wasn't exactly a recent sighting, but it was worth checking out.

It had been some time since Bolan had been in this part of the world, and the sights and smells of the bazaar hit him like a hammer. The pungent smells of dried spices, freshly butchered meat, charcoal cooking fires, donkey dung and closely packed humanity gave the marketplace an aroma one could only find in the Middle East. The crowd was also uniquely Middle Eastern and not all of the shoppers were Pakistani. At least a third of them wore traditional Afghan dress.

Even though it had been over five years since the end of the Afghan-Soviet War, the Western frontier town of Peshawar was still crowded with Afghan refugees, some of whom had been in the camps for more than ten years. Originally they had fled from the initial invasion of their homeland by the Red Army, but now they were being kept away from their homes by the factional fighting that had taken the place of the war against the Russians.

International refugee-aid organizations had tried to bring some order to the chaos caused by tens of thousands of refugees crossing the border and descending on Peshawar, but they had not been entirely successful. It had been hoped that once the Russians withdrew, the Afghans would be able to return to their own lands, but that hope had proved to be hollow. And there was no way of knowing when, if ever, they would leave the camps in Pakistan.

With his height and broad shoulders parting the crowd, Bolan made his way through the bazaar to a side street off the main plaza. Since street numbers weren't a feature of most Middle Eastern towns, he had to check each shop before he spotted what he thought was his man.

Under the awning across the front of the small but tidy shop, a middle-aged, bearded man in traditional Afghan clothing sat on a hassock smoking a cigarette. This was Ahmed Jamillur, the man Bolan had hoped to find. Once more Kurtzman's roving electronic eyes had proved to be accurate.

Jamillur smiled widely when Bolan walked into view. "I see that a merciful God, may his holy name always be praised, has let you live, my friend."

"He has smiled on me," Bolan replied as he glanced around the small shop. "And I see that he has allowed you to prosper, as well as live. This is a long way from the mountains overlooking Kabul."

"That it is." Jamillur shrugged. "But no man can tell what his fate will be. That is in the hands of God." The Afghan bowed his head. "It has been given to me that I would become a humble shopkeeper. It has also been given to me that I am to have another wife and even more children."

"You have been truly blessed," Bolan replied. Jamillur's first wife and two of his children had been killed in a Soviet Hind gunship attack on his camp during the war. Another son, his eldest, had been killed later in the fighting.

"Come inside where it is cool and we will talk of the old days."

"I would like that."

As was always the case in the Middle East, refreshments came before business. Jamillur clapped his hands and a young girl came out bearing a silver tea service. She was only about eleven or twelve, but Bolan could see the Afghan beauty she would someday become. He made no comment, though. In the Middle East a man of good breeding didn't comment on another man's female relatives.

After the tea was served, the girl left the two men to their business. After two sips, Bolan set his teacup down. Now that he had taken the customary refreshment from his host, he could talk about why he was in Peshawar. "I am here on business again."

Jamillur studied the warrior for a long moment. "I am not surprised, my friend. You are a man whose business will never end. How can I be of service to you this time? To be sure, I no longer have my ear to the pulse of my poor country as I once did, but I am not completely without my resources."

The man's understatement made Bolan smile. The old Afghan warrior's "resources" would probably put the intelligence services of many Western nations to shame. In a land where family and business connections could spread over several nations, his ears and eyes were big. That, of course, was why he had looked him up.

"You have heard, of course," Bolan began, "about the recent incidents in India and Pakistan where the airliners were shot down."

"I know about them." Jamillur nodded gravely. "But I wish that I did not. It is shameful to make war on helpless women and children that way. Even though two of the airplanes were killed in the name of my faith, as a follower of Islam I am deeply ashamed to have any connection with it."

"You won't mind helping me put an end to this, then?" Bolan asked. Even though he had worked with the Afghan before, in the Middle East, matters of religion dominated everything, including friendship, so he had to move carefully.

"I will help you," Jamillur said firmly, "even though I know that you will cause the deaths of many of my fellow believers. If you promise to put an end to this insult to Islam, I will do anything I can to help you."

"Thank you, Ahmed. I wouldn't have asked you were it not extremely important. I'm trying to keep the fanatics from causing a war to break out. A renewed war with India will kill thousands of people on both sides, Muslim and Hindu alike."

"I will help you. The problem, though, is that while I hear many things about the fanatics both here and back in Afghanistan, I do not hear the details of their doings."

"The only detail I need to hear about," Bolan said, "is where they're getting the missiles they used to bring those planes down. My mission is to take these weapons back under American control before more planes are shot down and a war is started."

"Blessed are the peacemakers," Jamillur mused.

"We need all the peacemakers we can get this time," Bolan told him. "Someone wants the war to be nuclear this time, and that's why it's so important that I find out where those missiles are being held."

"That will be a difficult thing to learn, but I have heard one thing that might be helpful in this quest. Do you know of the two countrymen of yours who were killed in Afghanistan and their bodies dumped back across the border?"

Bolan nodded. "They were CIA men trying to buy back missiles."

"I know," Jamillur said. "They were to meet with certain Mujahedeen leaders who had claimed to have some of the Stingers in their possession. Once they were there, though, they were shamefully killed."

"Do you know who these leaders are?"

"I know one of them," Jamillur admitted, "and I know where his main camp is. If he has the Stingers, they will be held at the camps where they can be easily guarded."

Bolan glanced at his watch, then stood. "I have to go now, but I'll come again this afternoon and bring a map so you can show me where the camp is."

"Where are you staying?"

"At the Ruby Gate Hotel."

"The innkeeper there is not an honest man." Jamillur shook his head. "You should stay here with me. I have a modest home, but there is always room for a friend."

Bolan smiled. "Thank you for the invitation, Ahmed, but it would be better if you weren't connected with me. I wasn't invited here this time and have to watch out for the Pakistani Intelligence Service, as well as the Islamic fundamentalists. Also, friends will be joining me here this afternoon."

Jamillur watched the tall American make his way back to the main bazaar and lose himself in the crowd. *El Askari,* the Soldier, had returned and death wouldn't be far behind him. The man he knew only as Belasko carried death around with him everywhere he went. Even so, most of the time the death that went with him struck down those who most deserved to die.

The problem was that Death often didn't have very good eyes. When he struck, he sometimes cut down the innocent, as well as the guilty. He just hoped that El Askari had a firm grip on his dread companion this time.

Stony Man Farm

BARBARA PRICE WAS in the War Room debriefing the three men of Able Team on the California operation. After uncovering the smuggling operation being run out of the Golden Palm Gallery's warehouse, Brognola had terminated their mission and ordered them back to Stony Man for a complete debriefing.

She had just started asking about what they had found in the warehouse when Cowboy Kissinger walked in.

"I hate to break in on this little gabfest, Barbara," the weaponsmith said with a curt nod to Lyons, Schwarz and Blancanales, "but have you come up with anything on those Stinger batteries I asked you about? I need to get that situation resolved before we're caught with our pants around our ankles."

Schwarz looked up at him. "What Stinger batteries?"

"The ones I need to bring our air defenses back up to combat-ready status. The Stingers we have in stock are all long overdue for a battery change."

A strange look came over Schwarz's face. "'Batteries not included.' That's what that was all about."

This was the first time that Barbara Price had heard the words *Stinger* and *battery* in the same sentence since her first conversation with Kissinger several days earlier, and she made the connection at the same time Schwarz did. "The raid on Century Microdyne in Modesto."

"Right. They took the Stinger batteries that had just been produced, and now we know why."

"What in the hell are you two going on about?" Kissinger asked, frowning. "All I asked about was replacement batteries for the missiles we have in the armory."

"You can't have any," Schwarz said, "because the people who make them are all dead."

"Say what?"

Price pushed her chair back. "You guys entertain yourselves for a few minutes. I've got to tell Mack about this immediately."

Kissinger looked puzzled. "Would someone mind telling me exactly what is going on around here?"

"And you can tell me at the same time," Lyons said, looking directly at Schwarz.

The electronics man leaned back in his chair. "Well, boys, it's like this. The target-tracking and acquisition systems in the Stinger missiles are powered by small but powerful batteries. And like all dry-cell batteries, even if they aren't used they run out of power after a while."

He looked at Kissinger and grinned. "And when they run out of power, the missiles don't want to track and fire. In fact, without fresh batteries, Stingers make damned good clubs, but that's about it."

"I know all that," Kissinger said. "But what got Barb all fired up?"

"Mack and Phoenix Force are trying to put a lid on whoever is using Stingers to start the next Pakistani-Indian war and—"

"I know about all of that. Just cut to the chase."

"Okay," Schwarz said, raising one hand. "What you didn't hear before you charged in here and rudely interrupted us is that we just had to clean up a mess in California where someone gunned down an entire assembly line in the company that makes the batteries for Stinger missiles. In fact, the only company in the United States that makes them. And after turning the assembly-line workers into dog meat, the raiders took all the batteries and disappeared."

"So you're telling me that there aren't any Stinger batteries in the entire United States military-supply system?"

"More or less. Apparently, in an attempt to cut down on supply inventory sitting in warehouses, the Pentagon decided go to with a manufacture-on-demand-only policy for several things, including these batteries. That's why you can't get any. They're not in the Pentagon's supply pipeline because they haven't been manufactured yet. And the batteries that were stolen in California are probably headed for the Indian subcontinent right now. It's been better than five years since the Afghan War ended, and all the Stingers that were sent there probably need new batteries before they can be used."

"So what am I going to use for air defense for this place in the meantime?"

"Why don't you ask the Air Force to loan you an F-15 Eagle? I'm sure Grimaldi would be glad to fly it for you."

"Smart ass."

"If I was so smart, would I be in this line of work?"

"Good point."

CHAPTER THIRTEEN

Peshawar, Pakistan

Back in his hotel room, Bolan opened his bag and laid out the carefully selected mountaineering and oil-survey gear that had been packed for him back at Stony Man. Even with their well-established cover, he expected that his room would be searched as soon as he left and he wanted everything to look as natural as possible. With the exception of the metal-detector-proof ballistic nylon fighting knife tucked in the back of his belt, he had come in-country completely clean so as not to compromise their cover.

The story was that they were a Canadian oil-exploration team looking for new sites for test drilling. As the team's Canadian, Gary Manning would pose as the expedition's leader and would do most of the talking so the accent would be right. British English was the region's universal language, and many Pakistanis spoke it well enough to be sensitive to accents, particularly American accents.

Even though Pakistan had been thoroughly searched for oil from one end to the other over the past fifty years, there were always new exploration teams bringing in new equipment to check the barren hills and valleys for more precious oil. It was known to be a long shot, but the government encouraged Western companies to continue their explorations. If oil were actually found, Pakistan would go from being a poor country to a rich nation almost overnight.

Usually on a mission of this urgency, Phoenix Force joined up with the American military for specialized equipment and support, and they often had links, even if unofficial, to the government of the country they were operating in. But due to the extreme political sensitivity of the situation this time, the Executioner and Phoenix Force couldn't expect any cooperation from either the Pakistani or Indian governments. In fact, if they were found out by either government, being thrown out of the country was the best they could possibly hope for. More than likely, they would be imprisoned and would eventually be executed. The U.S. government would not acknowledge them.

As soon as he had arranged his gear so that it could be easily searched, and reported on, Bolan went downstairs and found that the two Land Rovers he had leased had just arrived. After signing the papers and paying in advance for a two-week lease, he got into one of the rigs to drive to the airport to meet Grimaldi's incoming plane. The other Land Rover, driven by the man from the leasing office, followed behind him.

THE PESHAWAR CIVILIAN airport was more of an airfield servicing domestic flights than a full-fledged airport. Across the road, the Pakistani air force had a jet-fighter base that gained fame in 1960 when CIA pilot

Francis Gary Powers launched his U-2 spy plane from its runway for his fateful rendezvous with a SAM missile high over the Soviet Union. Now the base was home to the Number Fifteen Cobra Squadron, equipped with American-built F-16 Falcon jet fighters.

Military security prevented civilian aircraft from landing on the American-built fighter base, and a barbed-wire-topped chain-link fence separated the two facilities. Nonetheless, the concrete runway of the civilian field was long enough to handle the commercial variant of the C-130 Hercules transport plane that was carrying Yakov Katzenelenbogen and the men of Phoenix Force.

The Phoenix Force commandos were sharing the cargo hold of the aircraft with crates of machinery labeled as oil-exploration equipment. Enough of it was actually what it was labeled so that there wouldn't be a problem with the customs officials. The rest was the weapons and equipment for their operation, as well as the satellite-link communications gear they would use to keep in touch with Stony Man.

Bolan arrived in time to meet the Hercules when it touched down and taxied to the hangar that had been rented in the oil company's name for the operation.

"It looks like you could use a little more time driving Herkies," Bolan said in greeting to Jack Grimaldi when the man stepped out of the fuselage door. "That landing was a bit raggedy."

The pilot grinned. "Piece of cake. I just hit a bad crosswind on final approach."

"That's what they all say after they crawl out of the wreckage."

"He couldn't find a way to kill us in the air," Rafael Encizo muttered as he followed Grimaldi onto the tarmac. "So he thought he'd try to do it with his landing." He shook his head. "I'm going to start turning down missions that don't include first-class tickets on a major airline." He glanced over at Grimaldi. "And the plane must be flown by a rated pilot, not a talented amateur."

"Rafael thinks that he ought to ride in style," Yakov Katzenelenbogen stated as he joined them by the door. "He thinks that he's getting too old to be bounced around the sky for endless hours in a military-reject airplane."

"I saw our old friend Ahmed Jamillur," Bolan said.

"I'm glad to hear the old bastard's still alive."

"So am I," Bolan replied. "He's our only lead so far. He said that he knows where some of the Stingers are being held across the border."

"When do we move on them?"

"Probably tonight. I have to take a map to him so he can point out their location."

"Do I need to bribe these guys or what?" Grimaldi broke in when he caught sight of the Pakistani customs officials approaching in an open-topped jeep.

Bolan shook his head. "The Bear took care of everything when he set up our cover."

While a Pakistani passport-control official looked at their Canadian passports and stamped them, the two customs officials went over the plane's manifest with Grimaldi. After a cursory look at the sealed crates in the Hercules' cargo hold, they drove off. A few minutes later a rented truck and driver pulled up to the rear ramp to start loading the cargo for the short trip to the warehouse Bolan had leased for their operations center. Piling into the Land Rovers, the Stony Man warriors followed the truck.

The warehouse had been used to store spices back when spices had been worth importing. The wooden beams and flooring still carried the pungent odor of cinnamon and cardamom.

"Jesus!" James looked around when he walked in. "This place smells like a Lebanese health-food store."

FOR THE NEXT HOUR the men busied themselves unpacking the crates and setting up their command center in the warehouse. After retrieving their combat gear and individual weapons, they set up the satellite-link communications center. As soon as Manning established communications with Stony Man, Bolan slid in behind the keyboard to check in with Barbara Price.

She came on the line immediately and gave him a detailed account of the theft of the Stinger batteries and Able Team's raid on the warehouse after they had been shipped.

"Since that's the situation," Bolan said, "I'm going to make our first move tonight. I made contact with one of the names on the Bear's list, a Mujahedeen leader I once worked with. He says that he knows where some of the Stingers are being held across the border in one of the Afghan camps."

"Do you think it's wise to move on only one report?"

"Jamillur's report has a high probability of being accurate, so I want to hit this place as soon as I can. I'll be getting the exact location from him this afternoon, and I want to go in tonight."

"You might be giving the opposition an early warning that someone is after them," Price stated.

"There is a danger of that, true. But I'm willing to risk it. Since we have so little to go on here, I want to shake up the opposition a little. I want them to have to hurry the operation and get sloppy. That's the best chance we have to home in on them."

"That's a dangerous tactic," she replied. "If they get spooked badly enough, it might force them to step up their timetable."

"That's a risk I'm taking," he said. "But I'm afraid that if we wait until we've located their main base, if they even have one, they'll have gotten all the missiles operational and it'll be too late."

"Good point," she conceded. "I'll let Hal know that you're going tactical immediately."

"Also tell him that we could sure as hell use anything that any of the other agencies uncover as soon as they uncover it."

"He says that the President has given the proper orders to share everything that comes in. But," she added, "I've also got Aaron reading their mail. If anything comes up, I'll get it to you ASAP. Good luck tonight."

When Bolan cut the satellite link to Stony Man, he called Katzenelenbogen over. "Keep setting things up. I want to be completely operational as soon as possible. I'm going back into town to get that location from Jamillur so we can move out this afternoon."

"Since we're going tactical," Katz said, "take a com link in case I need to talk to you."

"Good point."

The com links were powerful miniature radios equipped with earplug phones and throat mikes. Their signal could reach for miles and was scrambled to prevent anyone from listening in. Since the warriors couldn't call on anyone for help or support this time, the com links were essential.

WHEN BOLAN CAME BACK two hours later, the inside of the warehouse had taken on the organized look of a proper command post. As long as they were in Peshawar, it would be their link to the outside world. Grimaldi had also set up the coffeepot and a hot plate so they wouldn't have to go out for meals. The less time they spent on the streets of Peshawar, the less exposure they would have to enemy action and the less chance to blow their cover.

"Okay," Bolan said. "Gather around, gentlemen, we have a mission tonight."

The warrior first recounted Barbara Price's message about the theft of the Stinger batteries and what it meant about the missiles in the hands of the terrorists.

"That means that we have a little more time, then," James said.

"Not really. That plant in California was hit several days ago and the batteries could be here already. They probably took a flight out of California the next day, and they could well be in-country by now."

"But won't it take them a while to deliver the things to whoever has the missiles, and even longer to replace them and run the checks to make sure they're working properly?"

"It might, but we have to act under the assumption that we don't have any time to waste."

"What I don't understand," Manning said, "is why they launched this campaign if they knew that the missiles needed fresh batteries."

"That's simple," Bolan answered. "I'm sure that they didn't know at first. They probably figured that the Stingers were like RPG rounds and could be stored forever until you needed to use them. It's to our advantage that we're dealing with a relatively nontechnical culture this time. Had they checked the missiles over before they started shooting them, we wouldn't be here right now."

"So it's a foot race," Manning said. "We have to find the Stingers before they can get the new batteries to them."

"That's about it." Bolan walked over to the map pinned on the wall. "And here's the first place we're going to go to look for them."

His finger reached out to the map and traced a small circle around a mountainous region some fifty miles inside the Afghan border. "I have information that there's a Mujahedeen camp here that has some Stingers."

"Do we have a recon photo of the camp?" Encizo asked.

"No," Bolan replied. "And I don't want to wait for Aaron to get them to us this time. My informant says that these guys have been shopping the missiles around, so I want to get in there before they disappear. We'll be leaving as soon as we can get suited up, and we'll hit them tonight."

"Bummer," James said. "We don't even get a chance to see the sights of Peshawar first? You know, the belly dancers, the camel races and the other cultural events."

"Believe me," McCarter said, "if you've seen one Pakistani town, you've seen them all. And the belly dancers are a bit too fat for my tastes. Plus they sweat a lot."

"Bummer."

"Also," Bolan added, "considering that we don't have a hell of a lot to go on this time, I want to try to snatch a prisoner for interrogation. Are there any questions?"

There was none.

"Okay," he said, "let's get going. Pull the vehicles inside so we can load them up."

Both of the Land Rovers Bolan had leased for their ground-transportation needs were painted tan, and while not intended as camouflage, the color would help them blend in well with the barren hills of the

Hindu Kush Mountains. After loading enough oil-surveying gear into the two vehicles to pass any cursory inspection they might run into, the team hid their long weapons up under the frames. Each vehicle kept one subgun ready in the back, and they all had pistols holstered inside their jackets in case they ran into trouble before they got into Afghanistan.

They donned combat blacksuits, then shrugged into tan safari jackets emblazoned with the logo of their cover company, Empire Oil Survey. Each man wore a blue baseball cap. The black pants and rubber-soled boots of their night-combat uniforms looked a little out of place with the civilian jackets, but they would have to do. When the Stony Man team ditched the vehicles and went tactical, the safari jackets would stay behind.

"Tell the Farm that we're on the way," Bolan told Grimaldi as he swung into the passenger seat of the lead vehicle. "We should be able to get back early tomorrow morning."

"I'll be here."

After seeing the team off, Grimaldi went back inside the warehouse. For the duration of the operation he would stay behind to guard their command post and act as their communications liaison.

He poured himself a cup of coffee from the pot plugged into the transformer next to the communications console and sat down to wait out the long night.

CHAPTER FOURTEEN

Peshawar, Pakistan

The roads leading north out of Peshawar were crowded, but it wasn't quite like the L.A. freeway. For one thing, many of the vehicles on the winding two-lane blacktop weren't motor driven, and few of the power vehicles were anything that would be seen in the United States. Three-wheeled, British-made light trucks were popular, as were horse-drawn wagons rolling on salvaged car tires and wheels. Nomads with camels and heavily laden donkeys shared the road, as well.

In the lead Land Rover, Gary Manning patiently wove his way through the traffic until they were clear of the crush and outside of Peshawar. Once they were in the open, Bolan broke out the map and guided Manning off the main road onto a side track that led to the north and the Afghan border. The road was little more than a goat track, but the Land Rovers handled it with ease.

There was a faint chance that when they got closer to Afghanistan they would come across a roving Pakistani army border patrol that would want to know what they were doing off of the highway. But they had their excuse ready. There was a purposely mismarked map, plus the oil-survey gear stacked in the back of both vehicles, to make their excursion off the more traveled routes look legitimate.

Crossing the high mountain border between Pakistan and Afghanistan unseen wasn't difficult even during broad daylight. As with most of the international boundaries in the Middle East, this border was more of a line on the map than any kind of physical demarcation on the ground. The only places between the two countries where one found border police or customs stations were along the main roads and highways. But since the Land Rovers didn't need to keep to the main roads, that wasn't a problem.

Once they were several miles inside Afghanistan, Bolan ordered the Land Rovers to halt in a hidden draw. "Okay," he said, "let's get tactical."

While the others freed their weapons from their hiding places, Bolan and Manning set up their military-issue Global Positioning System navigation equipment for the run into the target area. The GPS gear they were using was the new Slugger II system that had just been issued to the Army and was the most accurate land-navigation system ever developed.

GPS navigation worked by exchanging signals with the twenty-four NAVSTAR satellites orbiting the earth at a height of 10,900 miles. When the GPS receiver made contact with three of the satellites, it triangulated its location on the ground by using the satellites' precise locations in orbit at that particular split second. The grid location that was shown on the readout was accurate to within five meters of wherever it happened to be on earth.

If the Slugger II system had a fault, it was that the GPS gear worked only as well as the map that was being used with it. Along with the civilian oil-survey map that had purposely been mismarked, they also had the latest issues of the American military maps of the region. When concern about the renewed Pakistani nuclear-weapons program had arisen, the DIA had satellite-mapped the entire region in 1992 as part of the Pentagon's contingency plan to deal with an expected Indian-Pakistani nuclear war.

Once the weapons were readied and the GPS was up and running, the two Land Rovers moved out again. When dark fell they were still an hour away from their target, but since the GPS worked as well in the dark as it did in the day, they were able to continue on.

After driving for another hour with his night-vision goggles, Bolan found his jump-off point. The Land Rovers were well muffled, but sound carried far in the cool night air of the mountains. If old Jamillur's information was correct, the Mujahedeen camp was less than a half mile ahead on the next ridge line.

"Hold it up here," he said into his com link. "And turn them around so we don't have to back out later."

Once the vehicles were in position for a quick withdrawal, the team stripped off its civilian jackets to reveal the tops of their blacksuits. Their assault harnesses were already loaded with magazines and grenades, so once they were put on and combat cosmetics were applied to their faces and hands, the Stony Man warriors were ready for war.

McCarter, James, Manning and Encizo put out local security around the vehicles while Bolan and Katzenelenbogen went forward to recon the area. They didn't intend to move on the camp until the deep of night, so they had more than enough time to make a thorough recon.

Since Afghanistan was at peace, the camp was well lit by both fires and kerosene lanterns, and the two men had no difficulty locating it.

"That's it," Bolan said as he handed the laser range-finding night-vision binoculars to Katzenelenbogen, who was lying in the sand beside him. "I make it just a little over four hundred yards."

The Israeli took the glasses with his left hand and held them up to his eyes. The camp was spread out along the ridge in no particular order. There was, however, a tighter cluster of tents on the right side that looked to have sandbag bunkers around them as an interior perimeter. One of those tents, standing off by itself, had additional sandbags stacked around its base.

"I'd say that's it, all right," he stated, handing the glasses back. "It looks like we'll need to get all the way into that group of tents over to the right. From the sandbags stacked around that one tent to the rear, that's got to be where they're holding the Stingers."

Using a red-filtered penlight, Bolan marked his map to show the location of their objective, then folded it back into his side pants pocket before pulling back from their observation point.

THE APPROACH to the Mujahedeen camp went off without a hitch. Since the Afghans were deep inside one of their own mountain strongholds, they hadn't bothered to post sentries beyond the camp's outer boundaries. And since it was a fairly large camp, they thought they were safe from even the most foolhardy enemy.

Rafael Encizo was on point and was the first of the team to make contact. In the ghostly green glow of his night-vision goggles, he saw the figure of a sentry, awake and on duty, but with his AK-47 slung.

"Stony Alfa," he whispered over his com link to Bolan, "I've got a sentry off to my left."

"Take him out," came the message though his earphone.

The Cuban slung his Heckler & Koch assault rifle over his back and pulled the Tanto fighting knife from its sheath on his assault harness. With the exception of the sliver of its sharpened edge, the knife's chisel-pointed blade was parkerized mat black and was invisible in the dark.

His rubber-soled combat boots made faint scrunching noises on the sand as he moved in for the kill, but they were masked by the wind. He went wide, bypassing the guard before turning back to come in at him from behind. Matching his steps to the sentry's mindless pacing, he moved in close and struck like a snake. His left hand shot out to clamp over the man's mouth and jaw, jerking his head to the left while his knife hand flashed in over his other shoulder.

The point of the knife bit into the side of the man's neck, and Encizo ripped the razor-sharp blade forward, slicing through his windpipe and jugular vein. The guard made a hissing, gurgling sound as the air left his lungs, and his hands flew up to his neck. But the sudden loss of blood robbed all his strength, and they fell to hang limp at his sides.

The smell of the sentry's hot blood and voided bladder was strong on the cool mountain air as he went limp in Encizo's grasp. When the man stopped struggling, the Cuban lowered him to the ground and motioned the rest of the team forward.

Manning and McCarter were the first to reach his side. Pausing only long enough to sweep the dark camp with their night-vision goggles, they moved forward to their objective, the tent surrounded with sandbags. While Manning and McCarter went to find the Stingers, Encizo joined James and they went to find a Muji they could snatch.

Bolan and Katzenelenbogen moved up, too, but they halted at the edge of the perimeter by the sentry's body and stayed there to coordinate the operation and provide fire support when they pulled out.

Manning and McCarter had no trouble gaining their objective. They had expected to find a sentry posted at the tent, but found it unguarded. "You think this is the place?" Manning whispered. "There's no guards."

"There's one way to find out." McCarter slipped through the opening and immediately ran into crates of ammo. Snapping on his red-lensed flashlight, he saw seven Stinger launchers stacked against the end of the tent. "I've found them," he transmitted.

"Take them out," Bolan sent back.

James and Encizo also had no trouble finding their target. A man in desert camou fatigues stumbled out of one of the tents and headed for the nearby latrine. Encizo drew his knife again as he slid in behind him, but reversed his grip on the handle and smashed the butt of the hilt behind his victim's ear. The man slumped to his knees without making a sound. James reached down and grabbed him by the epaulets of his American-style field jacket, then jerked him upright and slung him over his shoulder.

"I'll carry him, you cover," he whispered to Encizo.

Turning to cover their withdrawal, Encizo swept the camp with his night-vision goggles. So far, so good. Now to get out of there.

Suddenly the silence of the night was shattered by a pop and a whoosh as a parachute flare was launched from the far side of the inner perimeter. The instant the flare came to life, the rattle of an AK on full-auto followed.

"This is Stony Alpha," Bolan transmitted over the com link. "Pull back with what you have now. We'll cover for you."

McCarter and Manning had just finished placing the quarter-pound demolition charges on the Stinger missiles when Bolan's call came. "Damn!" the Briton muttered. "I wanted to take the rest of this stuff out, too."

"Forget it," Manning said as he slung two of the Stingers over his shoulder by their carrying straps. "Pop the fuse and let's get the hell out of here."

McCarter pulled the fuse igniter and heard the primer pop. Nonetheless, he touched the fuse right behind the igniter to make sure that it was lit. "Let's do it," he said when he found that it was burning.

Crouching outside the tent, Manning scanned the tents in front of him. When two men ran from one of them, he didn't hesitate to stitch both with a long burst from his H & K.

"Get going!" McCarter grated. "That fuse is burning!"

THE FIRST BURST of AK fire woke Major Fuad's personal representative in the camp's command bunker. Since shooting at shadows was all too common with the Mujahedeen, the Iranian sergeant lay there for a moment until he heard return fire that didn't have the characteristic chatter of a Kalashnikov. Then he leapt out of bed, snatched up his Israeli-made 7.62 mm Galil assault rifle with the sniper's scope and ran out of the bunker.

Although the Galil was a Jewish weapon, it suited him far better then any of the Russian small arms that were standard issue throughout the Middle East. He had used the captured Israeli army rifle to good effect when he had been a young freedom fighter in Beirut.

Its full-size 7.62 mm NATO round carried much farther than the 7.62x39 mm assault-rifle cartridge of the AK family of weapons, and it hit harder.

He didn't have a night scope fitted to the Galil, but the day scope did capture the light of the flares and moon, and gave him a fairly clear sight picture at night. He spotted a black-clad figure fleeing for the perimeter and was bringing up his rifle when his eye was drawn to a group of three men moving much more slowly. Focusing in on them, he saw that it was two more black-clad men with a third man in between them. From the light-colored uniform worn by the third man, he realized that it was one of his own troops who had been captured.

He had no idea who these raiders were or why the camp was being hit, but he knew that he couldn't afford to have one of his men captured and possibly expose what he knew about Major Fuad's operation. Losing his life would be the least the major would demand if he allowed that to happen.

Centering the man's back in the cross hairs of his scope, the sergeant took up the slack on the rifle's trigger. He stroked the trigger softly, and the Galil's butt slammed back comfortably into his shoulder. When he acquired the target in the scope again, he saw that the man was down and the two black-clad raiders were pointing their weapons in his direction. He dropped behind the bunker as their return fire thudded harmlessly into the sandbags in front of him.

He was coming back up to see if he could take another shot when the ammunition storage tent behind him erupted in an ear-shattering explosion and a ball of flame. The blast drove him facefirst into the sand, and he covered his head with his hands as debris rained around him.

It was only when Manning's demolition charges exploded that the Iranian realized why the raiders had come. The seven Stinger missiles that Noor's agent had just purchased and delivered were stored in there. The major wasn't going to be pleased to learn that they had been destroyed.

"LEAVE HIM," Encizo snapped as James knelt beside their now-dead captive. "He's gone."

"Damn," the ex-SEAL medic said as renewed shouts behind them brought more men running in their direction.

"McCarter! Manning! Get a move on it!" Bolan ordered over the com links as he and Katz laid down a base of fire from their support positions.

"On the way."

Manning and McCarter joined up with Encizo and James, and the four commandos ran through the night. As soon as they were out of the range of small-arms fire, Bolan and Katz pulled back, as well.

When they got back to where they had left their Land Rovers, they climbed into the vehicles and were gone long before anyone from the camp could follow. Driving with only the night-vision goggles to guide him, Manning kept to the wadi leading away from the Muji camp. Several miles away, he found the main road, switched on his headlights and headed for the Pakistani border.

"I GUESS WE'RE BACK to square one," Encizo groused as they headed back to base.

"Not exactly," Katzenelenbogen replied over the com link. "In case you missed it, most of those guys were yelling to each other in Farsi. They're Iranians."

"Iranian or not, we still can't talk to the guy."

"Very true. But now that we know who's behind this, we'll just snatch the next Iranian we see and talk to him instead."

"Great," James said. "We'll go down to the bazaar tomorrow and ask if there are any Iranians in the crowd. When someone holds up his hand, we'll grab his ass and start slamming his head against the wall until he talks."

"Crude," McCarter said, grinning, "but as we all know, it can be rather effective at times."

Bolan ignored the banter on the com link, knowing that it was merely the adrenaline from the firefight talking. Even men as experienced as they were sometimes needed to talk themselves down from the adrenaline high that was a part of combat, particularly night combat.

"What I meant," Katz continued, "is that now that we know for certain that the Iranians are involved, we can look for Pakistanis who are associated with the Islamic Party."

"From what I understand," McCarter said, "that's about half of the population outside of those who are running the government, and even some of them are suspect."

"That makes it even easier," James stated. "We just grab the first dozen guys we see, have them count off and then talk to all the even-numbered ones."

"What if it turns out that it's the odd-numbered ones who are the bad guys?" Encizo asked.

James shrugged. "No problem, man. You just mix them all up and make them count off all over again."

CHAPTER FIFTEEN

Peshawar, Pakistan

"Sorry you didn't make the snatch," Jack Grimaldi said when Bolan recounted the raid to him over coffee hours later. "We could have used an informant."

"That's true," Bolan said. "But it wasn't a complete bust. We took seven Stingers out of action."

"Out of how many, though?" the pilot asked. "Considering that the CIA gave the damned things out like they were cheap hot dogs, there's got to be hundreds of them out there. At that rate, we'll be here through the end of the year."

Bolan had no answer to that. Grimaldi had put his finger on the biggest problem they were facing. It would make absolutely no difference how many missiles they captured or destroyed if there were more of them that they had missed. All it would take would be for one more to be fired, and the Northern Indian subcontinent could go up in nuclear flames.

"Let me see one of those things," James said as McCarter inspected the two missiles they had recovered from the Iranians. Since they hadn't been able to take the time to record all the serial numbers of the missiles destroyed at the camp, bringing two of them back was second best. There was a chance that Kurtzman could develop something from the two numbers.

"Here you go." McCarter handed him one of the thirty-four-pound missiles.

James swung the Stinger to his shoulder, and putting his eye to the optic sights, aimed it out the window. Across the road at the Pakistani air-force base, one of the F-16s was taxiing out to the end of the runway to take off, and its jet exhaust was pointed directly at the warehouse. The ex-SEAL aimed the missile's optic sight at the jet and went through the target-acquisition procedure, but nothing happened. The IR seeker didn't pick up on the jet's hot exhaust.

"It's dead," he said as he lowered it. "There's no power to the acquisition system, so it won't go active and track a target. You might as well throw the damned thing for all the good it is."

"That's what Barbara said," Bolan replied. "Most of them have been in the field for so long that they won't be any good until they get the new batteries."

"When did she say that those batteries were stolen?"

"About a week ago."

"That's enough time for them to have been flown in for sure."

"That's true," Bolan said. "But the real question is how long it will take for the opposition to get the batteries to wherever the missiles are being held. Then they'll have to install them, run the checks and then get them back out to the action groups. That's going to take some time, and I'm counting on it being time enough for us to find them."

Bolan finished his coffee and stood. "I'm going to go into town to see Jamillur again," he told Katz. "We're bound to have created some anxiety last night and I want to see if he's picked up anything yet. I know it's early, but bad news travels fast around a place like this."

MAJOR FUAD WOKE EARLY that morning to a report about the raid on the camp in Afghanistan. After reading through the document, he wasn't too concerned that the Stingers at the Afghan border camp had been destroyed in the night raid, nor was he concerned that his sergeant had been forced to kill one of his own men to keep him from being captured by the raiders. He was concerned, however, that someone had dared to make the raid. He had to know who had been so bold to have carried it out and he needed the answer immediately.

The Islamic Party wasn't without its enemies, even in the other Muslim nations. The rot of decadent Western temptations had spread far and wide among the faithful, particularly in nations like Pakistan, which had long been colonies of the Western powers. In fact, if the presence of him and his men in the country was to become known in official government circles, they would be in danger. Nonetheless, he was almost certain that it hadn't been the Pakistani army that had carried out the night raid across the border.

For one thing, had it been the army, it would have come with gunship helicopters and armored vehicles with their weapons blazing, not just two trucks. And second, from the reports of the camp's survivors, there had been only a handful of men in the attacking force, less than a dozen. The army would have sent at least a full battalion of troops.

The report sounded more to him as if the United States had dealt themselves into the game, as they had done so many times in the past. Regardless of what their President might say about seeking peace in the Middle East, the Great Satan stood in rigid opposition to the expansion of the glory of Islam. In everything from their unending support of the outlaw Jewish state, to their war against Saddam Hussein, to their efforts to keep Iran from developing modern weapons systems, the Americans had done everything in their power to keep the Muslim peoples living in the Dark Ages.

More important than that, though, were the actions the United States had taken over the years to foil the plans of Islamic freedom fighters to strike back at their enemies in other Muslim states. Their invasion of Lebanon and their massive aid to Egypt and Algeria to combat growing Islamic fronts were the actions of an implacable enemy of Islam. Those were purely Middle Eastern matters that the Americans shouldn't have become involved in, and by doing so they had shown their true colors.

If it was the Americans who had raided the camp, the question then was which American force had done it. It was certainly not the fools from the CIA. Under the new administration, they were no longer a threat to anyone. It was also unlikely that it had been the regular American military. Tehran had told him that there were no American mobile forces deployed anywhere within striking distance of the Indian subcontinent.

That left only the Americans of the shadow world of clandestine deep-cover units. They were a hard core of warriors who weren't acknowledged by any official agency. And that brought one man specifically to mind.

He had heard the stories of the American most often known in the Middle East as El Askari, the Soldier. Sometimes this man worked alone, but he was also known to associate with several other commandos. While the American government staunchly denied his existence, it was believed that he worked with the knowledge and approval of the President. But if he had actually done everything that was claimed for him, he would be the most famous man of this century, not a complete unknown.

Fuad only half believed that El Askari even existed. More than likely he was only a figment of someone's hashish-induced fantasies. It was true that the Americans had employed Special Forces units against Islamic freedom fighters on several occasions. The destruction of Moammar Khaddafi's secret desert "fertilizer" plant had been the work of Navy SEAL, and Green Berets had operated in Lebanon. But as good as those commando units were, they were merely men, not superhuman beings like those in the American children's comic books. And since it had been only men who had overrun the unprepared border camp, that pointed to it being an American Special Forces unit that was responsible.

Even though several of the Mujahedeen in the camp had been killed, it was apparent that the raiders' primary target had been the Stinger missiles that had been stored there. But the loss of the seven missiles wasn't critical to his operational plans. He had more than enough missiles on hand to hit all of the targets he had chosen. In fact, if events went as predicted, he wouldn't have to use even a quarter of the missiles he already had. With the schedule he had worked out, it would be a toss-up whether the Indians or the Pakistanis would be the first to take nuclear revenge on their enemy.

Either possibility was all right with him. His job was simply to start the war between the two nations. Others would come after him to bring Northern India and Pakistan under the umbrella of the Islamic Party once the fallout had blown away. The Islamic Guard would enforce order while the Imams sought out traitors to the faith and punished them. Those who had professed to be Muslims while pursuing the decadent ways of the West would serve as object lessons to the people.

Once the heretics were purged from the land, the barren hills would bloom under God's grace, but that wouldn't be the end of the struggle. There would never be an end to it until all of the world acknowledged

God's rightful rule and submitted themselves to it. Submission to God's will was what Islam was all about.

But for this to take place, he had to find out who was trying to foil the plan. And that meant telling his spies in Peshawar, Islamabad and Lahore to step up their surveillance of their subjects. If American commandos were in Pakistan, they wouldn't be able to stay hidden for long.

THE PESHAWAR BAZAAR seemed to be even more crowded when Mack Bolan went to see his Afghan contact later that morning. The cross-border raid had been close enough to Peshawar to have caused someone to be concerned, and he wanted to know what was being said about it, and by whom.

The old Afghan freedom fighter was seated in front of his shop again, and he smiled when he saw Bolan approach. "You have been busy, my friend," Jamillur said as he clapped his hands to signal his daughter to bring tea for him and his guest.

Bolan took a seat on the hassock across from the silver-inlaid table. "What makes you say that?"

"I have heard about the raid on the Mujahedeen camp across the border last night. The Iranians who were with them are not happy that they were surprised in their beds like children. They are saying that they will have vengeance on the infidel dogs who attacked them in the night."

Bolan smiled thinly. "I have heard that from Iranians before. It doesn't worry me."

The men fell silent as Jamillur's daughter emerged from the back of the shop with a silver tea service on a tray and poured pungent Afghan tea for them.

"It seems that I'm hearing of Iranians everywhere I turn lately," Bolan said as he reached for his cup.

"That is true. Now that the Russians are gone and the Afghan people have gone back to fighting one another again, the Iranians have taken the place of you Americans as the military advisers to the tribes. They are also the devils who are sponsoring the Islamic Party in both my homeland and here in Pakistan. They are very powerful now and are bad enemies for a man to have."

"I think that we can deal with them when the time comes," Bolan stated flatly.

"Be careful with them, old friend. They are demons because they think God is with them. I think, though, that when God looks down on us and sees what they are doing, he wants to vomit."

The old Afghan drained the last of his tea and placed the cup on the table. "Enough of talking about those dogs. What can I do for you today?"

"I do need to talk more about the Iranians, though," Bolan said. "I need to know who is known to be linked to them. Now that I have proof that they're involved in this business, I want to follow that track."

Jamillur thought for a moment. "You may be right. Though a real man would never make war on women and children that way, the Iranians would. They have done it before and can do it again. I will do what I can to learn who their contacts are, my friend."

Bolan stood to go. "I can come back tomorrow if you think that you'll have any information by then."

"I think that it may not be safe for you to come here again," Jamillur said evenly. "There are eyes in the bazaar that not even I can see, and they are not friendly eyes. I will send a man to your hotel with any information I receive. He will say that his name is Ali and that your tea has come in."

Taking a small cardboard box from behind the counter, the Afghan filled it with paper-wrapped packages of tea and tied it closed with string. "I remember that the Jew liked our Afghan tea, so he will enjoy this. Also, it will look better if you have a package when you walk away from here. Not that I have seen anyone watching me, but this is Peshawar."

Bolan took the small package. "I'm sure Katz will enjoy this."

"God be with you, my friend."

"And with you," the warrior replied.

BOLAN'S LEAVING Jamillur's shop was noted by a young man dressed in the rough clothing of an impoverished Afghan refugee. He wasn't an Afghan, though. He was Iranian. He had been trained at one of the terrorist camps in Afghanistan that had become known as the University of Jihad. He had done so well in his studies as a terrorist that he had come to the attention of Major Fuad and had been recruited into the service of the Islamic Party as a spy.

For his first assignment, Major Fuad had sent this young man to follow the old Afghan leader who had left the Mujahedeen gathering when the two American CIA spies had been killed. Anyone who didn't have the manhood to witness the execution of two enemies of Islam wasn't to be trusted. And anyone he associated with would also be a traitor to the true faith.

The spy had followed the Afghan leader to a tea shop in Peshawar that was owned by another old Afghan, Ahmed Jamillur, who was also a known enemy of the Islamic Party, and noted that he had stayed for two days. When he reported this information to Fuad, the major had ordered him to continue his surveillance on the shop to see what other enemies of Islam visited there.

He had seen Bolan go into the tea shop the day before yesterday, and now the Westerner had come back. The first time, he could have simply been a tourist. But to go to the shop twice made him a person of interest. Getting on his Honda motorbike, he was able to track Bolan as he made his way back out of the market to where he had parked his Land Rover.

The Westerner's height made it easy to keep him in sight. Something about the way he carried himself, though, made the spy keep well back even though he knew that he wasn't seen. This infidel, whoever he was, moved like a man who was trained to war, a man who would know that an enemy was behind him without turning his head.

While his orders were to keep Fuad informed of the Afghans who visited Jamillur's shop, the appearance of this Western infidel had to be important, as well. And if it was, maybe the major would reward him by giving him a more important assignment. Watching old men drink tea in the shade wasn't his idea of the glories of Jihad.

CHAPTER SIXTEEN

Peshawar, Pakistan

As part of his quest to learn who had attacked the Afghan camp, Major Fuad flew Noor's private helicopter into Peshawar. He wanted to check in personally with his spies and government contacts to see if they had any information about who his enemies might be. Identified enemies he could deal with, but the last thing he needed right now was to have an unknown opponent working against him.

Because of its proximity to the Afghan border, Peshawar had long been a gathering point for action groups, spies, thieves and smugglers. While the Islamic Party had a well-established network of agents in the city, Fuad had added several more who answered directly to him. Information, both concrete and mere rumor, was as much a staple of the main bazaar as was rice and curry powder. That was why he had placed two of his best agents there to keep their eyes and ears open.

"Tell me what you know about this infidel that you followed," Fuad ordered the young spy he had placed to watch over several reactionary Afghan leaders, including Ahmed Jamillur. The Iranian was in civilian clothes and was meeting his agent in a small café off the bazaar.

"He is staying at the Ruby Gate Hotel with five other men. The manager of the hotel says that they are a Canadian oil-company survey team that plans to be in town for two weeks. He says that they are fools because they are exploring for oil even when it is well-known that there is no oil in the Hindu Kush or eastern Pakistan. He also told me that the man told him that they would be climbing mountains in the Hindu Kush." The spy shook his head. "Only crazy foreigners could find pleasure in climbing the Hindu Killer Mountains."

"What does he look like?" Fuad prodded the spy to get the interrogation back on track.

"He is tall, even for an infidel. His hair is black and is cut short like a soldier. His eyes, they are blue, and when he moved through the crowd, they seemed not to miss anything that was going on around him. Also, he did not smile except when he was talking to the old Afghan."

The more the spy spoke about this man, the more Fuad became interested. He didn't really believe the stories that were told about El Askari. But if they were true, this man easily fitted the description. But then, he could also be only what he said he was, a Canadian oilman.

Nonetheless, the infidel had gone to the tea shop twice. And since the old Afghan was known to be an enemy of the party, it was logical to assume that his visitor was an enemy, as well. The fact that the shopkeeper was also a friend of the old Afghan who had ridden away from the execution of the two CIA men meant that Jamillur might also have known of the Stingers that had been used to lure the American spies to their deaths. If so, the shopkeeper could have given the location of the border camp to the Canadian. If he even was a Canadian and not an American secret agent.

The real questions were, if the infidel was a spy, did the other Canadians know who he was? Or were they all spies and not really Canadian oilmen at all? Those questions would have to wait, however, until the Afghan shopkeeper was taken care of. Rather than wait until he had more information, Fuad decided to act immediately. Once Jamillur was in Noor's fortress, the answers to many of those questions would be at hand.

"Does the old Afghan live at his shop?"

"Yes, Major, with his wife and his two daughters."

"I will see to the shopkeeper tonight," Fuad said. "Go back to the marketplace and continue your surveillance. Particularly keep on the alert for the infidel. I want to know where he goes, what he does and anyone he talks to."

"Yes, Major."

As the spy faded into the market crowd, Fuad realized that even when he picked up the old Afghan, there was always the possibility that he wouldn't talk. Some of those old men were stubborn to the point of death. Suddenly a thought occurred to him. There was a way that he could find out if the Canadians were who and what they said they were.

It would be simple, and, with his contacts in the Pakistani police in Peshawar, wouldn't have to expose any of his men. It might cost Noor a couple of his gunrunners, but they were scum like their employer and were completely expendable. As was Noor himself when the operation was finished.

He quickly finished his tea and left the café for a meeting with a local police official on his payroll. If he got to the officer soon enough, the plan could be put into operation before the day was out.

Stony Man Farm

"WE'VE GOT A HOT ONE." Aaron Kurtzman was beaming as he wheeled his chair into Barbara Price's private office.

She spun to face him. "What's that?"

"I just intercepted a Pakistani Intelligence Service report on a border incident that happened only a couple of hours ago. One of their army patrols on the Afghan border ran into a smuggler's vehicle and fired on it when it tried to flee. When they examined the wreckage, they discovered two Stinger missiles hidden in it."

"They were heading into Pakistan with the missiles, not taking them to India, right?"

"Right," he answered, seeing her line of reasoning. "If they're still gathering missiles, it means that we might have more time than we thought."

Not knowing how much time was left before the re-energized missiles started moving into India was the main piece that was missing from the puzzle. But, barring a miracle, there was no way they would learn that critical piece of information. Since Kurtzman didn't believe in miracles that didn't originate inside his computers, he welcomed any indication that the clock hadn't run out yet.

"The best thing, though," Kurtzman added, "is that the Pakistanis captured one of the smugglers unhurt, and he's being held in Peshawar."

"You're kidding!" Price could hardly believe what he had said. With only the few leads Bolan had uncovered, they were still far from being locked on a firm target. This could be the break they needed to zoom in on the situation.

"What do you have on the Peshawar slammer?"

"Great minds." He grinned as he laid a printout on her desk. "Since it was built during the days of the British raj, I thought I'd check with the archives of the historical-architecture department at Cambridge. Sure enough, they had a copy of the floor plan on file."

"I knew that computer of yours was going to come in handy someday."

"Don't it just," he said with a grin.

"Send all this information to Mack immediately and tell him to do what he thinks is right about that guy in the slam."

"On the way."

Peshawar, Pakistan

BOLAN WAS SCROLLING through a list of known Afghan Mujahedeen camps when Kurtzman came on the line with the information about the Stinger intercept on the border and the captured smuggler being held in the Peshawar jail. "Send it," he transmitted, and the fax machine started humming moments later.

The warrior pulled the faxed plan out of the machine and studied it for a moment. "Katz!" he called out. "Come over here a minute. Aaron's sent us a hot one."

The Israeli hurried over. "What did he come up with?"

"It seems that the Pakistanis fired up some smugglers coming across the Afghan border with a couple of Stingers in their vehicle."

"And?"

"One of them survived the firefight and is being held in the jail downtown."

"That's real convenient."

"Maybe too convenient," Bolan replied thoughtfully. "But Barbara thinks that we ought to spring the guy and talk to him." He held out the fax copy. "She even sent us a copy of the floor plan of the place."

"But," Katz cautioned, "if we do that, if something goes wrong, we run the risk of exposing our operation to the Pakistani authorities. Aren't you a little suspicious of their nabbing a smuggler so soon after we hit that camp?"

"Could be that our attack spooked them and they want to hurry and get the missiles to their destination. Or it could be a way for someone who knows about the opposition's operation to let us in on it without revealing himself, maybe somebody who's had second thoughts and doesn't want to see a nuclear war in his backyard."

"Don't you think that's a stretch?" Katz asked. "For that to happen someone would have to know that we're here and what we're trying to do. And if that's the case, we'd better give some thought to getting on the plane and getting the hell out of here before we end up in the Peshawar jail in the cell next to the smuggler."

"You've got a point," Bolan agreed, laying the floor plan of the jail aside. "Let's pass on this guy for now and continue to see what Jamillur can come up with. If he can't develop anything, we can get back to him. If he actually is a smuggler, the Pakistanis won't be in any great hurry to let him out. And since they don't have the ACLU here, he won't be going anywhere anytime soon."

IT WAS ALMOST MIDNIGHT when Major Fuad, following the spy's directions, had his driver halt the four-wheel-drive Toyota at the entrance to the side street off the main bazaar. A second vehicle pulled up behind him as he stepped out. At this time of night the plaza was deserted. He knew the danger of his personally taking part in this operation. He was the commander of a great plan, not a common soldier. But Inman

Fuad was first and foremost a dedicated Islamic warrior, and Islamic warriors had to destroy the enemies of Islam wherever they found them. Jamillur didn't follow the tenets of the Islamic Party so that made him an enemy to be destroyed.

The six men with the major silently checked their weapons and pulled down their face masks before following him into the alley that ran behind the row of shops. Jamillur was sleeping the sleep of the just when Fuad's commandos burst through his back door. Before the old man could clear the fog of sleep from his mind, two men grabbed his arms and jerked them behind his back and drove his face into the dirt floor.

"Don't kill him," a tall man commanded in Farsi as the strong hands held the Afghan immobile while another man bound his wrists. As soon as the knots were tied, a gag was slipped over his mouth and he was jerked to his feet.

When he saw the intruder's leader, Jamillur recognized him as being the Iranian fanatic his Afghan friend had told him about. He couldn't see the color of his eyes, but this had to be the Iranian who had killed the two American CIA agents who had tried to buy Stingers.

"What do you want me to do with the women?" one of Fuad's sergeants asked as he led Jamillur's wife and two daughters from their sleeping room. All three had been stripped naked and gagged with their clothing. Jamillur lunged toward them, but one of the Iranians slammed the butt of his AK into his belly and stopped him.

Fuad looked the family over. The elder girl was young, but she was already a dark-haired Afghan beauty. "Take the older one," he commanded. "We will give her to Noor."

The Iranian holding the girl laughed. "We can find a good use for her before we do that."

"Not her," Fuad snapped. "I need her intact for the interrogation."

As the Iranian dragged the girl over beside her father, Fuad pulled the Makarov pistol from the holster on his belt. Flicking the safety off, he looked at the Afghan's wife. Her dark eyes were glittering with raw hatred as she ignored her nakedness and tried to put her body in front of her younger child. When he aimed the pistol at her, she didn't cringe or fall to her knees, and only the gag in her mouth kept her from attacking him with her teeth.

Shifting the muzzle of the pistol to the head of the little girl, he stroked the trigger. The woman's muffled scream almost covered the report of the 9 mm round. A second round cut off her scream, and she fell beside her daughter.

"Move them out," he ordered the men holding his struggling captives as he took a pair of grenades from his assault harness. As soon as the two captives were marched out into the alley, he stopped at the rear door and waited until his men and the captives were at the mouth of the alley. He then pulled the pins on both grenades, tossed the bombs back inside the shop and ran for the vehicles.

ONCE THE TOYOTAS CLEARED Peshawar and headed into the open country to the east, the Iranians in the second vehicle relaxed. The old man's arms were bound, and he wasn't a threat. They even removed his gag. The Afghan had heard the Iranian mention Ali Noor, as if the two were allied in this operation. If that was the case, he knew that he would never escape from the stone fortress known as the Snake's Skull.

As the vehicles approached the sprawling refugee camp on the east side of the city, Jamillur knew that this was the last chance he had to try to escape. There was nothing beyond the camp but desert and nowhere for him to hide. If he could get free here, he could take refuge with his own people who would protect him. His daughter was in the lead truck with the Iranian, but he would lead a Mujahedeen band to Noor's fortress to rescue her once he was free. But to save her he first had to save himself.

The Iranian who had leered at his daughter's nakedness was wearing U.S.-issue hand grenades on his assault harness. But the man hadn't known how to properly attach them and had tied them to the harness straps with a nylon cord passed through the grenade pull ring.

If he could get hold of one of the grenades and pull hard enough, the pin could come out of the fuse, releasing the safety spoon and igniting the fuse train. It would detonate five seconds later, but in that time he could throw himself free of the vehicle and escape the blast. It was risky and the only way he could pull on the grenade was with his teeth, but it was the only chance he had.

Gathering his feet under him, he lunged forward, throwing himself on the Iranian and slamming him against the back of the passenger seat. The other guard didn't shoot for fear of killing his comrade. The Afghan's teeth clamped around the pin of the grenade, and he jerked his head back. The pin pulled free of the fuse and the spring-driven safety spoon snapped free with a metallic twang. The striker hit the detonator and the grenade was live.

In a blind panic the Iranian pushed him back down, but it was too late. The live grenade fell free.

"God is great!" Jamillur shouted right before the grenade detonated.

The explosion blasted the Toyota and the three Iranians. The driver took a piece of shrapnel in the base of the skull and was killed instantly. Jamillur took some of the concussion that wasn't blocked by the other two Iranians. He grunted in pain as he felt the razor-sharp bits of metal penetrate his stomach and chest.

The Toyota lurched as the driver's dead body fell against the steering wheel. The left front wheel hit a boulder on the side of the road and was slammed over to the right full-lock position at the same time that the outside rear wheel bounced in a deep rut. The back end of the Toyota came up and it rolled over onto its left side, spilling its passengers, dead and dying, into the dust.

Jamillur was thrown clear of the wreck, but couldn't move. His legs didn't answer his commands and he knew that his back was broken. He heard shouts from the refugee camp and turned his head far enough to see the men running toward him. He felt a wet warmness flowing down his belly and he knew he was dying, but he had to stay alive long enough for them to reach him.

His gamble had failed, and now it would be up to his friend El Askari to avenge him and his family.

CHAPTER SEVENTEEN

Outside Peshawar

Major Fuad looked back when he heard the explosion and saw the Toyota roll over. He ordered his driver to stop and was about to tell him to turn around when he saw the Afghans from the refugee camp running to the overturned vehicle with their illegal AK-47s ready in their hands.

"Wait!" he said as he watched the scene unfold. He wanted to go back and rescue his men, but the last thing he needed right now was to get into a firefight with two dozen angry Afghans. The Pakistani authorities had tried to disarm the refugees, but separating an Afghan from his gun meant that you had to take his life first. After several firefights the police had learned to ignore the openly carried weapons.

When he saw their curved knives flash as they slit the throats of his men, the major ordered his driver to move out. He wouldn't be able to question Jamillur about the Canadian he had been seen talking to, but he still had the girl and there was a chance that she would know something about her father's visitor. Even if she didn't, though, she still might have her uses. And he could always sell her to Noor when he was done with her.

IT WAS AFTER MIDNIGHT when a double knock sounded on the door of Bolan's hotel room. Katzenelenbogen had his pistol ready in his left hand before the sound of the knock echoed away.

The Executioner signaled caution. "Who is it?" he called out in English.

"I am a friend of Jamillur and I have a message for you," a young voice replied in heavily accented English.

Drawing his Beretta 93-R, Bolan thumbed off the safety and flicked the selector to the 3-round-burst position. "Wait a minute."

As soon as Katz was in position to back him up, the warrior opened the door. The messenger couldn't have been more than fifteen or sixteen and was dressed in the typical patched clothing of an Afghan refugee. His hands were held open in front of him, and he didn't move as Bolan looked past him to make sure that the hallway was clear.

"Come in," he said, motioning with the pistol.

The youth moved slowly as he entered the room. He was young, but he knew not to make any sudden moves around men with guns. It was something every male had to know if he wanted to live long in that part of the world. He stood stock-still while Bolan patted him down for hardware.

"What is your message?" the Executioner asked when he came up clear on the search.

"I am Ali. I am to tell you that your tea is ready," the young Afghan said in schoolboy English. "And I have an important message for El Askari."

Bolan frowned. The code wasn't exactly right, but the boy had used the name he had become known as among some of the Afghan tribes.

"Give me the message," he said.

"Are you El Askari?"

"I am Ahmed Jamillur's friend," Bolan declared. "You can give me the message, and I will see that it gets to the right man."

The youth took a deep breath and plunged into his story. "Ahmed Jamillur has been captured and his family has been killed."

Dropping a grenade in the room couldn't have produced a more shocked reaction.

"What happened?" Katz asked, now coldly awake.

"Men with Kalashnikovs came to his shop and they captured him. Then they killed his family and took him away."

Bolan's mind flashed back to the slender young girl with the dark eyes who had brought him tea. "Did they kill all of his family?"

"I think so," the young Afghan answered. "They put a bomb in the shop when they left, and his relatives are digging there now to look for the bodies."

"Did anyone follow you here?"

"No. I was very careful."

"Good," Bolan answered. "Go now. I'll do what I can for Jamillur."

As quietly as he had come in, the youth left.

"I'll take David and check this out," Bolan said as he shrugged into his shirt. "I want you to take Calvin, Gary and Rafael and go to the command base.

Pack up everything here and take it with you. We just checked out, but don't bother to tell the manager. We'll meet you there when we're done."

"Do you want me to have Jack get the plane ready?"

"Not yet. We still might be able to salvage something from this. But it sure as hell looks like our cover's blown."

"Doesn't it."

WHEN BOLAN AND MCCARTER arrived at Jamillur's tea shop, the Pakistani police were already there. So was a small, but growing crowd of Afghans crowding the narrow side street. The old man had been an important leader in the refugee community, and the attack threatened all of them.

Bolan parked the Land Rover on the main street in case they had to make a run for it. "Keep out of sight," he told McCarter as he closed his windbreaker over the holstered Beretta. "I'll go in and check it out."

"Watch yourself."

On the opposite side of the street from the shop, Bolan saw two bodies, one large, the other small, a child, lying under colorful Afghan blankets. He knelt and pulled the blanket from the smaller body to see which of the children it was. The body was that of a younger girl, not the one who had served him tea, and she had been shot once in the chest. He carefully laid the blanket back over her.

"What are you doing here, mister?" the voice behind him asked in educated English.

Bolan looked up to see a Pakistani police officer in fresh khakis standing a few feet away, his hand resting on the butt of the .38-caliber revolver holstered at his belt.

"Ahmed Jamillur was a friend," Bolan said as he slowly got to his feet. "I was told that there had been an accident and I came to see about him."

"This is a police matter," the officer said. "Tourists are wise not to get involved."

"I just wanted to see if there was anything I could do to help his family."

"They will be taken care of. There is nothing for you to do here."

The cop was wrong, there was a lot that he could do. But there was no way that it was going to happen now that the police were involved in the matter. To insist would only earn him a trip to the police station and maybe a night in a jail cell.

"Yes, sir."

The policeman stood and watched as Bolan made his way to the edge of the crowd. As soon as he was in the open, an Afghan went up to his side and walked along with him. "You are the friend of the one-armed Jew?" he asked quietly.

"Yes, I am," Bolan answered without looking at the man as he signaled for McCarter to hold back.

"I need to talk to you about Jamillur," the Afghan said. "I talked to him right before he died."

Bolan was surprised, but kept on walking. "He's dead?"

"Yes. The Iranians were taking him away, and he was able to explode a grenade in the truck. They all died when we ran out of the camp," he said dryly. "But though Jamillur was badly wounded, he was still alive when I got to him. He told me who had done this to him and his family."

"Come with me," Bolan said when he reached the Land Rover. "We'll talk."

"Where are we going?"

"To a safe place."

MCCARTER KEPT the Afghan discreetly covered while Bolan drove to the warehouse, and the man said little on the way. When the Executioner arrived he saw that Katz and the rest of the team had taken up security positions while they waited for him. The Afghan stepped down and submitted to a frisking.

"He's clean," James said as he stepped back.

"Okay," Bolan said. "Why don't you tell me who you are and everything that happened tonight."

"I am Hassen Kader," the Afghan said with the air of a man who thought that his name should mean something even to complete strangers. "Ahmed Jamillur was my uncle and the head of our clan. Now that he is dead, I am the head of the family."

"How did you learn what happened tonight?"

"I was visiting some of our people in the camp when we heard the trucks drive by very fast going east. Then there was a grenade explosion and we thought that we were being attacked. Grabbing our weapons, we rushed out in time to see one of the trucks go out of control and turn over. The other one kept going, though. When I reached the overturned truck, I found my uncle lying on the ground with his hands bound behind him. Three other men in desert-camouflage uniforms were lying on the ground around him. One of them was dead, but the other two were only wounded. When I heard one of then cry out in Farsi—" he paused to ritually spit on the floor "—I knew they were Iranians and I slit their throats.

"My uncle was badly hurt. The grenade had torn into his chest and belly and his back was broken when the truck turned over. But he could still speak and he told me what had happened to him. He said that Iranians burst into his house, overpowered him and tied him up. Then he said that they killed his wife and younger daughter before taking him and the other girl away."

"Do you know who these Iranians were and why they would have done this to him?"

"All I know is that he said Ali Noor had sent the Iranians. He heard them speaking of him when they took his daughter away."

"Do you know who this Noor is?"

Kader nodded.

"Tell me what you know about him."

"Not too long ago," Kader said, "Ali Noor was only a small-time heroin smuggler working the China-Middle Eastern routes. He bought the raw poppy across the Afghan border and had it refined here in

Pakistan. Later he branched out into selling Indian women to the oil sheikhs and then he started running guns. It was then that he became wealthy.

"This wealth has allowed him to acquire a private army and a stronghold in the mountains of eastern Pakistan close to the Afghan border, where he holds wide power. One rumor has it that he is connected with the Islamic fundamentalists in Iran. Others report that he has ties to the hard-liners in Red China. The one thing that is certain is that he has contacts across the border who could easily supply him with the Stinger missiles you are looking for."

"Maybe I should pay this man a visit."

"If you do, be very careful. Not only does he have a private army, it is well armed. And as tonight proved, he has Iranian friends, as well."

Bolan pulled the map out of his pocket and opened it on the table. "Can you show me where Noor has this fortress?"

The Afghan studied the map for a moment. "It is here," he said, pointing to a mountainous region in eastern Pakistan, "at a place called the Snake's Skull."

"What can you tell me about the place?"

"It is very old," Kader said. "It was built during the Mogul times with the labor of their infidel prisoners. It is said that it has never fallen to an enemy as long as the garrison inside had the will and the ammunition to fight. Now it has been rebuilt, but I cannot tell you how. Noor does not encourage visitors. I hear fantastic things, though. It is said that he has antitank missiles and other modern Western weapons, but I have not seen them myself."

"I'll have to see this fortress of his."

"I want to go with you when you visit Noor."

"I'm sorry," Bolan replied. "Jamillur was a good man and I will miss him, but I can't get involved with private missions of vengeance."

"Jamillur told me that you were interested in getting back the Stinger missiles that your country gave to the freedom fighters."

"That's right. They're being used to kill civilians in both India and Pakistan, and my government wants them back under its control."

"If you want the missiles, then you will have to go after Noor."

"Why is that?"

"Where else would you go?" Kader shrugged. "It is well-known that he has been asking to buy them from the Mujahedeen and he is offering top prices."

"Why didn't Jamillur know that Noor was trying to buy Stingers?"

"My uncle was an old-fashioned Afghan of great honor, and his honor was well-known. He did not listen to the talk about pimps and drug dealers, and the men who knew of their dealings did not speak of them around him."

Bolan should have thought of that himself and used an informant who was a part of the shadow world, not an honorable man. If he had done that, old Jamillur and his family might still be alive.

"I talked to him and endangered him and his family. For that I'm sorry."

"You went to him as a friend," Kader said. "There is no dishonor in that. But as a friend, you have an obligation to help me avenge his death."

"Yeah, I suppose I do. But I have to take care of the missiles first. When that's done, I'll do what I can to avenge his death."

"That is good enough for me."

"It'll have to be."

"DO YOU THINK we can trust that guy?" James asked as soon as they were alone again.

"We can trust him," Katz answered. "He's an Afghan and the leader of his clan has just been killed. Until Jamillur's death has been avenged, Kader isn't going to do anything to compromise his chances to get vengeance. Apparently he thinks that we can help him so he'll play ball with us for now."

"It'll be easy enough to check out his story about the fortress," Grimaldi said. "In the morning I can grab a chopper, fly a recon mission over that place and see what shakes out. We can slap the Canadian oil-company logo on the bottom of the bird and no one will notice. I'll take David along with me for company."

He turned to McCarter. "You can sound like a geologist, can't you?"

"Righto, mate," McCarter said, letting his Cockney accent loose in full force. "Petroleum, drilling stations and all that rot."

"You'd better hope that you don't have to talk to anyone," Katz said. "Because if you do, that means you'll be on the ground, and you don't want to be on the ground in that area."

"It'll still look better if I have another man in the chopper when I fly over, more like we're an oil-company survey flight."

"Okay," Bolan said finally. "But you'd better make sure that you give that place a wide and fast pass, and only make one run. Take pictures instead of trying to eyeball everything. If that place is what we think it is, they'll have more than enough antiaircraft missiles, and they're likely to shoot you down and ask questions later."

"I'll be careful," Grimaldi stated. "Believe me. I'd hate to have to walk all the way back here. I didn't bring my sun block."

"Okay," Bolan said. "Everyone get some sleep for now. We can't do anything until morning. Rafael, you take the first watch."

CHAPTER EIGHTEEN

Peshawar, Pakistan

There was a flight service at the far end of the civilian airport, and they were more than happy to lease one of their helicopters to an oil company. Playing the part of a man who was spending someone else's money, Bolan didn't haggle much about the steep price for a three-day rental. While he finished filling out the paperwork, Grimaldi went out on the flight line to take possession of the aircraft.

The chopper Bolan secured was an old military-surplus Bell UH-1D Huey converted to civilian use. Like the military C-47 Gooney Bird transport plane of WWII fame, the Vietnam-era Huey had made a very successful transition to civilian use. All over the world veteran Hueys were flying as everything from aerial ambulances to freight haulers and mail carriers.

Slipping into the pilot's seat and fastening his shoulder harness, Grimaldi started running through the chopper's prestart checklist. Since the pilot knew the Bell aircraft, he didn't need to open the copy of the checklist that had come with the ship. After the hundreds of hours he had spent in the right-hand seat, the start sequence for a Huey was burned into his brain.

As his hands moved over the controls and switches, he recited the checklist under his breath. "Battery, on. Inverter switch, off. RPM warning light, on. Fuel, main and start, on. RPM governor, decrease. Throttle, flight idle."

Reaching down with his right hand to the collective control stick, he twisted the throttle open to flight idle and rested his finger on the start trigger on the collective. Glancing over both shoulders, he saw that the path of the main rotor was clear.

"Cranking!" he yelled to let any gawkers know that he was starting the turbine and to clear the circle cut by the main rotor.

The electrical starter whined and the big Lycoming T-33 turbine in the rear burst into life with a screeching roar and the smell of burning kerosene. Over his head, the forty-eight-foot, two-bladed main rotor slowly began to turn. As the turbine rpm built and the rotor blades picked up speed, he released the start trigger. Holding the throttle at the idle position, he quickly checked the instruments to make sure that everything was in the green.

When he saw that it was, he slowly rolled the throttle open. The *wop-wop* sound of the two-bladed rotor coming up to speed let him know that it was spinning fast enough to lift him off the ground. Ever so gently he pulled up on the collective control in his right hand to feed pitch to the rotor blades. Without looking at his tachometer, he felt the blades slow their building revolutions as they bit into the cool morning air. He backed down on the collective just a hair to flatten the pitch to let the blades accelerate faster under load.

When the rotor rpms were back up, he pulled more pitch with the collective and the Huey lifted off the ground. Once he was high enough to be free of the ground effect, he nudged forward on the cyclic control in his left hand. The Huey's tail came up, and he started to move forward.

He stayed low as he flew the quarter mile to the warehouse. Executing a pedal turn to line up the Huey's side door with the building's main entrance, he set down and killed the fuel to the turbine.

"It looks like you're back in the saddle again," Encizo commented when he saw the pilot open the cockpit door and step to the ground.

Grimaldi patted the Huey's dull skin. "She's a little worn, but she's a good bird."

IN NOOR'S FORTRESS, Major Fuad woke early that morning to take care of the day's business. Even though he had slept only a couple of hours since returning from Peshawar, there were things that took priority over his physical comfort. His latest message from Singapore said that the shipment of batteries had been delayed because of a problem with the aircraft.

Fuad was anxious to put the final phase of the plan into operation, but he also knew the virtue of patience. The cause of Islam had waited four centuries to triumph again, and it could wait a few more days until an aircraft could be repaired. All he had to do was to ensure that he would have the time he needed to get the batteries in and make the missiles fully operational. To do that he needed to ensure that Noor's fortress was protected from his enemies.

But, with the man who had been killed in the raid on the Afghan camp and the three who had been killed the previous night, he needed reinforcements to do that job. Until they came, he could either send his men out with Noor's smugglers on their Stinger-buying missions or guard the fort, but not both.

Who would have thought that the old Afghan would have had the courage to do what he had done. Though Jamillur had been an enemy, it was an act worthy of the highest praise. Nonetheless, it left Fuad shorthanded.

With that in mind, he radioed an order to the Islamic Party training camp closest to the border with Afghanistan, demanding that two dozen men be sent to him immediately. That should be enough to do what had to be done.

WHILE THE STONY MAN TEAM was tying down the last of the oil-exploration gear in the back of the Huey in preparation for the flight, Grimaldi climbed into the pilot's seat and fired up the still-warm turbine. As soon as the rotor was up to speed, McCarter climbed into the copilot's seat and strapped himself in. "Let's get this show on the road."

Grimaldi grinned as he put his sunglasses on. "One low-level, high-speed oil-survey flight coming up."

The pilot pulled pitch on the collective, and the Huey rose into the air. Feeding in a little right pedal, he went into a circling climb well out of the way of both the fighter base and the civilian airfield. Once he was clear, he pointed the nose of the Huey toward the east and settled down for the long flight.

McCarter did the navigating as they flew low past the mountains, deserts and small villages below. Since they were flying so low, it was more like following a highway map than real aerial navigation.

"If our information is correct," McCarter stated, looking up from the map, "it should be about two miles in front of us behind that hill mass."

Grimaldi twisted the throttle hard against the stop as he nudged forward on the cyclic control stick at the same time that he pushed it all the way to the right. The old Huey went up on one side as it nosed even lower to the ground at well over a hundred miles per hour.

"You drop this damn thing any lower," McCarter growled, "and we can just get out and do the damned recon on foot. We're supposed to be a geological-survey team, not a damned gunship crew."

Grimaldi grinned broadly. Seeing a ridge line approaching, the pilot pulled back on the cyclic and sent the chopper rocketing up over the top.

"Bingo!" he called out when he saw the rock walls of the fort clinging to the outcropping in the distance. "Get the camera ready."

INSIDE NOOR'S FORTRESS, the Iranian radar operator had picked up Grimaldi's chopper when it was several miles out. When it became apparent that it was heading in their direction, he called up the Iranian commando on air guard in the north tower. The major's orders were that all approaching aircraft were to be shot down without warning.

As Grimaldi racked the ship around to get into position for his run past the fortress, the rotor tips hit a hot-air pocket and made the unmistakable *wop-wopping* sound of a helicopter. Echoing off the wadi walls, the noise alerted the Iranian commando with the Stinger missile in the north tower.

Swinging the missile launcher toward the noise, he locked the image of the approaching aircraft in the launcher's optical acquisition sight and pressed the track button. The missile dumped its pressurized nitrogen coolant to the seeker head and spun up its internal gyro. In less than a second he heard the launch-lock tone in his headset and pulled the firing trigger past the stop.

The boost charge ignited, pushing the missile out of the launcher. Twenty meters out of the tube, the main rocket motor kicked in and accelerated the missile past Mach 2 in an instant. The small triangular fins on the front of the missile swiveled to make a course correction to follow the chopper as it started its run toward the fortress.

"OH, SHIT!" Grimaldi yelled when he spotted the smoke of the launch signature. "They're shooting at us!"

He slammed the cyclic over to the far right and stomped down on the left pedal to let the torque of the main rotor help spin the chopper around. Knowing that the missile had to be a heat seeker, his only hope was to face into the sun and let the missile seeker head lock on to the only heat source in the sky that was hotter than his jet-turbine exhaust.

He hauled back on the cyclic control, jerking up the nose of the ship almost vertically, aiming it at the sun. If the IR trace of the blazing desert sun couldn't break the lock, then nothing could. Holding his course for thirty long seconds, he slammed the control stick to the right side and shoved it all the way forward at the same time. The Huey made another snap turn to bank from the sun and dive toward the ground below.

Had the missile been a Russian Strella or even the older American Redeye, that tactic would have worked. However, the missile closing in on him was a Stinger, and one of the features that made it the most deadly of the world's shoulder-fired antiaircraft missiles was its ultraviolet-radiation discrimination feature.

The heat-seeking head did lock on to the sun since it was the hottest object in the sky in front of it, but the ultraviolet-detection circuit told the heat-seeking head that it was also receiving ultraviolet radiation, so it couldn't be an aircraft that it was locked on to.

Obeying its electronic master, the IR-seeking head unlocked from the sun and sought out the next-hottest thing in its flight path, the exhaust of the chopper's jet turbine. When the ultraviolet circuit told the seeker head that this target was big enough to block out the UV spectrum, and was therefore an aircraft, the IR seeker went into the final lock and rode it into the target.

This change in course took place in microseconds and doomed the Huey.

IN THE COCKPIT, Grimaldi was just about to congratulate himself on having evaded an aerial disaster when he saw the Stinger missile abruptly change direction and head for him again.

Moments later the Stinger hit right under the chopper's turbine exhaust. The missile's warhead was also an advanced design, a semishaped charge that fired a cluster of diamond-shaped pellets. Traveling as fast as machine-gun bullets, the tempered-steel pellets tore the guts out of the Huey, smashing the transmission and rotor controls.

Grimaldi just had time to cut the fuel feed to the turbine when it declutched from the damaged transmission and screamed on overrev as it self-destructed. "We're going down!"

The pilot frantically tried to establish autorotation with the plunging ship, but he was too low for the rotor blades to come back up to speed and lift. At the last possible second he pulled full pitch to the blades with his collective to try to cushion the impact, but it barely slowed the fall.

The helicopter hit a glancing blow against the ridge line and rolled onto its right side, the main rotor blades snapping off and flying away. The skids dug into the ground abruptly, stopping the ship and sending McCarter and Grimaldi slamming against their shoulder harnesses. The tail boom snapped off and careered over the canopy while the shattered remains of the crew compartment came to a rest right side up only a hundred yards from the top of the ridge.

CHAPTER NINETEEN

Eastern Pakistan

McCarter woke to the feeling of someone roughly jerking him out of the wreckage of the downed chopper. His hand automatically went over to his shoulder holster, only to discover that it was empty. He was reaching down for the fighting knife in his boot top when a stunning blow to his shoulder numbed his right arm.

An Arab wearing desert-camou battle dress stepped into his line of sight and raised the buttstock of his AK-47 assault rifle for another blow if he continued to resist. McCarter let his body go limp and allowed himself to be dragged out of the wreckage and stood on his feet. He shot a quick glance back at the cockpit and saw that Grimaldi was jammed up against the instrument panel. It looked as if he was still breathing, though, and he didn't show any blood, so he could be okay. For now he had to concern himself with his own survival. If he could stay alive, he could try to rescue the pilot later.

He stood stock-still and faced the half-dozen AK-47 muzzles aimed at him as hands roughly patted him down for hardware and took the knife from his boot-top sheath. The gunmen were speaking in what he thought was rapid-fire Arabic. But even though he had a small working knowledge of the language, they were speaking too fast for him to follow what they were saying. He knew, though, that whatever they were saying wouldn't bode well.

As soon as they found that he was clean, his arms were pulled behind his back, his hands were bound and he was hustled to a waiting sand-camouflaged truck and shoved into the back. Two of the gunmen joined him for the short trip to the fortress perched on the rock. A narrow trail that was cut into the rock led up to the main gate. The deep crevasse in front of the gate was traversed by a heavy planked bridge, but it didn't look as if it could be raised drawbridge-style.

The vehicle drove through the arch of the gate and stopped in the paved courtyard inside. From the outside, the fortress looked like something out of a thirties foreign-legion movie, but the inside was modern. The walls had been plastered and painted white to reflect the harsh sun. A cooling fountain and small garden were situated in a portico against the back wall.

He didn't have long to enjoy the scenery, though. The guards dragged him out of the truck and, prodding him with the muzzles of their AKs, forced him through a stone archway in the inner wall and into a corridor. At the end of the hall, heavy wooden doors opened into a plush, air-conditioned office decorated with tasteful, expensive furnishings and Middle Eastern artwork.

Waiting for him was a tall, golden-eyed man wearing pressed desert fatigues and a Makarov pistol holstered in his field belt. McCarter didn't need an introduction to know that this was the man in charge.

"I am Major Inman Fuad," the man said in almost unaccented English. "And who are you?"

McCarter noticed that the "major" didn't wear rank badges and didn't mention the organization that he was associated with. But the Briton knew that he wasn't in the Pakistani military—there was nothing of the Pakistani about him, including the accent. This guy had upper-class Iranian written all over him.

"My name is David Green," McCarter replied, allowing a note of indignation to enter his voice, "and I'm a petrol engineer with the Empire Oil Survey, a Canadian company. We were doing a geological-survey flight before we were shot down." He looked Fuad up and down. "I assume by your men?"

"You flew over a sensitive area, Mr. Green," Fuad stated, as if that explained the shooting down of a civilian helicopter. "I had to take precautions."

"What's going to happen to me and my pilot?"

"That depends on if you are who you say you are."

"I think that should be evident. A look at the equipment and documents in the helicopter should confirm who we are."

Fuad discarded with a gesture the evidence of the maps, manometers and other oil-exploration equipment. "The fighting knife in your boot, Mr. Green. That is what doesn't ring true about who you say you are. The pistol is understandable, and I would believe a folding knife in your pocket or a utility knife in a case on your belt. But you had a fighting knife, a man killer, and it was strapped to your boot top like a commando. Why is that?"

"It doesn't mean anything. It's just a habit I picked up when I did my national service in the British army."

"It does if the part of the British army you served in was the Special Air Service. They wear their knives tied to the tops of their boots. Maybe you were in the SAS or even the parachute regiment?"

"No," McCarter, the ex-SAS man, replied. "I was in an infantry regiment, the Glosters, and we tied our knives to our boot tops, too."

"Tell me about your pilot," the Iranian demanded, switching topics. "What did you say his name is?"

McCarter tried to remember what Grimaldi's cover name was for this mission, but his head still wasn't working properly. "His name is Jack."

"Ah." The Iranian flipped open Grimaldi's wallet. "Jack what?"

"I don't remember. I just met him a couple days ago and everybody just calls him Jack."

"It seems that your pilot has two last names. Most of his cards are in the name of Jack Bennett, but there is one here that says Jack Grimaldi. Which one of them is his real last name?"

"Like I said, I don't remember his last name."

Fuad changed tracks again. "Why were you and Jack flying in this area?"

"I already explained," McCarter said, "we're an oil-exploration team and we were doing a survey of the region."

"That is odd," the Iranian said. "This area has been gone over several times and no oil has ever been found. Why has your company come here to search it again?"

"Damned if I know." McCarter didn't have to fake his frustration this time. "They ordered us to run a survey here, and that's what we were doing."

"That's a little stupid on their part, don't you think?"

The Briton shook his head. "The company doesn't pay me enough to think, mister. I just take my paycheck and do whatever I'm told to do. I don't know how things are done around here, but where I come from, a man has to do what he's told if he wants to make a living."

"I know all about following orders. The question is, what orders were you two following when you tried to fly over this fortress?"

"We were on an oil survey when we spotted this place. We don't have stone fortresses in Canada and we simply wanted to see what it was. Curiosity, you know?"

Fuad stared at him for a long moment before motioning for the guards.

"You and your pilot will be my guests here until I have a chance to check out your story. If you are engineers, then you will be free to go."

"What about the helicopter?" McCarter said. "How do I explain that to my boss in Toronto?"

"That is a problem, isn't it?"

JACK GRIMALDI AWAKENED to find himself lying on a hard bed in a dark, damp room. When his eyes adjusted to the gloom, he saw that he was alone in a small stone cell and the only light was coming from a small opening high on the wall by the ceiling.

Since McCarter wasn't in the cell with him, he could only assume that the Briton had been killed in the crash. He would mourn him when he had time later. Right now he had to figure out a way to get out of this place before he joined him in a lonely desert grave. If this Noor guy didn't hesitate to blast a civilian chopper out of the sky with no warning, it wasn't likely that he would treat survivors much better.

Since the first thing Grimaldi had to do was to recon his surroundings, he painfully got to his feet and waited for the room to stop spinning. The left side of his face and head hurt and he was having trouble focusing his eyes. Both shoulders were sore where he had been thrown against his harness. He didn't feel any internal pain, but from the superficial damage, he knew that he was lucky to have survived the crash.

The cell itself was a typical stone dungeon about ten feet square. The stones were large and well-set in ancient but uncrumbling mortar. Since he didn't have a hammer and stone chisel with him, he wouldn't be cutting his way through the walls anytime in the near future.

The cell door was old-fashioned, ironbound and wooden, and it looked to be at least a hundred years old. Knocking softly on it told Grimaldi that it was very thick. The only good thing was that it didn't have a window, which meant that he couldn't be watched while the door was closed. That might work to his advantage later.

He had finished his inspection and was sitting on his pallet when he heard the sound of approaching footsteps. He was on his feet and ready when the door was opened, but when he saw the AKs in the hands of his captors, he instantly decided against trying anything rash. Plus, in his condition, he wasn't sure that he could even run, much less fight.

"Hey! Take it easy," he said when his arms were jerked behind his back. The AK butt that slammed into his ribs told him that it was best to keep his mouth shut. As battered as he was from the crash, he didn't need a rifle-butt massage.

After being taken down corridors and up a number of flights of stairs, he was led into a well-furnished modern office where a man in desert fatigues and a pistol at his belt stood silently. Since it was the other guy's nickel, Grimaldi waited for him to speak.

After introducing himself, Fuad got straight to the point. "You are the pilot, correct?"

Grimaldi nodded. "Yep, that's me."

"What were you doing flying over this fortress?"

He shrugged. "We saw it and just wanted to check it out. We don't have anything like this where I come from."

"And where is that?"

"California."

"What is an American like you doing working for a Canadian oil company?"

"They pay well." Grimaldi shrugged. "And I fly for anyone who pays me."

"You are a mercenary, then?"

"No. I don't have anything to do with that. I'm a civilian pilot."

"Why do you have credit cards with two last names in your wallet?"

"I'm on the run from my ex-wife's lawyer," the pilot replied with a grin, "and I needed another name to go on my paycheck so he couldn't get his hands on it."

Fuad didn't think that the pilot was as stupid as he seemed to be, but that didn't matter. Even though he had already arranged for reinforcements to be sent, the appearance of the helicopter changed everything. There was no doubt in his mind that the pilot and his passenger had been making a recon of the fortress, not an oil survey as they claimed.

According to the spies in Peshawar, there had been seven men on the survey team, counting the pilot. Since he now had two of them in his cells, that left five to contend with. Normally five men wouldn't be a worry, but he wasn't so sure that these five were no danger. Not after the raid on the Mujahedeen camp.

"I will find out who you really are," Fuad said, "and you will stay here until I do."

"I hope it won't be too long," Grimaldi replied. "I have bills to pay and the company is going to chop me from the payroll if I don't show up."

Stony Man Farm

"WE'VE GOT A PROBLEM," Barbara Price said as she walked into the computer lab and dropped into the empty chair next to Kurtzman's computer console. "Jack and David are down somewhere in eastern Pakistan."

Aaron Kurtzman spun in his chair. "What happened?"

"Mack doesn't know yet. They went on a chopper recon flight over Noor's fortress and they didn't come back. They also aren't answering the radio."

"If our information is correct about Noor being in the Stinger business, he would have no trouble knocking down a chopper if he wanted to. He'd certainly have enough missiles to use."

"That's what Mack figures happened to them."

"What's the next move?" he asked.

"Manning has reported the disappearance of the aircraft to the Pakistani authorities as a routine exploration flight that didn't return, but their air force doesn't have much in the line of search-and-rescue capability."

"There's also the good chance that they wouldn't rescue them even if they knew where they were."

"There is always that," she acknowledged. With the exception of Iran and Libya, Islamic terrorism wasn't a state industry in most nations of the Middle East. But it was allowed to exist because the countries involved didn't have either the will or the resources to shut it down. The chances were good that the hard-line Islamic element in the Pakistani government knew all about Noor's activities and were protecting him. His smuggling networks would be very useful to them, and they wouldn't want nosy Westerners snooping around.

"What did Mack say he was going to do now?"

"He's still evaluating the situation, but he says that he wants to try to keep the cover in place for now and keep to the mission plan. He did say that he wants you to make a satellite run over the area and see if you can pick up the crash site before he moves on Noor's fortress. If they went down from a mechanical failure, he doesn't want to move on Noor prematurely."

Kurtzman's fingers flashed over his keyboard, bringing up the classified menu for the NRO, the National Reconnaissance Office. Once he was in he called up the Keyhole series spy-satellite flight-path schedule. The KH-11 series recon cameras had a twelve-inch resolution, and if the helicopter was down in the mountains, the satellite would be able to see it.

He studied the map showing the satellite flight paths for a moment. "You can tell him that I should be able to get a run scheduled within the next twelve hours. Keyhole Sierra Three will be coming on-line then, and I can program it to make a slight diversion to cover that area."

"This is what I was afraid of about this mission." Price closed her eyes and leaned back in the chair. "The guys have no backup, and now that Grimaldi is down they don't have a pilot to fly them out if they need an emergency extraction."

She abruptly stood and thought for a moment. "I'm going to talk to Hal and see if there's any way that he can line up some military support for me to call on if they need to get out of there in a hurry."

"With the situation as touchy as it is there," Kurtzman cautioned her, "there's no place in the vicinity that an American rescue force could use as a staging area. In fact, the mere presence of the American military anywhere in the region could easily be misunderstood and could touch off the war they're trying to prevent."

"I know," she replied. "But I don't want to leave them hanging without trying to set something up."

"Do what you can, of course," he counseled. "But remember that those guys have gotten themselves out of tighter spots than this without any help from the military."

"I still want to have some kind of backup available," she insisted. "I have a bad feeling about this one."

CHAPTER TWENTY

Peshawar, Pakistan

After thoroughly considering their options, Bolan did as Kurtzman expected he would and decided to get the team off center stage and out of the line of fire. He could feel the clock ticking down and knew that time was running out. Now that McCarter and Grimaldi were missing and either dead or captured, he couldn't risk staying in Peshawar any longer. Their cover might not be completely blown, but it was ragged around the edges. Being a sitting target was out of the question.

"Katz," he called out, motioning for the Phoenix team leader to join him, "we need to talk."

"What is it?"

"I want to move our operation into the field," he said. "All of it."

"You mean close down the warehouse and the hangar?" Katz asked.

"Yeah. I want to get as far away from Peshawar as we can. If this Noor guy is our opposition and if he's working with the Iranians, he has far too many eyes in town. I want to be someplace where we have a little more freedom of action while we're trying to sort this out."

"What do you have in mind?"

"I think we should take our oil-exploration act on the road. I think the opposition is inside our cover, but there's a lot of eastern Pakistan we can pretend to be looking at while we're trying to get more information on Noor's operation."

"If we do that, though, we'll lose the ability to fade into the background that we have here in town. If we run into a border patrol and can't answer their questions, we'll have to be ready to fight our way out."

"I think it's still better for us to have our enemies out in the open where we can see them and not hiding in the crowds around here."

"You've got a point," Katz agreed. "I'll get the men going on it right away."

"While you're doing that," Bolan said as he turned to the communications console, "I'll let Barbara know what we're going to do."

Barbara Price wasn't happy with Bolan's decision to move the team out of Peshawar. If the situation turned critical, being in the field made their extraction even more complicated. But she thoroughly understood Bolan's reasoning. With the situation still as fluid as it was, he needed his freedom of action more than he needed a base camp.

"I'm still going to try to get Hal to set up an emergency-extract option through the military," she told Bolan. "Hunt says that the indicators are all as high as they can be, and the next incident will definitely be enough to start the war."

"Go ahead and try to set it up," Bolan said. "But I don't think that it'll fly. If they start popping nukes over here, I don't think the President would dare risk even sending in a plane for us. It would be seen as taking sides. If we can't fly our Herky out, our best bet will be to try to get out overland through Afghanistan and try to come out in Tashkent. The GPS gear will let us go overland most of the way, and we'll stay away from the cities."

"I'll let Hal know what you're doing," she said. "Good luck."

"I'll be in touch."

IT TOOK LESS than an hour for the team to pack up their oil-survey gear, portable satellite com link, GPS navigating system, mountaineering equipment, rations for five days and their weapons. The rest of their supplies would be left behind, even though they knew that they would more than likely disappear before they had even driven out of sight. Along with being famous for its smugglers, Peshawar was also well-known as a city of thieves.

They were putting the last of their supplies into the two Land Rovers when Hassen Kader drove up in a battered old truck. "You are going after Noor now," the Afghan leader stated flatly as he stepped out of the vehicle.

"We'll be seeing him sooner or later," Bolan admitted, "but we're leaving Peshawar because there are too many eyes and ears here. I sent two of my men out in a helicopter to take a look at Noor's fortress and they didn't return. I think that someone figured out who we are and shot it down."

"I am sorry to hear about your men," Kader said. "But I think it is a wise move for you to move out of Peshawar. You should bring your men into my camp. I can assure you that there are no spies there."

"I appreciate the offer, but I think it'll be better for us if we're out in the open where we can have more freedom of movement."

"Where are you going?"

"We'll be heading east so we'll be in a better position to hit Noor's fortress once we can confirm that it's our target."

"What more confirmation do you need?" the Afghan asked. Jamillur had said that these men were America's greatest warriors, but he hadn't seen it in them. "You already know that his men have been buying the missiles. You know that his Iranians killed Jamillur, and now you tell me that he shot down your helicopter. What more information do you want?"

"I still don't know if Noor has thc missiles at his fortress," Bolan answered. "My only mission here is to stop the missiles from being used against civilian airliners. If I have to kill Noor to stop them, I'll do it, but he isn't my main target."

The Afghan shook his head. "I will continue to get more information on the missiles for you. But in the end, it will still be Noor that you will have to stop."

A HALF HOUR OUT of Peshawar, Bolan ordered the team to break out their weapons and go tactical.

"This is more like it," Encizo said as he brought his H&K from under cover and laid it across his lap with his finger hovering by the trigger. "I'm no good at skulking around back alleys. I like it better when we can let it all hang out."

Manning looked off at the barren hills on either side of the rutted dirt road they were following. The only vegetation on the khaki-colored landscape was scrub brush, and it grew as though there were a rule that said at least twenty feet distance had to stretch between plants. It wasn't a true desert, but it was close.

"We sure as hell have it all hung out, all right. We've got no cover, no concealment and no place to duck if the shit hits the fan. I like it better in the woods where there's someplace to hide."

"That's just because you grew up in Canada and you're more comfortable in the woods."

"Don't tell me that the Cuba you grew up in looked anything like this."

"That's for sure," Encizo agreed, grinning. "There are no palm trees or cool sea breezes anywhere around here."

"There *are* some palm trees," Manning said as they topped a rise in the road. "Look over to the right front."

The palm trees the Canadian pointed out were three hundred yards ahead at the bottom of a draw where the road turned down into what looked like an oasis. Calvin James, in the lead Land Rover, was heading toward the watering hole and Manning turned to follow him.

James's vehicle braked to a halt under the trees, and Bolan and Katz got out to recon the area as a possible base-camp site.

"It doesn't seem that this place gets much traffic," Katz said after they toured the area. "We can lay up here until Kurtzman sends us the recon photos of Noor's fortress."

"At least we'll be able to post security and know that we won't have someone watching us all the time."

ALL THAT Barbara Price's latest call to Hal Brognola accomplished was to get the big Fed to fly down from his Washington office.

"Have you heard from them lately?" he asked Kurtzman as he entered the computer lab thirty minutes later.

The computer whiz wheeled his chair around slowly. He didn't have to ask which "them" Brognola was referring to. "Not since they left Peshawar. They're heading east to recon that smuggler's fortress they reported earlier."

"They haven't said that they were planning to attack it?"

"Not yet."

"Damn! Do you have communication with them?"

"On the portable unit."

"Get Bolan on the line."

The Executioner came on-line almost immediately.

"This is Brognola," the big Fed said into the mike. "The President is concerned that you haven't made any more progress than you have. He's managed to drag the Pakistanis and the Indians kicking and screaming to the conference table, but he's afraid that the talks will break down if there's even one more Stinger incident. The rabid anti-American factions in both countries are angry that the talks are even taking place. They want blood, not more negotiations. The President needs assurances at this point that you are making progress on your end so he can decide whether he should continue the talks or explore his other options."

"Give the Man our regards," Bolan said, "and an invitation to send in the Marines anytime he likes. As far as our making any progress here, as soon as we locate a firm target, we'll be glad to hit it for him. As it is, though, we're still in the information-chasing stage."

"What are you doing about McCarter and Grimaldi?"

"Nothing right now," Bolan replied. "Like I said, I need to develop more intelligence on Noor's fortress before we can move on it. If they're being held there, I don't want to move too soon and blow it."

Like it or not, Brognola had to agree with Bolan's assessment. "I'm going to be staying at the Farm until further notice, and I want you to keep me updated on a regular basis."

"I'll be sure to call when I have something to report," Bolan promised.

THE WARRIOR'S conversation had done little to sweeten Brognola's mood. His feet were being held to the fire and he wanted some relief now. Bolan said that he needed more intelligence on Noor's fortress, so that's what he would get.

"Bring up the Keyhole flight schedule," Brognola told Kurtzman.

A few keystrokes later Kurtzman had the information displayed on the monitor. Brognola studied the data on the screen for a long moment.

"Now get me the orbital command sequence. The entry code is Lewis Carroll with two *r*s and two *l*s."

"I know."

A few keystrokes had him in the classified menu that was used to realign the orbiting satellites. "I'm in."

"Now," Brognola said, "direct Keyhole Delta Six to change orbit."

"Where are we going with it?"

"Pakistan."

"Wouldn't it be easier to have the NRO send the Aurora over? It takes quite a while for the Keyhole birds to change orbit."

The Aurora project was the Pentagon's latest aviation ultrasecret. Designed as a successor to the aging SR-71 Blackbird high-speed spy planes, the Aurora was straight out of a science-fiction movie. It was a hybrid spyplane-spaceship capable of flying over twice as fast as the old SR-71, which held the world's official speed record for an air-breathing aircraft. That record would instantly fall as soon as the Pentagon decided to declassify the Aurora project.

"They've already been ordered into the air," Brognola said. "In fact they're being launched right now. But the Man wants more continual coverage and wants the satellites moved in, as well. And don't think that all of this is being done in support of the Stony team. He wants the recon birds overhead when those idiots start popping nukes at each other. The whole NRO is on alert for this one."

The National Reconnaissance Office was the little-known and highly classified branch of the National Security Agency that supervised the operation of the Keyhole and other intelligence-gathering satellites. In an age of ballistic missiles, they were America's front line of defense against an enemy sneak attack. The NRO also operated the still-secret Aurora space planes. If the NRO was focusing on the Pakistani-Indian situation instead of keeping an eye on North Korea and the Russians, the situation was more than serious, it was critical.

"Now," Brognola said after Kurtzman plugged in the spy satellite's new orbital information, "maybe I can get some real information about what the hell's happening over there and get the Man off my ass."

If there was anyone in the world who appreciated high-tech intelligence gathering, Kurtzman did. His life was devoted to squeezing usable data from the electrons and microwaves that were the neuronal circuits of modern technology. Nonetheless, he also knew the value of the bare-eyeball observations of the man on the ground.

The satellite and Aurora recon runs would most certainly provide Bolan and the team with invaluable information about the fortress and the region around it. But in the end it would be the Mark One human eyeballs of the Stony Man team that would make the difference. No computer had ever been designed that could sift through information as fast as the human brain. And no sensor or detector could pick up the nuances of the information that a well-trained man on the ground could. The satellite information would be helpful, but the men in Pakistan would still have to make the tough decisions based on what they saw with their own eyes.

CHAPTER TWENTY-ONE

At the Oasis

Right at that moment, it was the well-trained eyes of Rafael Encizo that warned Bolan of the danger heading toward them. He, James and Manning had taken up security positions around the oasis while Katz and Bolan set up their camp.

"We've got visitors," Encizo transmitted over the com link. "I've got three or four men on foot in the hills, and another dozen in two jeeps coming toward us from the north. They're moving in the open, but I can't ID them."

Bolan looked beyond the ring of palm trees around the oasis and saw the vehicles. They were too far away to positively ID, but they looked like Mujahedeen to him.

"Keep down," he sent back. "Let them get in closer."

There was no time to move their Land Rovers to a safer place, so the men took cover away from the vehicles so as not to draw fire on them. If they were damaged, the team would be on foot miles from the nearest town.

"It's okay," Katz transmitted over the com link as he lowered his field glasses. "It looks like Kader's in the lead jeep."

"I thought I told him that we wanted to keep to ourselves for a while," Bolan said. "We don't need anyone drawing attention to us."

"Let's hear what he has to say before we run him off," Katz suggested. "He did say that he was going to try to locate more of the Stingers for us."

The two jeeps stopped several yards from the oasis, and if the Mujis were armed they were careful not to show their weapons. Bolan stepped out to meet the Afghan warrior, but kept the H&K ready in his hands. Kader claimed to be an ally, but in this part of the world, it didn't hurt to be cautious.

"El Askari," Kader greeted him, "I have news of the Iranian dogs you seek."

"Come and tell us the news, Hassen Kader," Bolan said, inviting him into the shade of the oasis. By the unwritten law of the Middle East, the first man at an oasis owned it until he left. Others wanting to use its shade and water had to have his invitation.

Also knowing the local customs, Katz took a canteen from the inside of the Land Rover and offered it to the Afghan. "Share our water."

Kader took the canteen and downed a short sip of the stale water. "Thank you for your hospitality."

Now that the formalities had been seen to, they could get down to business. "I have a new report from my people in Afghanistan," the Muji leader said. "They have told me that more Iranians are moving into Noor's fortress. They are coming from one of the terrorist training camps in the mountains and will cross the border into Pakistan tonight. If you like, I will lead you to them."

Katzenelenbogen and Bolan locked eyes and Katz nodded. Stopping the reinforcements before they got to the fort might pay big dividends when it came time to storm its rock walls. Each gunman they could take out while he was still in the open was one less that they would have to dig out from behind thick stone walls.

Bolan picked up the map from the seat cushion of the Land Rover and laid it on the hood. "Where are they supposed to be coming from?"

Kader studied the map for a moment. "Here," he stated, stabbing his finger at a low pass through the hills that started in Afghanistan and ended up in Pakistan. "The Pakistani army patrols have been ordered out of that region tonight so there will be no chance encounters."

That was the first Bolan had heard of collusion between Noor and anyone in the Pakistani government. It could add a new dimension to the problem. "Do you know who in the army is supporting Noor?" Katz asked.

"They are supporting the Iranians rather than him," Kader said. "I have also learned that Noor seems to be under the control of the Iranians, as well, rather than just working with them."

"What do you mean?"

"Noor's men do not go anywhere now without an Iranian with them and they take their orders from the

Iranians. Also, Noor has not been seen at any of his usual haunts for several weeks now, and no one has been allowed inside his fortress."

That wasn't surprising news. Since the start of this, one of the biggest questions had been why a drug dealer and gunrunner would want to provoke a war between India and Pakistan. For the ruling Iranian Islamic Party, however, nuclear war fell under the category of state policy.

"In return for this information," Kader said, "I want to go with you if you move against these butchers. I will send a dozen of my best fighters and our best weapons."

"What do you think?" Bolan asked Katz.

"This might be the break we need," the Israeli replied. "If we take out those reinforcements, it won't be so difficult for us to get into that place. Also, with McCarter and Grimaldi gone, we're going to need some help taking them out, so I say that we let them come with us."

"I agree."

AFTER CONSULTING his superiors in Tehran, Major Fuad was even more convinced that Green was at the very least a mercenary working for the Americans, if not an outright American CIA agent. A man fitting his description was known to have been involved in several actions against Islamic freedom fighters over the past several years. Now the question was what he was going to do with him.

He knew that he could torture Green and force him to reveal what he knew about his mission. In the end, though, all he would have left would be carrion not even fit for the dogs to eat. All he would learn was what he already believed—that the Americans were moving against him.

There might be a better use for this prisoner than merely torturing him to death for the information he held inside his head. He could be of much greater use to the plan if his body were to be found in Northern India with a loaded, American-made Stinger missile launcher at his side. The fact that it would be one of the missiles that wouldn't fire until it had a new battery would be of no importance.

The Indians would be able to identify him as an American agent and would assume that the United States was somehow involved in the crisis on the side of the Pakistanis. The American government would say that they knew nothing of him, of course, but since the American President was negotiating with Pakistan, the denial wouldn't be believed.

Even if it did nothing else, it would make the Hindus feel that they were again being betrayed by the Americans. Not only that, but it would help in another area. Ever since the first airliner shootdown, the Indian border-security forces had doubled their patrols along the border with Pakistan and were making it very difficult for anyone to cross over. Finding an American with one of the missiles instead of a Pakistani might make them relax their vigilance.

He didn't bother checking in with Tehran to have this idea approved. He knew that if he did, they would insist on his putting Green to the question. They were always eager to torture their prisoners, even if they knew what they would say before they started in on them. He understood their passion, but he thought that it was sometimes a waste of resources. A living man, or even a corpse, as in Green's case, could be very useful if he were placed in the right spot.

And even if he sent Green south, he would still have the pilot, whatever his name was, left to question.

Calling for the guard outside his door, he told the man to find Sergeant Hussein and have him report to him immediately. The sergeant was one of the Hindi speakers assigned to the group that would take the missiles into India. He knew the secret smuggler's route through the Kashmir Pass that would let him get past the Indian border patrol.

As soon as Hussein appeared, Fuad quickly briefed him on what he wanted to have done. The sergeant saluted and hurried to do as he had been ordered.

MCCARTER WAS DOZING when the door to his cell slammed open. He opened his eyes to see four Iranians with AKs charge into the room. Moving slowly so as not to set them off, he got to his feet, being very careful to keep his hands in plain view. Two of the guards grabbed his arms while the other two kept their weapons trained on him.

"Where are we going, guys?" he asked.

Instead of an answer, one of the Iranians jammed the muzzle of his AK into McCarter's back, so he started to walk.

The Briton blinked to clear his eyes when he was led out into the bright sun. One of Fuad's Toyota four-wheel-drives was parked in the courtyard with several of his men standing around it. It looked as if he was going for a ride.

Two of the guards pressed him facefirst against the hood of the vehicle while the other two jerked his arms behind his back and bound his wrists tightly with what felt like a braided leather rope. After double-checking the knots, they lifted him into the back of the vehicle and pushed him onto the floor. One of the major's men, wearing civilian clothing instead of his desert fatigues, got behind the wheel.

A few minutes later another Iranian wearing civilian clothing came out and loaded a long crate into the back with McCarter, then he slid into the passenger seat. After a word to the driver, they drove out of the fort, and, after reaching the main road, headed for the hills to the south.

As he lay with his face pressed against the steel floor of the Toyota, McCarter tested his bonds. They were tight and the rough rope cut into his wrists. Even so, he continued working against it, feeling the blood start to flow as his skin tore. If the rope was braided leather as he thought it was, it should stretch slightly when it got wet, and his blood was all he had to wet it with.

Going into an almost meditative state, McCarter moved the pain from his wrists into a small corner in the back of his mind and shielded it from his conscious awareness. He had to concentrate on what he was doing and didn't have time to experience the pain. There would be time for that after he had freed himself.

A little more than an hour later the Toyota pulled into a village and stopped. McCarter was grateful for the relief from the pounding he was taking in the back of the vehicle. No matter how he tried to brace himself with his hands and shoulders, the damned thing was beating him half to death. So far, though, he had worked his bonds enough that he thought the leather rope felt a little looser. But his hands and wrists were so numb that it just might have been loss of sensation instead of slack in the rope.

As soon as the Toyota came to a halt, the sergeant dismounted, and the Briton caught what he thought was the Farsi word for water in what he said to his driver. The driver stepped out, and leaning over the side of the Toyota, grabbed McCarter by the collar and jerked him upright into a sitting position. Slowly drawing the canteen from his field belt, he unscrewed the cap and extended it toward him.

McCarter's mouth and throat were more than dry, and caked with dust. He was parched, and he could almost taste the water he was being offered. It would be hot, stale and metallic tasting from the canteen, but it would be wet and welcome. He was thirsty, but he wasn't dehydrated yet and he had a better use for the liquid.

Leaning forward awkwardly with his mouth open, he slammed his chin against the canteen, knocking it from the Iranian's hand. The water spilled out onto the floor of the Toyota. The driver cursed, but then laughed when he saw the carefully staged expression of horror on McCarter's face.

"Lick it up, infidel," he spit in Farsi as he snatched up the canteen and fastened it back on his belt before walking away.

As soon as the driver was out of sight around the corner of a building, McCarter twisted around and leaned back until his bound wrists were resting in the spilled water. He could feel the moisture on his skin as he twisted his hands against the rope. Slowly, as he tugged against his bonds, he felt the leather soften and stretch.

The question was, would the rope shrink tight again when it dried? He didn't know what it would do, but he hoped that he would be able to keep enough pressure against the rope as the water evaporated so that it wouldn't tighten up again and he could keep the precious slack he had gained.

He had just sat up again against the side of the rear compartment when the two Iranians returned. With a single glance back to make sure that he was where he should be, the sergeant climbed into the passenger seat and ordered the driver to start the engine. The Toyota pulled out on the road leading south out of the village and quickly picked up speed.

With the muscles in his arms tensed to keep the tension on the loosened bonds, McCarter checked the sun and saw that he was being driven south toward India.

BROGNOLA RAN toward the communications room when he was told that Bolan was on the line. The White House had just called for an update, and he didn't have anything new to tell the Man.

"Why don't you go ahead and hit Noor's fortress immediately?" the big Fed asked after Bolan explained his plan to take out the Iranians.

"If the Iranians are reinforcements headed for the fort," Bolan explained, "I don't want to have to deal with them after they get inside those stone walls. That place is going to be difficult enough to take as it is."

"But you're putting your force at risk without going after the primary objective," Brognola said. "The President isn't going to like that."

"This is a tactical decision that affects how well we'll be able to do later when we try to take that fort. The last thing I need right now is a politician dictating my options. I have a feeling that we don't have much time left, and if we don't get into that fortress the first time we try, we'll never get a second chance."

CHAPTER TWENTY-TWO

Inside the Fortress

As soon as the prisoner had been driven away, Major Fuad got back to the most pressing matter at hand—the new batteries for the defective Stinger missiles waiting in his armory. According to the fax he had just received, they were finally being flown out of Singapore and would be arriving in Peshawar at noon the following day. That would have them delivered to the fortress before the day was out, and the technician could finally begin installing them. The man had said that it would be only a matter of two days at the most before all twenty of the missiles would be ready for use.

Fuad was certain that he could accomplish his mission with only three or four of the missiles hitting their targets in each country, but he wanted to have more than that ready for use, particularly in India. The Islamic Party agents in the northern provinces had reported that both the Indian army and the border-security forces had stepped up security around the airports, as well as along the border regions between the two countries. He expected to lose at least half the missiles and gunners to the Indian patrols when they tried to infiltrate their targets.

He didn't, however, have to allocate extra missiles for the targets in Pakistan. Even though troops were guarding the airports he intended to hit, his connections in the Pakistani army high command would make it easier for his men to infiltrate their targets there. The same connections that were allowing his reinforcements to come into the country unmolested would work to let his gunners get into position around the Lahore and Islamabad airports. A Stinger or two later and the entire population of Pakistan would be ready to march south.

Noor's fax machine started to hum with another incoming message. When he took the hard copy from the tray, he saw that the message was from the spy he had left to watch over the Canadian oil-survey team in Peshawar. The report was short: the suspect Canadians had suddenly left Peshawar; they hadn't bothered to check out of their hotel and their warehouse had been abandoned without a guard being placed over the equipment they had left behind; they had last been seen driving east in two Land Rovers.

The message was short, but that was all the information Fuad needed. The Canadians, or Americans, as he had suspected them to be all along, had to be the enemy who had raided the Afghan camp. The chopper that had been shot down had been on a reconnaissance mission as he had thought, and, when it didn't return, the Americans suspected that they had been discovered and had run from Peshawar.

The question now was how far they were going to run and where. If they were abandoning their mission to try to track down the Stingers, he wouldn't have to worry about them. But he didn't expect that it would be that easy. Though he had no respect for the Americans as a people, or for their corrupt government, he knew that many of their warriors were men of grim determination. If they believed that he was holding the helicopter crew captive, they might try to rescue them. While they would never succeed, an attack might draw unwelcome attention to the Snake's Skull, and he couldn't afford that.

He already had his reinforcements coming in, and they should arrive early the next morning. When they did, he would send them out to put up a defensive perimeter around the fortress. But even before they showed up, he could start running defensive patrols in the hills around the fortress with the men he had on hand. He also wanted to get the ground-surveillance radar set up in the hills surrounding the fortress to give him even more warning of anyone approaching.

He briefly thought about contacting the Islamic Party's top agent in Pakistan, army General Sajad Balik, and asking him to provide an army unit to help protect the fortress. That, however, would be too risky. While Balik and several of his key officers were all loyal Muslims who supported the plans of the Islamic Party, not all of the army's junior officers and sergeants were party supporters. Were they to start asking questions or to talk about being sent on such an unusual assignment, it might arouse suspicions.

Plus he didn't want to have to share the glory of the plan with anyone. Balik was positioned to bring the army in on the side of the party once the missiles started to fall, but the credit for causing that to happen was to be all his. When the plan was successful, he would be responsible for bringing more territory under Muslim control than any man since the sixteenth century. He would become a prince among the faithful, and men would remember him for a thousand years.

That was a great prize he wouldn't willingly share with anyone.

ALI NOOR ALSO KNEW that the missile batteries were finally being flown in. But unlike his uninvited Iranian guest, he wasn't rejoicing to hear that particular piece of news. Even though Fuad had said that he would be left in peace as soon as the major's operation was completed, he had no faith in that promise. He knew what Fuad thought of him personally, and it wasn't much. Even more important than that, though, was the fact that since he was aware of many of the details of the Iranians' operation, he was a liability to the ayatollahs. For their scheme to work the way they had planned it, they couldn't leave anyone alive who could point the finger at them.

There would be great international outrage when the nuclear exchange between Pakistan and India finally occurred. The great powers would be poised and ready to punish whoever they thought was responsible for the carnage. For the ayatollahs' plan to work the way they wanted it to, no one could know of their part in causing the war. For them to survive, they had to appear completely uninvolved.

When the Iranians moved into Pakistan and Northern India, it would have to appear to the international community that they were simply offering humanitarian aid to their fellow Muslim survivors of the nuclear tragedy. Then, when they took over the governments, it would have to appear that the people themselves had freely chosen to declare their countries to be new Islamic republics. None of that would be possible if there was a witness to the treachery of the Iranians. That meant that he was expendable, as were all of his staff and employees. And since the batteries were on their way, his time on earth was quickly running out.

The only way he was going to survive this would be if he disappeared before the missiles started delivering their deadly warheads. He hated to abandon the fortress palace that he had lavished so much money on, but it would be of little use to him if he was dead.

The major had put one of his Iranian guards in charge of watching over Noor's communications room, but he hadn't stopped the dealer from conducting his routine business affairs with the outside world. It was necessary for everything in Pakistan to seem normal, even the dealings of a gunrunner and drug smuggler. In the Middle East, business was business and someone would notice if he completely dropped out of sight.

Going into his communications room, Noor powered up his powerful computer and modem. Clicking into his financial menu, he transferred the contents of his bank accounts out of Pakistan, even with the guard looking over his shoulder. To keep Fuad's watchdog from sounding the alarm, he transferred the money to the national bank of Saudi Arabia. Even though the Saudis had sided with the Westerners in the Gulf War and sold their oil to them, they were still considered to be the keepers of the faith and therefore loyal to Islam. When he later got the chance, he would transfer the funds to Morocco, but he didn't want to alert Fuad by even mentioning one of the Islamic Party's staunchest enemies.

Once his money was safe, he went back to his personal quarters to prepare to abandon his fortress. Along with the money he had stashed away in his bank accounts, he also had a great deal of ready cash on hand. In the Middle East, money in the hand was worth far more than a letter of credit or a bank check. So were jewels and precious stones, and he had a stash of those, as well as a supply of gold coins. He had no idea how much these solid assets were worth, but he knew that he wouldn't be able to carry them all with him. So the problem was to sort through them and make up a small bundle of only the most valuable items.

He sighed when he thought of having to leave the rest of his valuables behind, to say nothing of the fortress's furnishings and artworks. It had taken him years to gather them, but while he enjoyed these things, he enjoyed his life even more. And once he reestablished himself in Morocco, he could buy new things.

The question now was, how was he going to make his escape? While Fuad hadn't put him under a constant guard, he was in fact confined behind the fortress walls. The Iranian guards had replaced all his own men on the gates and the sentry posts, effectively preventing him from leaving without the major's permission. He also couldn't try to bring any of his own men in on his plan to escape. He had thought that they were loyal to him, but from what he had seen, the major now had most of them eating out of his hand.

But, while Fuad's guards were in control of the fortress's gates and walls, he didn't think that they had discovered the ancient bolt hole that had been cut deep in the rock under the walls. As with most of the fortresses in the Middle East, the original builders had engineered a secret way out for the inhabitants, in case things looked bad outside the stone walls.

Later occupants had built over this underground escape route, but he had uncovered it during his extensive remodeling and rebuilding. Using men he brought in specifically for this one job, he had the tunnel opened again and cleared all the way to the end. Even back then he knew that for a man in his line of work, it never hurt to have a way out.

The tunnel was barely tall enough for a man to walk upright and went deep into the outcropping the fortress was built on. Once under the rock, when the tunnel was in complete darkness, there was a pit to trap an enemy who didn't know where it was. During the rebuilding, he had wisely left the trap in place in case someone was following him when he had to make his break.

The tunnel came out almost a half kilometer away on the back side of the hill. The opening was blocked by large stones and was overgrown with brush, so it was hidden from casual observation. He had prepositioned enough tools in the tunnel to be able to break through from the inside.

The tunnel would be his way out, but once he was away from the fortress he would be on foot and it was a long way to the nearest civilization or an airport. He would have to make his way to the village five kilometers away and try to get a vehicle there, or even better, a horse. It had been years since he had ridden, but it was a skill that no man ever forgot. And maybe being on horseback would be better than trying to escape in a jeep.

Once Fuad discovered that he was missing, he would send his men out in their four-wheel-drive Toyotas to look for him. And with the major's contacts in the army, he could probably get motorized military patrols to join in the search for him, as well. On horseback, however, he could go places that no motor vehicle could. It would be slower, to be sure, but time wouldn't matter as long as he was alive.

BOLAN INVITED KADER to have his men come into the oasis so they could plan the attack on the Iranians.

The Muji leader had said that he had assembled his best men and weapons, and the Executioner wanted to see what his best was before he got into this any deeper.

It was no surprise to see the weapons carried by Kader's Mujahedeen warriors. To a man, they all carried Russian-made AK-47s captured during the Russian-Afghan war. Two of them had RPG-7 antitank rocket launchers also of Soviet manufacture. There wasn't a single backyard copy of the old British bolt-action .303 SMLE that had been the Afghans' favorite before the Soviets brought in tons of modern weapons and then conveniently lost most of them on the battlefield.

The surprise was that Kader had somehow acquired a Russian 30 mm automatic grenade launcher. Mounted on a tripod, the 30 mm weapon resembled a comic-book belt-fed machine gun with a short, fat barrel. Even with Kader's men joining them, they would still be outnumbered, so the grenade launcher was a welcome addition. It could fire the deadly antipersonnel grenades eight hundred meters with great accuracy.

The fighters were all mature men, not teenagers, and they looked as if they had been in combat before. They weren't Rangers, but they would have to do.

With everyone gathered around the map, Bolan and Kader went over the terrain and picked the two most likely routes the Iranians would take to reach the pass. While they talked, one of Kader's men translated for the Mujis who didn't speak English. Once everyone knew what he was supposed to do, the strike force mounted their vehicles to move out.

Bringing up the GPS navigation system, Bolan set their course for the pass and led the convoy away from the oasis.

CHAPTER TWENTY-THREE

In the Mountains

The sun was low in the sky when Bolan and the Phoenix Force warriors arrived at the base of the mountain pass right inside the Afghan border. If Kader's information was correct, this was the route the Iranians would use to cross into Pakistan on their way to join their comrades in Noor's fortress. His information about the Pakistani army pulling back seemed to be correct because they hadn't seen any indication of border patrols.

Halting the vehicles, Bolan dismounted and went to talk to Kader. "This is the start of the pass," he said, "and it doesn't look like there are any recent vehicle tracks, so I think we got here before them."

"Even though the Pakistani army has left the area," the Afghan stated, "the Iranians will wait until dark before they make the crossing. They do not want even civilians to see them because they might talk."

"Get your people formed up and we'll sweep down the side of the pass. If we don't find them, we'll set up an ambush and wait for them."

Taking up a tactical formation, Bolan put the Phoenix Force commandos up front on point and let some of Kader's Afghans pull the flank security.

Keeping well back from the crest of the ridge, they started up the pass.

"STRIKER," ENCIZO'S controlled voice said over the team's com link, "we have contact."

For thc past half hour the Cuban had been up on point with James in his slack position. At the moment the two men were several hundred yards ahead, waiting for the rest of the team to join them before leapfrogging ahead.

"Where are they?"

"There are three four-wheel-drive rigs right below me with two dozen men in desert-camouflaged uniforms clustered around them. I don't see any heavy weapons with them, but it looks like they're all packing AKs."

"I'm coming up," Bolan replied. He wanted to check this out for himself before committing to battle.

"Affirm," Encizo answered. "But keep low. They're in position to bring fire on us if they spot you."

Keeping to the rocks, Bolan made his way to the reverse slope of the ridge and joined Encizo. The troops in the draw below seemed to be taking a break while they waited for orders to move out again. Their three vehicles were parked close together instead of being spread out, and they didn't seem to be expecting any trouble. Best of all, the only heavy weapons he could see were two RPG launchers.

"Let's nail them," the Cuban growled.

Bolan hesitated, scanning the high ground that surrounded the draw. "I want to check in with the Afghans on the flanks first. They might have some friends in the area we can't see. We don't need any interruptions once we start in on these guys."

Kader's Afghans and the rest of Phoenix Force had deployed along the back side of the ridge and were ready to go to work as soon as Bolan gave the signal. James had mounted his sniper scope on his H&K and had taken up a well-concealed firing position on the far left flank, covering the Iranians' only avenue of retreat. With the ranging scope fitted to the assault rifle, he could bring accurate single-shot fire out to a range of eight to nine hundred meters.

"Okay," Bolan said. "The Afghans say they're alone, so let's do it."

Encizo flashed the attack signal, and James's finger took up the slack on the trigger. His first shot took out the Iranian guard seated in the lead vehicle who looked to be the man in charge. At least he was the man with the pistol on his belt and a map in front of him. The high-velocity 7.62 mm round took him high in the middle of his chest and knocked him backward out of the seat.

The echo of James's shot hadn't even died away before the rest of the Phoenix warriors opened up on the remaining Iranians. With their weapons set on full-auto, they sent a deadly rain of fire into the draw, taking the Iranians completely by surprise.

Even though they had been caught off guard, the Iranians were professionals. They scrambled for their weapons and returned fire quickly. But most of them were too late and were completely exposed to the deadly rain of fire from the ridge. The ones who were able to make it to cover behind their vehicles fared not much better than the ones who were caught out in the open.

The Russian 30 mm grenade launcher the Afghans brought with them also added to the carnage of the small-arms fire. Though it didn't pack the range of the American 40 mm grenade launchers, it had the same kind of antipersonnel warhead and did the same kind of damage. The grenades reached behind the vehicles and sent their deadly shrapnel into the men hiding behind them.

It was over in seconds, and the two dozen men lay scattered around their shot-up vehicles.

"Cease-fire!" Bolan called out.

The gunfire echoed into silence, and for a second all was quiet again.

"Clear the kill zone," Bolan ordered.

Their weapons held at the ready, the Afghans and the Phoenix Force warriors cautiously moved down into the draw. Kader, however, ran on ahead of the rest, eager to get closer to his enemies. The first Iranian he came to was dead, his chest torn open by shrapnel. Several bullet holes pierced the upper body of a second man. The third one, however, had only a grazing head wound and moaned when the Afghan rolled him over.

Reaching down, the Muji grabbed a handful of the front of the man's camouflage jacket and pulled him to his feet. When Bolan glanced over, he saw the Afghan's left arm around the Iranian's neck and the fighting knife poised in his other hand.

"Kader!" he yelled. "Don't! We need him!"

The warning came too late.

The Afghan's knife blade flashed. Burying it to the hilt in the soldier's lower belly, Kader gave it a savage twist. But he wasn't content to release the man and let him die. In those few brief seconds before the Iranian's brain shut down, he looked deep into his dark, panicked eyes.

"This is for my uncle and his family," he said as he ripped the knife upward. The blade tore through the man's intestines, stomach and lungs, separating the ends of his ribs from his sternum, as Kader drove for his objective, the Iranian's heart. When the blade bit into the still-pumping organ, the man's pupils dilated completely and his eyes faded into a dull glaze as he went limp in Kader's grasp.

When Bolan reached his side, Kader had withdrawn the knife and was poised to stab him again. "Kader!" he said sharply, grabbing the Afghan's shoulder. "That's enough, he's dead."

The Muji turned toward Bolan and seemed to blink back into focus. The pupils of his dark eyes were wide and glittering, and his lips were drawn back from his teeth.

"That is only the first one of these dogs who will pay for Ahmed's death," he snarled. "My uncle will be avenged."

"If you can't take them prisoner next time, Kader," Bolan snapped, "I can't have you working with us. I need prisoners to interrogate and I can't talk to dead bodies."

"I am sorry, El Askari, I did not think." Kader sounded sincere. "Now that my knife has been bloodied, I can wait to take the rest of my vengeance."

"You had better. I need information more than I need dead Iranians."

As soon as all of the bodies had been checked, the Afghans counted their own casualties. Two of them had been hit, but neither was seriously injured. While their wounds were being bandaged, the rest of Kader's men quickly salvaged the weapons and ammunition from the Iranians' bodies and the trucks.

Even though Kader's information about the Pakistani army purposely pulling away from this sector of the border had proved to be correct, Bolan didn't want to risk running into a patrol. Sound carried far in the mountains, and if the Pakistanis had heard the gunfire, they would come to investigate.

"Let's get them back in the vehicles and get out of here," Bolan told Katz. "We don't want the army to come back and find us here."

Two of the Iranians' vehicles were too badly shot up to be driven away, but the third was quickly loaded with the newly acquired weapons, and the Afghans clambered aboard to drive it back to where the other vehicles had been left. Once they had rejoined their vehicles, Bolan took a heading from the GPS and led the strike force back into Pakistan and turned east toward Noor's fortress.

Brognola wanted him to hit the fort and he was ready for it now.

THE SUN WAS SETTING as the Toyota carrying the two Iranians and David McCarter sped into the southernmost foothills of eastern Pakistan. The driver and officer had kept up a steady chatter for most of the trip, but it had meant little to McCarter. He had caught a few words of their conversation, including one or two words that he thought might be place names. But it didn't mean diddly to him without a map.

All the way up from the village, McCarter had kept his wrists tensed against the leather rope. The rope had dried, but the hard-won slack he had gained was still there. As soon as the driver was completely occupied trying to keep the speeding vehicle on the unpaved mountain track, the Briton started twisting the rope against his wrists. Now that he had the slack, he needed a lubricant to help ease his hands through. Again his blood would do nicely.

He winced as the rope cut into his bruised flesh again and reopened the dried scabs, but he forced the pain back and persisted. Struggle and tug as hard as he could, however, his hands were simply too big to pull through the slack in the rope.

Slumping back against the side of the Toyota, McCarter calmed his mind and searched for an alternative. He refused to accept that there was no way for him to get free. He had to keep trying because he knew that as soon as he got to wherever those two goons were taking him, he would be a dead man.

An image in a movie he'd once seen popped into his head. The hero had had his hands tied behind his back, but he had been able to slide his bound wrists down over his feet and bring them around in front of him. It had looked easy in the film, but then, the hero always had it easy in the flicks.

McCarter was tall and fit and endless hours of unarmed combat practice had made him as limber as an acrobat. He had long arms, as well as big hands, so maybe he could do it. The thing was, he didn't know if it was possible while he was wearing his combat boots. The molded rubber cleats on the bottoms of the soles might catch and hold the rope, but he had to give it a try.

Rolling onto his side, McCarter extended his arms behind his back as far as they would go. Pointing the toes of his boots until his feet ached, he drew his heels up until they were pressed tightly against his buttocks and brought his bound wrists down over them. His hands slipped down over the heels of the boots, but the rope caught when he tried dragging it up onto the soles.

Rocking his wrists from side to side, he worked them halfway up the soles, but the rope caught again in between the mud cleats. He arched his back and strained to pull one of the boots through. The rope cut deeper into his skin and the thin muscles over the bones of his wrists as he tugged and twisted, but he felt the rope ride up over one of the boots. Pushing as hard as he could and giving a final jerk, the one foot was free. The other followed immediately.

Not waiting an instant in case one of the Iranians turned around, he rose to his knees, clasped his still-bound hands together and swung them against the side of the sergeant's head as if they were a sledgehammer. His clenched fists struck right above the Iranian's left ear, and he heard a dull crack over the noise of the Toyota as the man's skull was crushed. His head lolled on his neck as he slumped forward in his seat, dead.

Recovering before the driver could go for his weapon, McCarter turned and, opening his arms wide, slid his hands down over the Iranian's head and around his neck. With his bound wrists on each side of his throat, he hugged the driver to him in a deadly embrace, squeezing his windpipe.

The driver's hands frantically tore at McCarter's as the Iranian fought to breathe, and he lost control of the vehicle. The Toyota edged off the side of the road, and the driver made a wild grab with one hand to try to correct the slip, but was too late. The vehicle headed down the side of the mountain.

Gathering his feet under him, McCarter tried to throw himself clear as the Toyota rolled over. The side came up and slammed him in the back as he jumped clear, knocking the wind out of him. He crashed into the rocks as the truck went end over end into the chasm.

The Phoenix Force commando was stunned by the fall, but he twisted around and raised his bound wrists to his mouth. His sharp teeth made short work of the leather rope, and the minute it parted he got to his feet. Ignoring the pain in his wrists and the battering he had taken in the fall, he headed downhill for the wreck. His first order of business was to make sure that the two Islamic commandos were dead. But even more important, he needed to strip the bodies if he was going to survive.

Both the driver and the sergeant had been thrown clear of the Toyota in its wild ride down the mountainside. He came to the sergeant's body first and stopped. The man didn't have a canteen on his field belt, but he was armed with a Russian Makarov 9 mm pistol, which he took, along with the pistol belt and holster.

Farther down the hill, he came upon the driver's corpse, lying next to his wrecked vehicle, where an AK-47 assault rifle was clipped to the back of his seat. He appropriated it, as well, and stuffed the extra loaded magazines into the side pockets of his field pants.

The driver's canteen, however, was less than half-full. The man hadn't had a chance to refill it after McCarter had dumped it in the back of the vehicle at the village. It wasn't much water for this kind of terrain, but it would have to do. Neither of the Iranians had had any rations, but he wasn't concerned about food. He knew that he could last a hell of a lot longer without eating than he could without water.

Now that he was armed and at least had some water, it was high time that he got out of the area before someone came down the road and spotted the wreck. Before he left, though, he had to take care of the Stinger that had been loaded into the Toyota with him.

Untying the thirty-four-pound missile, he hefted it like a baseball bat and slammed the optic sight against the Toyota's bumper. Bits of plastic and glass flew, and the housing cracked. Grasping the other end, he slammed it against the bumper repeatedly until the tube was destroyed. Finally he hurled the missile as far down the hill as he could. Someone might find it down there, but it would be of no use to them now.

Before McCarter set out, he had to decide on a direction. Without a map, he had no way of knowing where he was, but he figured that there was a pretty good chance that he was already in India. That left him with a problem—should he continue south, deeper into India, or should he try to get back across the border to Pakistan and make for Peshawar?

Since he didn't have his passport or identification documents with him, either way he ran the risk of being picked up by the local authorities and held until he could prove his identity. But since he at least had a legitimate reason to be in Pakistan and could prove it with a phone call to the team's communications center in Peshawar, he decided to head north.

CHAPTER TWENTY-FOUR

On the Border

Once they were an hour away from the ambush site, Bolan called a halt so he could contact Stony Man Farm. It took only a minute to plug in the portable satellite com link and bounce the signal off one of the military com sats orbiting overhead. Brognola was on the line in seconds, and Bolan gave him a quick rundown on the ambush in the pass. He concluded by telling Brognola that they were going to hit Noor's fortress next.

"Since none of the Iranian vehicles was carrying Stingers," he said, "I'm convinced that Kader's information was correct. Rather than them being a strike force that had been targeted against a Pakistani airport, they were reinforcements for Noor's fortress, as he claimed."

"I would concur with that," Brognola said.

"And," Bolan continued, "since Kader was right about that, I'm going to let him in on the rest of the operation against Noor. Now that the odds have been cut down a little, we're ready to take on the fortress."

"I'm glad to hear you're finally making your move," Brognola replied. "The Man's been on my ass to produce results and I haven't had much to tell him lately. I can assure you that he'll be very glad to hear this. The disarmament talks aren't going well, and we're all just waiting for the next terrorist incident to blow the lid off."

"We'll move on from here tonight," Bolan said, "and find a safe place to lager tonight. Tomorrow we'll move on in and recon the area and then go over the walls tomorrow night. I'll be taking a dozen or so of Kader's men with us to create a diversion while we climb up the walls. I'll talk to you again before we make our move."

"Sounds good," Brognola replied. "The Bear wants to talk to you. He's got something you'll need."

"I've finally got your recon photos," Kurtzman said when he came on the line, "and I made a computer-enhanced blowup of the fortress and the area around it. I also found the chopper crash site. The crew compartment is pretty well beat-up, but it looks like the crash was survivable. But even on max enhancement I didn't see any signs of bodies or graves in or around the wreck. They either survived and walked away from the wreck or their bodies were taken away for burial somewhere else."

Bolan also knew that they could have been taken captive and held at the fortress, but at least there was a chance that they were still alive. "I've got the fax ready," he said. "Send them."

Once the faxed photos were received, Bolan headed out across country again. With the GPS system guiding them, even at night it was easy for the convoy to make its way directly over the hills for Noor's fortress. After several hours of driving across the barren terrain, he called a halt a little less than an hour's drive away from the fortress. Not knowing what kind of patrols the Iranians were running around the stronghold, he didn't want to get too close.

"There is a village not far from here that has been settled with refugees from my clan," Kader said. "We could spend the night there and be among friends."

That sounded like a good idea to Bolan. Now that he had acquired an armed Afghan escort, it would be difficult to have their cover story believed if a patrol happened across their camp and started asking questions.

"Do you know the way or do you need me to locate this village on the map?"

"Even in the dark, I can find my own people."

KADER RECEIVED a warm welcome in the village. The people knew that Jamillur was dead and that Kader had taken over as the head of the clan. Jamillur had been well loved by his people, but though Kader was young, he was known to be a wise man, as well as a strong leader.

Even though the villagers were dirt-poor, they hurried to prepare a meal for their leader, his warriors and their American guests. They might have been poor, but they knew the ancient code of hospitality. The hot, spicy food was a welcome change from the freeze-dried rations the Stony Man team had been eating lately.

After dinner Bolan motioned for Kader to join him. "What do you know about Noor's fortress?" he asked the Afghan.

"Only what is being said about it. I have not seen this place in many years myself."

"Maybe these will help refresh your memory," Bolan said as he showed him the recon photos.

The portable fax didn't have the fidelity of the bigger units, but it still produced usable copies of the satellite photographs. The photos were good enough to clearly show the dishes of the ground-surveillance radar units in the hills around the fortress. They also revealed the antitank missile launchers and heavy machine guns in their sandbag bunkers on top of the walls. Kurtzman had thoughtfully circled each threat and had given it a number. Even if they had had twice the number of men that they did, this wasn't going to be an easy job.

"These pictures were taken from an airplane?" the Afghan asked.

"No," Bolan answered. "They were taken by one of our orbiting spy satellites."

"You mean the fast-moving lights in the night sky?"

"Yeah. They have cameras on board, and they can radio the pictures they take to our ground stations."

Kader shook his head in amazement. "For a people who are powerful enough to put high-flying lights in the night sky, I do not understand why you cannot put an end to a people like the Iranians. They are not powerful at all except in their hatred of those who do not believe as they do."

"We could easily kill them all," Bolan agreed, "but that's not the way my government does things. If we did that, we would be no better than they are. It might not make much sense to you, but it's the way my people think."

"Much of the evil in this part of the world would go away if the Iranians were not in it."

"I can agree with that," Bolan said honestly. "But I can only deal with things as they are, not how I would like them to be. Our problem now is the Iranians in that fortress."

The Afghan studied the photos for a long time. "I do not remember anything that you cannot see in these pictures, except that the walls are very well made and they are smooth. They will be difficult to climb."

"We'll check the place out tomorrow," Bolan said, "and maybe you'll remember it better then."

When Kader went back to his people, Bolan and Katz watched the villagers entertain their new leader. These were poor herdsmen and there was only one motor vehicle in the village, a broken-down truck of indeterminable manufacture. There was, however, a herd of magnificent horses that provided the villagers with both transportation and their main source of income. An Afghan man might be able to afford a four-wheel-drive truck, but he still measured his personal wealth in horseflesh.

Katz watched as an Afghan thundered into camp on a spirited stallion. The Muji reined in the horse and jumped down from the saddle to present the horse to Kader. "How far did you say we are from Noor's fortress?" the Israeli asked Bolan.

"Twenty-five miles. Why?"

Katz nodded toward the rider and his mount. "I was thinking that if we left our Land Rovers here, we might have an easier time getting past the ground-surveillance radar Noor has in the hills. In a place like this, those units are likely to be tuned to pick up vehicles rather than animals so they don't go off every time a herd of goats walks by."

"You're thinking of riding in the rest of the way instead of driving?"

"Why not? We could be there in three hours and we wouldn't have to keep to the gullies to evade the radar."

"You might have a point there," Bolan said. "It looks like they've got enough horses around here to carry us all. Let me talk to Kader again and see what he says."

DAVID MCCARTER WAS dog tired as he guided his steps toward the lights coming from the small village in the valley below. He had been on the march for the past two hours, and the rugged terrain was taking its toll on him. Before the sun had gone down behind the horizon, he had taken a sighting and had headed due north. The problem was, without a compass it was proving difficult to navigate at night in this part of the world using just the stars. With the mountain peaks blocking out much of the night sky on the horizon, it was nearly impossible to get and keep his bearings.

The other problem was that he didn't know if he was in Pakistan or India, so he had no idea where he was going and could only hope that it was north back to Peshawar and the rest of Phoenix Force. When he saw the lights of the village below, he decided to take the risk and go down to try to find out exactly where he was. Once he knew, he could set out again with a better plan of action.

As he got closer, he saw the spires of a small mosque at the edge of the village, but that didn't necessarily mean anything. If he was in India, he would probably be in the Kashmir region and there were more Muslims in Kashmir than there were Hindus, and mosques were common.

A hundred yards out of the village, he stopped and undid the buckle of his field belt. Unhooking the captured Makarov's holster, he hid it under a prominent rock. The AK and magazines he laid under a bush a few yards away. Marching into town with a piece at his side might not be a wise move. He could come back and retrieve them when he left.

The tinny sound of a small radio playing Arabic music, the bright lights and the smell of stale beer identified the small building at the edge of the town as a bar. Since he didn't even have pocket change on him, there was no way that he was going to get a beer, but the smell was overwhelming. At least, though, he should be able to get information from someone in a bar.

It didn't occur to him that because of the Muslim prohibitions against alcohol, not too many bars were found in Pakistan.

He took a long drink of the warm stale water in his canteen to reduce his thirst before he walked in. Every head in the place turned to watch him as he entered the open door. He was heading for the bar to see if the bartender spoke English when he heard a voice behind him call out, "McCarter! David McCarter! Is that you?"

He turned to see three Europeans seated at one of the corner tables, and one of them was motioning him over. He squinted against the glare and recognized the man as being an Australian SAS trooper he had known a long time ago, Peter Browning. They had spent two weeks together on a hares-and-hounds exercise in the Welsh mountains, and you could get to know a man real well under those circumstances.

"David!" the man said. "It is you! What are you doing in this godforsaken part of the world?"

"I could ask the same thing of you, Peter."

"I'm with CNN now," Browning explained, nodding to the two other men at his table, "and we've been sent from the Melbourne office to cover the war."

"What war?" McCarter was stunned. He didn't know so much had changed in the short time since he and Grimaldi had been shot down.

"The one that's about to start, or don't you keep track of the news anymore?" Browning said. "By the way, you haven't told me what you are doing here."

McCarter flashed an SAS tactical hand signal to indicate that he was under observation by the enemy. "Buy me a beer first, Peter. I'll tell you the story later."

The newsman nodded slightly to indicate that he had caught the signal and waved to the bartender. "One more beer over here, mate."

AFTER FINISHING their beer, Browning's two companions left the bar and McCarter leaned closer to the newsman. "We're in India, right?"

Browning looked startled. "Of course we are. Where did you think you were?"

McCarter ignored the question and asked one of his own. "Do you happen to have a sat-com link anywhere around here?"

"Not here," Browning replied. "It's back at Jammu with the production crew. We came up here without it to make a few quick background shots."

"Can you take me back to it and let me use it to make a call?"

A slow smile spread across Browning's face. "You're still in the game, aren't you, David?"

"I left the SAS a long time ago," McCarter said as a way of not answering the question.

"You're piquing my newsman's professional interest." Browning was all-business now. "How about a little quid pro quo here for old times together and all that rot? Give me a hint about what you're doing here, and I'll see what I can do to help you."

"I can't do that, Peter." McCarter pushed his chair back. "You remember how it works. Look, if I can't use your phone, I'd best be moving on."

"Sit back down, for Christ's sake," Browning growled. "Don't get your knickers in a bloody knot. I haven't laid eyes on you for years and you want to kip off without a word. But then, you always were a secretive little bugger, weren't you? I remember a couple of my old SAS bunk mates saying that they had run into you in Laos and some other places not quite on the map, and you wouldn't say boo to them."

"It's no use, Peter," McCarter said. "I can't talk to you on or off camera about why I'm here."

Seeing that he was getting nowhere with that approach, Browning changed tactics. "Where do you need to make this call to, Whitehall?"

"Virginia."

Browning's ears perked up at that. "Langley?"

"Bite your tongue," McCarter snapped. "You ought to know better than to think that I'm working for the bloody Company. I need to call my sainted old mum. She married a Yank, and she's in a retirement home in Virginia."

"And mine's the queen of Spain." Browning shook his head. "All right, David, I give up. We're going back to Jammu in the morning and I'll let you make your call then. But you're going to owe me for this, mate."

"Can I owe you a tenner, as well?" the Briton asked. "I'm completely tapped and could use a bit of the roast goat or whatever they're serving around here."

Browning reached into his wallet and pulled out a five-hundred-rupee note. "If I were you, mate, I'd make it the lentils tonight. The goat's gone off."

McCarter laughed. "Thanks for the warning."

CHAPTER TWENTY-FIVE

Inside the Fortress

Major Fuad tore open the long-awaited air-freight carton that had finally arrived from Peshawar. One hundred and thirty-seven Stinger batteries, each in its own protective package bearing the Century Microdyne logo, were packed inside. The batteries were unimpressive-looking devices, but he knew that they were vital to the plan. Now he could finally start overhauling the Stingers.

Stuffing the batteries back into the box, he hurried over to the other wing of the fortress, where the technician was waiting in the makeshift armory that had been set up to service the missiles.

Fuad was so excited about the delivery of the batteries that he completely forgot that the reinforcements he was expecting had not yet arrived. The only thing on his mind was the image of Stinger missiles streaking into the skies and airliners falling in flames.

THE TECHNICIAN from Tehran who had been sent to check out the Stingers was also more than ready to go to work. In the weeks he had been in the fortress, he'd had nothing to do since he discovered that the batteries in the missiles were defective. To make matters even worse, while he had been waiting the major hadn't let him out of the stronghold, claiming security reasons. It was true that he had been allowed to amuse himself with Noor's girls and the hashish brought by the Islamic Guard troops, but he still missed civilization.

In fact, one of the reasons he had volunteered for this assignment was that he had hoped that he would be able to break away from Fuad, lose himself in Pakistan and make his way back to France and real civilization. He had been a third-year student in a French technical university in 1979 when the Shah's regime fell and Ayatollah Khomeini took over Iran. He had been young and had returned to Iran because he was worried about his family. But once he was back in his native land, he hadn't been able to leave again.

Since his education had been in a technical field, he soon found himself put to work for the new regime. After the initial orgy of cleansing those from Iranian society who had been "tainted" by the West, even the God-mad ayatollahs had come to realize that a modern city couldn't function without having enough technicians on hand to keep the machines running. Prayers alone weren't enough to keep the power-generating plants or radio stations functioning.

When the war with Iraq started a year later, the young technician found himself immediately drafted into the army in a signals unit. Being in communications instead of the infantry was probably responsible for his having survived the war. Well over a million Iranian men had died in that long war, and nothing of significance had been accomplished. But now that he was a civilian again, he still had no freedom in the repressive society of the Iranian republic.

But while he had quickly learned how to play the game of the new regime, and to play it well, he longed to return to the freedom of the West. When he had been younger, he hadn't thought that being a follower of the Prophet was a soul-killing thing. Now, however, after fifteen years under the bloody rule of the joyless ayatollahs, he was more than ready to be a free man again. He was even ready to give up his religion if it meant that he could once again live like a human, not an unthinking puppet for power-mad men.

Even though he had no idea that Noor was planning to escape from the fortress, he also had come to the conclusion that he would have to make his escape right after the last of the missiles had been serviced. The holocaust Fuad intended to unleash would disrupt what civilized life there was in Pakistan and would make his escape to Europe even more difficult, if not impossible. It was a stroke of luck in his favor that Noor's fortress was close to Peshawar rather than being outside Lahore or Islamabad. It wasn't very likely that the Indian military would think that the frontier city was worth expending a nuclear bomb on.

He had come to Pakistan well prepared to make an escape if the chance presented itself. He had a thick packet of Western currency sewn into the lining of his jacket, and most of it was American dollars. They might not buy as much as they once did, but they were still more widely accepted in the Middle East than most of the other currencies. He was lucky that he hadn't hoarded Russian rubles as many of his friends had—they were completely worthless now.

Before he could make his escape, though, he had to complete his assigned task for the major. It would be only after all the missiles were ready to use that he would no longer be so closely guarded.

Opening one of the foam containers marked CLA-219A, he took out the first of the batteries. Hooking the leads of his voltmeter to the battery terminals, he was satisfied to see that the gauge registered a full eighteen volts. But since the batteries were new, he had expected that they would have a full charge.

Taking one of the Stingers from a stack on the floor, he placed it on the table in front of him and opened the housing of the tracking unit, exposing the battery holder. It took only a short time to remove the old battery, clean the terminals inside the housing and fit the new one in place. Once it was hooked up, he ran the circuit tests and saw that the missile was fully functional again. Closing the housing, he put the launcher aside and reached for the next one.

This Stinger wasn't in as good a condition as the first one had been. When he opened the housing, he discovered that a thick film of fine sand covered everything. Moisture had also got in, and he saw that the battery connections were badly corroded. He pulled a small vacuum brush from his toolbox and started cleaning out the dust.

As the technician worked, he wasn't at all concerned about what the missiles were going to be used for. Fifteen years in revolutionary Iran had taught him that personal survival had to be his only concern. The fact that the missiles were going to be used to kill civilians and possibly cause a nuclear war wasn't his problem. As far as he was concerned, the rest of the world had sat back and allowed the ayatollahs to take power in his country, and now they would have to suffer the consequences of their inaction.

Maybe when this was all over they would think twice before they allowed religious fanatics to take over a nation again.

DAVID MCCARTER HAD awakened that morning thinking that he had found the solution to his problems. According to Browning, it was only a two-hour drive to the town where the production van with its sat-com link was parked. Once there, he would make his call back to Stony Man and that would be the end of his odyssey. Barbara Price would get a set of documents to him so he could get out of India and rejoin the others for the remainder of the mission. A day or so at the most, and everything would be back to what passed for normal with the Phoenix Force.

He hadn't counted, however, on having to deal with Indian lease-agency vehicles. After a quick bread-and-beer breakfast with the CNN guys, he joined them in their Toyota for the short ride to Jammu. A half hour out of the village, however, the Toyota sputtered to a halt at the side of the road.

McCarter was under the hood in a flash, but couldn't find anything wrong with the engine. One of the CNN men headed back to the village on foot to see if there was a mechanic there or another vehicle they could hire.

In the front seat, Browning reached down into the foam cooler tucked in by his feet and pulled out a bottle of local beer. "Here you go, mate. As long as we're stuck here, we might as well make good use of the time."

McCarter had other ideas about what he should be doing. But considering the situation, he had no option and accepted the lukewarm beer.

WHILE THE TECHNICIAN busied himself with the Stingers, Fuad called his launch teams together for a final briefing on their individual assignments. He went over each of their infiltration routes and targeted airports one at a time, having the men recite the details back to prove that they knew their assignments intimately. He could allow no mistakes at this point. The delay with the batteries had put the plan well behind schedule.

Once he was satisfied that the teams were ready to go as soon as the missiles were, he released them to change into their civilian clothing and to load their vehicles for the trip. It was only when the briefing was over that Fuad remembered the reinforcements he had requested. After checking with his second-in-command to make sure that they hadn't arrived and gone unnoticed, he hurried to the radio room to call the Iranian camp in Afghanistan.

When he got through to the training camp, he was informed that the men had been dispatched on time, but hadn't been heard from since they had reported that they were ready to cross the border. Fuad had no idea why they had been delayed and was concerned. Without those additional troops to bolster his defenses, once he sent the launch teams out he would be seriously short of personnel to defend the fortress. Nonetheless, he had to send the teams and their Stingers on the way as soon as he could.

He put in another call to the camp and ordered the commander to make another two dozen men ready to leave at a moment's notice. If the first group of reinforcements still hadn't arrived by nightfall, he would have the second group sent to him immediately.

FROM A DISTANCE the two dozen horses and riders making their way over the barren hills looked like something out of a Western movie. Only when they got closer could it be seen that most of the riders were dressed as Afghans, not cowboys. The others were wearing black combat suits with civilian windbreakers.

"I thought that we were supposed to be a high-tech strike force," James said as he inexpertly guided his horse through the scrub brush. "This is like being in some Western movie. Remember the one where those mercenaries go into Mexico to try to rescue a rancher's wife?"

"This is high-tech, man," Manning said with a grin. The Canadian was as comfortable on a horse as he was in a vehicle. "Since the opposition has all the approaches covered with radar and long-range antitank missiles, we are infiltrating on four-legged stealth vehicles. If Katz is right, they won't be able to pick us up."

"These are some kind of stealth vehicles, all right," James groused. "They won't need their radar to spot us. They'll be able to smell us coming for miles."

"I know you're a city boy, but where I come from, horse sweat is considered to be a manly aroma."

"I know," James said. "'Way up north where men are men and smell like horses.' You'd fit in real well with Kader's boys. They smell like more than just horses."

"But they have nice guns," Manning reminded him. "And that's why they were invited to join the party."

"I'd still feel better about this if we had our Land Rovers with us. I don't think this animal can get me out of here at sixty miles an hour if something goes wrong."

The two vehicles had been left behind at the Afghan village with drivers from Kader's force and a radio. The Land Rovers wouldn't be brought up until Bolan called for them after the fortress was secured.

An hour later the lead riders of the column entered a deep ravine at the base of a massive ridge line. Kader brought his horse to a halt and turned to Bolan. "We should stop and leave the horses here, El Askari. The fortress is just beyond that ridge."

Bolan quickly checked his map and saw that the Afghan was right. This would make a good jumping-off point for an approach on foot. He signaled to dismount and swung down out of his saddle. There was little noise as the Afghans dismounted and readied themselves for the short march to the fortress.

The three herdsmen who had ridden with them from the village readied the horses for the return ride. The animals had served their purpose, and the villagers had earned a good rental fee in the transaction. It would be a disaster for them, however, if the horses were to get caught up in the cross fire.

As soon as the horses were herded off, Bolan's makeshift strike force set out for the ridge line. At least three hours of daylight remained, and he wanted to make a complete recon of the target area before he made his final plans. Planning an attack from maps and photographs alone was a good way to get killed. Cracking something as tough as a stone fortress required a thorough, personal reconnaissance.

BY MIDAFTERNOON Fuad's technician had repaired eight of the Stinger missiles. When the major came to check on his progress and found them ready to go, he had his men take the missiles down to the vehicles waiting in the courtyard.

Six of the Stingers were wrapped in plastic sheeting and secured for transport. Three of them were fitted up under the frames of the first two Toyotas that were scheduled to go. Those teams were both targeted to hit airports in Northern India. Since they had a longer distance to travel, as well as having to penetrate the border and evade the Indian patrols, he wanted them to leave first.

Fuad felt a surge of pride as he watched the three-man teams mount their vehicles and drive through the gate. "God is great!" he shouted.

The plan was under way at last, and he would soon join the list of the greatest Muslim warriors of all time.

IT TOOK TWO HOURS for the Stony Man commandos and Kader's Afghan warriors to move in close enough to spot all of the enemy sentry posts and weapons positions. When they had been located and marked on the photos and the map, Bolan left two lookouts and pulled everyone else back behind the hill.

Gathering Kader and his men and the Phoenix Force commandos around the photos, he laid out the plan of attack. "Like we thought," he said, "we've got to go over the walls. There's no way we can storm the gate. It's too heavily defended."

"It's a good thing that we have the mountaineering gear," Katz said. "Those walls are almost as smooth as concrete, and they're not going to be easy to climb. Whoever built that place made sure that there are no good footholds."

"I can use hand spikes and clamp-ons to get up here," James said, pointing to the part of the photo showing the angle in the wall where the north tower jutted from the wall. "The cracks between the blocks are enough to let me get up. Once I'm on top I can secure the ropes and toss them down to you."

Bolan turned to Kader. "The most important part of this is going to be the diversion I need your men to make while we go up the walls. If we're detected before we get to the top, we'll be sitting ducks."

"What is a 'sitting duck'?" the Afghan asked. "I do not understand."

Bolan smiled. "It's American for an easy target, a dead man."

"I see," he said. "You want us to draw their fire away from you."

"That's it." Bolan nodded. "I want at least half of your men on the south side. It will be a dangerous assignment because they will have to make them think that you are attacking them in force."

"We are not afraid of those dogs," Kader stated. "We will make them think that we are storming the Snake's Skull, because we will be."

"I don't want your men to take any unnecessary risks," Bolan cautioned. "We'll need them later to help us with the garrison inside the walls. Once we're on the walls, we'll try to make our way around to capture the gate and let your men inside."

By the time they had finished discussing the details of the assault, the sun had gone down behind the hills. "If no one has any questions," Bolan said, looking around the group, "I want everybody to get as much rest as they can before we move out tonight."

CHAPTER TWENTY-SIX

Inside the Fortress

Now that night was falling, Ali Noor prepared for his departure. Since the first of the launch teams had finally been dispatched to India with the refurbished missiles, Fuad had allowed his men to celebrate with the girls and hashish. They would be so busy that they wouldn't be keeping a close eye on him. It was a Godsent opportunity that he intended to take full advantage of.

That afternoon he had put together a selection of valuables and had stowed them in a small nylon bag. It had been difficult for him to decide what to take and what he would have to leave behind. He ended up packing the bag with bundles of currency, both Western and Pakistani bills. For the transactions where paper currency wouldn't work, he had taken several pouches of his better precious stones. He had wanted to take gold coins, as well, but because of their weight he had taken mostly silver instead.

All told, the bag weighed over twenty pounds, but that, a flashlight and a water bottle was all he was taking. He didn't even bother with food or clothing. Anything that he needed he would buy along the way. After changing into dark clothing and a jacket for the night chill, he waited impatiently to give the guards a little more time to relax.

When Noor finally decided that the time was right, he left his quarters and made his way to the dungeon beneath the walls. He was surprised to find that even the Iranian who was supposed to be guarding the cells was upstairs with the girls. That made this tricky part of his escape a great deal easier. He had been prepared to give him a message that Fuad wanted to see him, but he knew that when the guard discovered that it wasn't true, it would arouse suspicion. This way he would have a longer head start before anyone realized that he was gone.

Noor thought briefly about releasing the remaining Canadian Fuad was holding in the cells and taking him with him, but he quickly dismissed the thought. He had no idea of the man's condition, and if he wanted to make good on his escape he would have to move fast. The pilot would have to take his chances like the rest of the Pakistani population.

The old storeroom at the end of the corridor wasn't used for much anymore, but the door opened easily. Noor had made sure that the hinges to his secret escape route were kept well oiled. Turning on his flashlight, he shut the door behind him and turned to face the rear wall. A rough shelf made of planks covered most of the rear wall, but it was merely camouflage to cover the entrance to the tunnel.

The middle of the shelf held a few empty tins and pots, and he quickly stacked them out of the way on the floor before taking down the shelf itself. More ancient planks covered the stone wall behind the shelf, but pulling them aside, Noor quickly uncovered the opening in the stone wall behind them. Clutching his bag of valuables to his chest, he squeezed through the tight opening.

Once in the darkness of the tunnel, he pulled the planks back in place so as not to leave an obvious trail. Fuad probably wouldn't notice that he was missing until the morning, and it would take his men some time to search the fortress completely and find that he was nowhere to be found. By then, he intended to be far away from the Snake's Skull.

AFTER HIS EVENING PRAYERS Fuad went to the makeshift armory to check on the technician's progress with the rest of the missiles. Now that he had put the plan into action, he was anxious to send the rest of the Stingers on the way to their targets.

"I am very sorry, Major," the technician said, "but it will be tomorrow morning before I will have the rest of them finished."

"Why is it taking you so long?" the Iranian asked. "You said that it would take less than an hour apiece to put the new batteries in and test them. I do not understand what is taking you so long."

"Many of these launchers are in bad condition," the tech replied, defending himself. "They have been out in the open and have not been stored properly. Many of them require more than just a fresh battery. I have to clean the sand out of them and polish the corroded terminals before the circuits will work. These are sophisticated weapons and they have been in the hands of barbarians, not trained soldiers."

"But you are a trained technician and are supposed to know how to do this kind of work."

"I know how to do the work, Major, and I have been at it all day now without rest. Right now I am going to have my dinner, but I will come back as soon as I can and finish my work for the glory of God. I am just as anxious as you are to see this mission completed."

Realizing that he needed the technician's best efforts, Fuad backed off. "I understand. Eat and refresh yourself, but try to get the work finished tonight if it is at all possible. The rest of the missiles must go out tomorrow morning without fail."

"As you command, Major."

The technician vowed that he would stay awake all night if that was what it took to finish his work.

BOLAN AND KATZ were watching the fortress with their night-vision field glasses while James, Manning and Encizo checked over their mountaineering gear to get ready for the assault. Climbing at night was dangerous enough, to say nothing of climbing under fire, and they didn't need any problems with their gear.

Kader came up to them with a short, plump man dressed in dark clothing in tow. The man looked like a merchant or town dweller, and Bolan wondered what he was doing in these barren hills miles from a town of any size.

"This piece of diseased dog excrement is Ali Noor," the Afghan announced. "Pimp, drug dealer and gunrunner. I believe that you wanted to talk to him."

"Where did you find him?" Katz asked.

"He was stumbling around in the dark like a man from the city and walked right into one of my men. Luckily for him, my man didn't slit his fat throat."

"Does he speak English?"

"I speak English quite well," Noor answered for himself. "How may I be of service to you, sir?"

"A helicopter flew over your fortress two days ago," Bolan asked. "What happened to it?"

Noor shrugged. "Fuad shot it down with a missile."

"Who is this Fuad?"

"He is Major Inman Fuad of the Iranian Islamic Party. He took over my fortress several weeks ago and has been holding me prisoner since then."

"What happened to the two men who were in that chopper?"

"They were both captured."

"Are they alive?"

"One of them is," Noor said. "The other one, I don't know."

"What do you mean?" Encizo asked.

"Fuad sent him south to India with one of the defective missiles."

"Why did he do that?" James asked.

Noor shrugged. "I am just a pimp and a drug runner. He doesn't tell me his plans."

Encizo stepped up to him. "You'll be a dead pimp and drug runner if you don't watch your mouth."

"I am dead anyway." Noor looked the Cuban straight in the eye. "You can't make me any deader than I will be as soon as Fuad catches up with me."

He looked at the men surrounding him. "Or any deader than you will be if you are foolish enough to think that you can attack the Snake's Skull. Fuad has enough men and heavy weapons in there to hold off an army."

"I can't speak for you," James said, "but we might be a little difficult to kill. We aren't old men or women sleeping in our beds. We've seen this Fuad guy's work before and we aren't impressed."

"That may be. I am obviously not a manly warrior as you are, so I do not know about those things."

"But you do know about what has been going on in there since Fuad arrived, right?" Bolan asked.

"I know some of it, yes."

"Has Fuad been collecting Stinger missiles from the Mujahedeen tribesmen?"

"That he has been doing," Noor confirmed.

"How many of them does he have on hand now?"

"I do not know the exact count. I do know that he has at least two or three dozen."

"And," Katz added, "have the new batteries for them come in yet?"

Noor nodded. "They arrived early this morning and Fuad's technician is working on installing them in the missiles right now."

"Where is the girl?" Bolan asked.

When Noor looked blank, he added, "The girl who was taken from Peshawar when Jamillur was captured and the rest of his family killed."

"She is safe," Noor hurried to say. "Fuad has kept her in a cell since she was captured."

"She had better be safe, pimp," Kader said harshly. "She is my cousin."

"I had nothing to do with her kidnapping. Your fight is with the Iranian, not with me. I do not kidnap women and children."

"You buy and sell them."

"That is different." Noor sounded indignant. "That is a business, not crime. I pay good money for my women and I feed them well before I sell them."

"But you hold them captive until you sell them."

Noor shrugged. "They are an investment and they must be kept safe."

"Speaking of captives," Katz asked, "if you were being held captive yourself, just exactly how did you manage to escape?"

"In exchange for my life," Noor said, "I can show you a way to get into the fortress without being seen. There is a passageway that runs under the rocks."

"You are in no position to bargain, pimp," Kader snarled. "You will tell us what we want to know or you will regret the day that your diseased mother met your unknown father and slept with him."

"Wait a minute," Bolan said. "You're talking about a tunnel, right?"

Noor nodded.

"Where does this tunnel of yours come out inside the walls?"

"Do I have your word?"

"I won't kill you," Bolan said, looking at Kader, "and I will see that the Afghans do not, either."

"I can take you to the tunnel. It is not far from here."

"Where does it come out inside the walls?" Bolan repeated.

"In the lower level on the north side."

"What is on that level?"

"Storerooms and the cells."

"Is that where the man from the helicopter is being held?"

"And the girl?" Kader added.

"Yes."

Bolan turned to Katz. "What do you think?"

"It's worth a try. I really don't want to try to go up the outside of those walls and fight our way inside. Even with Kader's men to give us cover and a diversion, it wouldn't be easy that way."

"Show us where this tunnel of yours is," Bolan said, "and you'll live. But if you're leading us into a trap, I'll give you to Kader to dispose of."

Noor shot a glance toward the Afghan leader. "I will keep my word," he said. "Even pimps and drug dealers have their honor."

Bolan doubted that, but this wasn't the time to get into a discussion of ethics and the criminal mentality.

WITH THE CHANGE IN PLANS, the Executioner held another quick briefing with his Afghan allies. "Since we'll be going in the back way now, Kader, I'm changing the attack plan. I want half of your men to come with us into the tunnel. The other half I want to attack the same spots we talked about as a diversion."

Kader and the other English-speaking warriors quickly translated for the others.

"Since I don't know how long it will take us to get into place," Bolan continued, "I can't plan a timed diversion. Your men will have to listen carefully, and when they hear the first shots fired, that will be the signal for them to start firing, too. Even though we'll be inside, it will still be important that they draw the troops to the walls.

"Are there any questions?" Bolan asked.

There was none. The Afghans were experienced fighters and knew how to improvise once the first shots were fired.

"If everyone knows what they're going to be doing, let's get at it."

KADER ACCOMPANIED Noor as the gunrunner led the strike force around the hill behind the Snake's Skull to his secret tunnel. The Afghan didn't trust the man as far as he could spit and was ready to cut his throat at the slightest sign of treachery.

"Where is this tunnel of yours?" Kader snarled. "If you are betraying us, pimp, I swear that I will—"

"I hear your threat, mighty warrior," Noor interrupted. "But threats do not make the trail any shorter. It is not much farther now."

A few minutes later, Noor stopped and pointed to the ground. "Here is the opening," he said.

Bolan saw a small opening in the ground where the boulders had been moved to one side and fresh earth was showing around a dark hole. Someone, or something, had recently emerged from the ground.

"There is a trap halfway through the tunnel," Noor said. "I will have to lead you past it."

The opening to the tunnel was tight, and each man had to have one of the others hold his weapons for him so he could wiggle down into it. Once inside, they spread out to make room for the others. Though the tunnel was wide enough for two men to walk side by side, the ceiling was too low for the Americans to walk upright. Suddenly the tunnel widened and the ceiling was taller and Noor stopped.

"This is the trap," he told Bolan. "There is a deep pit dug into the floor, but there are hand- and footholds cut into the wall on the right side. If your men do exactly what I do, they will be safe."

Motioning for the others to follow in his steps, Noor reached up on the right wall and sought the handhold. Once he had it he swung his foot up and found the foothold. More notches carved into the wall let him quickly traverse the unseen pit.

Once everyone was on the other side of the trap, Noor turned to Bolan. "I have done all that I can do for you," he said. "Will you let me go now?"

"Not yet," Bolan answered. "You're going to take us all the way into the fortress in case there are any other traps or surprises you failed to mention."

"You are not a trusting man."

"You don't live long in my business if you trust strangers."

"May you live forever."

"I fully intend to," Bolan stated.

CHAPTER TWENTY-SEVEN

Inside the Fortress

At the end of the tunnel, Noor showed Bolan how to pull the planks apart to get into the small storage room. When the Executioner pushed his way through the opening, he saw a dim light showing around the edges of the ill-fitting wooden door closing off the other side of the room. Putting his eye to the crack, he saw a long, high-arched stone corridor leading away from the door. The curving stone stairwell off to the right apparently led up to the upper levels of the fortress. If he could get the strike force into the corridor without their being seen, they would have a better chance of getting up the stairs before they had to start fighting.

The corridor appeared to be empty. But as he watched, an Iranian in desert fatigues with an AK slung over his shoulder came down the stairs. After walking the length of the corridor, he took his position on a wooden bench by the base of the stairs. With a guard now in the picture, Bolan signaled for Katzenelenbogen to come forward and join him. This was a job for the Israeli's silenced Uzi.

Motioning for him to take a look, Bolan stepped back from the door. Katz put his eye to the crack, saw his target and nodded. As the Israeli snapped his Uzi off safe, the Executioner put both of his hands on the door.

At Katz's silent count of three, Bolan shoved the door open and the Phoenix Force leader stepped out into the corridor. The muzzle of his silenced Uzi flashed in the dim light, but the only sound was the tinkle of the subgun's empty brass falling to the stone floor.

The Iranian was halfway to his feet and grabbing for his AK, but he went down without a sound as the 9 mm slugs stitched him across the chest.

Katz rushed into the corridor with Bolan on his heels, but there were no other sentries. As soon as the Israeli signaled that the dungeon was clear, the rest of the Phoenix Force commandos poured in through the tunnel, followed by Kader's twelve Afghan warriors, who still had Noor in tow.

James raced past the dead guard for the cell doors while the rest of the team spread out and took positions in the corridor. The first two cell doors were unlocked and the cells empty. The third door was locked, and after pulling the bolt, he looked inside the dim room and saw Jack Grimaldi sitting on a narrow bunk.

"Jack! You okay?"

"'Bout time you guys got here," Grimaldi growled as he got to his feet. "What kept you?"

"The horses wouldn't go any faster," James said.

"What horses?"

"I'll tell you later." James handed the pilot his pistol. "We have work to do in here first. Are you up for storming a castle from the inside?"

"Sounds good to me," the pilot answered. "By the way, have you found McCarter yet?"

"He isn't here," James said grimly. "Noor told us that he was sent out of here in a Toyota yesterday."

"But he's still alive?" Grimaldi's voice showed his concern.

"As far as we know. Noor seems to think that he was sent to India with one of the missiles."

"Why?"

"He says he doesn't know."

The pilot shook his head. "This thing is getting crazier and crazier by the minute."

"Tell me about it."

The door to the cell at the far end of the corridor was also locked, and Kader opened it. Looking inside, he saw a small figure sitting on the bunk and called out. The girl ran to him, her dark eyes wide. "Uncle Hassen," she cried out. "Where is my father?"

In hushed tones Kader told the girl what had happened to her father. Tears welled up in her eyes, but she didn't cry. She knew that the men had come to fight, and as an Afghan, she also knew that they didn't need a weeping woman on their hands. She would grieve for her family when she got back to her aunt's tents.

"Is she okay?" Katz asked.

Kader spoke softly to her again and the girl shook her head. "God be praised," the Afghan said solemnly. "She says she has not been molested."

As with all the peoples of the Middle East, Afghan rape victims were forever tarnished. Even the daughter of a man as honored among his people as Jamillur wouldn't be able to find a husband if she had been raped.

"Give her to one of your men," Bolan said, "and have her taken out the way we came in. I don't want her to get hurt in the fighting."

"She will be well taken care of," the Afghan answered. "I can assure you of that. She is Ahmed Jamillur's daughter."

One of the Mujis took the girl and led her back into the tunnel. As soon as she was out of danger, the strike force made one last check of their weapons before moving out. Once they climbed the stairs leading to the upper levels of the fortress, they would be committed.

"Is everyone ready?" Bolan looked around at his strike force. Grimaldi had commandeered the dead guard's AK and ammo-magazine carrier and was ready for a little payback. The others had their weapons at the ready.

"We are ready to fight, El Askari," Kader said.

"Let's get up there and kick some ass," James added.

SINCE HE HAD the only silenced weapon, Katz led the way up out of the dungeon. His rubber-soled combat boots made no noise as he climbed the worn stone steps, keeping tight against the right-hand wall. When he heard the click of hard-heeled boot against the stone steps, he flashed a signal for the others to halt and swung the muzzle of his Uzi subgun to cover the left.

People usually hugged the right-hand side of a staircase when they descended and kept their eyes focused directly in front of them. If that was the case this time, he would have the drop on this guy. Katzenelenbogen patiently waited until he saw a pair of combat boots coming down the stairs before he made his move.

The Iranian's eyes grew wide when he saw Katz step out in front of him, but he didn't have time to unsling his AK before he was cut down by the silenced burst of 9 mm slugs from the Uzi. His rifle clattered against the stone as he fell, and Katz froze. When no one seemed to have noticed the noise, he signaled that he was moving out again.

The top of the stairs opened out into a covered portico that overlooked the courtyard. The strike force spread out along the portico as they came up and they waited until everyone was present.

The Iranian who walked into sight had his AK in his hands. When one of the Afghans stepped out to intercept him, he triggered his weapon without hesitation. The round missed and he went down under the Afghan's knife, but that one shot had been enough to signal the attack.

THE SECOND that the first AK shot sounded, the Afghans outside the main gate opened fire on the sentries walking their posts on the battlements. For a few seconds the Iranians were caught off guard. Several of them went down to the sharp-eyed Afghans and their blazing AKs. A few seconds later, however, the Russian-made 12.7 mm DShK machine gun behind its sandbagged bunker started hammering, and the Mujis had to duck for cover.

The machine gun kept the Afghans' heads down. Even the 30 mm grenade-launcher gunner had to lie flat behind his weapon as the heavy-caliber slugs chewed into the rocks around him. They had faced this formidable weapon before in the hills of their homeland and had learned to respect it. The Afghanistan war had also taught them the remedy for a 12.7 mm weapon, though. Hunkering, they yelled for the RPG man to come up.

The RPG gunner didn't have to be told what to do. He had been up against such weapons before. Checking the rocket loaded into the front of his launcher, he thumbed the firing hammer back and nodded to his comrades. When they laid down enough gunfire to make the Iranian machine gunner let up on the trigger for a second, he raised up, aimed and triggered the launcher. At such short range the RPG-7 rocket was still accelerating when it impacted right below the blazing muzzle of the DShK.

The detonation of the 85 mm shaped-charge warhead of the antitank rocket sent a jet of white-hot molten metal and explosive gases though the sandbagged bunker as if it weren't even there. Designed to penetrate twelve inches of armored-steel tank turret, it had no trouble taking out the machine gun and the two Iranians crewing it.

Giving a howl of victory, the Afghans raced for the walls and the main gate. Behind them, the 30 mm gunner swept his deadly grenades along the top of the wall, adding to the chaos.

THE FIRST BURST of AK fire brought Major Fuad wide-awake, and he grabbed for his uniform and boots. By the time he was dressed, it sounded like a full-scale firefight had developed. He didn't know how the Americans had managed to get a strike force in close enough to attack him, but they had. And from the sounds of the battle, it was a sizable force, not just a commando raid. With the men he had lost in battle and those he had sent south with the missiles, he wasn't sure that his guard force was large enough to beat back a determined attack.

Even if the Yankees were successful, though, they were too late to stop the plan. Six of the reenergized Stingers had already left for their targets in India. That left him needing the missiles for the Pakistani incidents. Two of them were already loaded into one of the Toyotas parked in the courtyard outside. If he could make his escape in the vehicle, he could drive to Lahore and fire those two missiles himself and complete the plan.

One way or the other, though, the Iranian had no intention of dying inside these ancient stone walls.

After chambering a round in his pistol, Fuad cautiously opened his door and saw that the portico outside his room was clear. Keeping close to the wall, he made his way to the stairs at the end of the corridor. Looking down, he saw that one of his men lay dead at the bottom of the stairs that led to the courtyard.

Keeping to the shadows, he made his way down the stairs and knelt beside the corpse. Holstering the Makarov pistol, he took the AK and chest-pack magazine carrier from the dead guard. Cracking the bolt on the assault rifle, he checked to make sure that there was a round in the chamber before flicking the assault rifle's selector switch to the full-auto position.

Slinging the magazine carrier over his shoulder, he undid the catches on two of the pouches so he would have instant access to the magazines. Now he was properly armed.

Keeping close to the inner wall, he made his way around the courtyard until he was close to the Toyota. When he saw muzzle-flashes from the other side of the yard by the stairs leading into the lower levels, he fired a full magazine in that direction. When the bolt locked back on the empty magazine, he smoothly dropped it and clicked a full one into place.

Snapping off short bursts, he dashed the last few yards to the Toyota that had been loaded with the two extra Stingers and the personal effects of the launch crew. Sliding into the driver's seat, he fired up the engine and slammed the gearshift into first. Dropping the clutch, he stomped on the throttle.

"Open the gate!" he yelled at the guards as he cranked the steering wheel around to head for the main gate.

Trained in blind obedience, two of the Iranians drew back the massive iron bolt that kept the two heavy wooden gates locked and pushed them open far enough for the Toyota to pass between them.

The Afghans charging the gate were surprised to see the massive wooden doors of the fortress swing open. They were rushing toward the open doors when the Toyota four-wheel-drive roared out, coming directly at them. They moved off to the sides of the road to let it pass. But by the time they recognized that the driver was one of the enemy, the vehicle was lost in the cloud of dust thrown up by its wheels.

That was only one enemy, though, and they could afford to let him go. There were more than enough inside the fortress, and now that the gate was open they could get to them without having to climb the sheer rock walls.

Shouting their war cries, the Afghans rushed the still-open gate before it could be closed again.

The Snake's Skull was theirs.

JACK GRIMALDI HAD teamed up with Calvin James, and they were fighting their way along the south wall toward the main gate. So far the Stony Man commandos and their Afghan allies weren't having an easy time of it. The advantage of surprise they had gained by attacking from under the walls hadn't lasted long.

Even though the Iranian guards had been smoking hashish, within seconds of the first shots they had reacted quickly to the threat of the intruders within their walls. Rushing to their posts along the tops of the walls, they were bringing accurate fire down into the courtyard.

James and the pilot were crouching behind a stone pillar when they saw the main gates being pulled open. They were surprised because they didn't think that any of their men had made it that far yet. But when they saw the Toyota race through, they knew that the Iranians had done it. No sooner had the dust of the vehicle's wheels cleared than they saw the Afghans storm through the open gate.

Now the battle was on.

BOLAN AND KATZ WERE hunting down the Iranians with methodical precision. The trick, though, was to flush the enemy from his hiding place without getting jumped first. It was the most difficult and dangerous kind of combat, but they were veterans at it. Even so, fighting in a stone fortress wasn't easy.

For every Iranian they spotted, two more were hiding in the shadows, their AKs ready. Since a hand grenade was a man's best friend in this type of combat, the two men used them as if they had expiration dates stamped on them. One man would provide a covering burst while the other tossed a grenade and ducked back. As soon as it detonated they would rush the position.

They had just finished sweeping the north wall when they ran into Grimaldi and James coming the other way.

"We're clear over here," James called out.

"Pull back and let the Afghans go after them," Bolan called back.

ENCIZO AND MANNING HAD linked up at the top of the stairs. When the rest of the team headed for the courtyard they took the stairs leading to the second-level portico of the inner wall. They were two steps from the top when an Iranian stepped out onto the landing, his AK blazing.

With the 7.62 mm rounds clipping the wall next to his head, Encizo dropped to one knee and sent a burst from his H&K into the guard's chest. Manning snatched a grenade from his assault harness, pulled the pin and tossed the bomb in front of them to clear the landing.

The grenade shrapnel was still singing through the air when they charged up the last few steps, their assault rifles blazing. At the stairs at the other end of the second-story portico they saw two of Kader's Afghans signal that the way in front of them was clear.

They waved back and turned to see if there was any business for them in the courtyard below, but it seemed to be fairly well in hand. Except for an occasional burst, the firing had ceased and the fortress was theirs.

CHAPTER TWENTY-EIGHT

Inside the Fortress

Dawn was breaking as the Afghans sought out the last of Fuad's Iranians in the nooks and crannies of the old stone fortress. Sudden flurries of shots indicated that even though their leader had abandoned them, true to their fanaticism, they preferred to die rather than surrender. It was brutal fighting, but Kader's people were more than willing to oblige them. Not only were the Afghans getting revenge for the death of Jamillur, they were getting payback for the repressive Iranian-sponsored regime that was preventing them from returning to their homeland.

As soon as the last of Fuad's men were down, Bolan had the Afghans secure the fortress walls while he and the Phoenix Force commandos went looking for the Iranian terrorist leader and his Stinger missiles. After a thorough search, however, Fuad was nowhere to be found, dead or alive. Both Noor and Grimaldi had checked each of the corpses for the tall, golden-eyed Iranian, but to no avail.

"My men say that a truck broke out through the main gate right after your assault started," Kader said. "There was only one man in it, but that might have been Fuad. They could not tell in the dark."

Bolan didn't like to hear that news. Fuad had proved to be a dangerous opponent, and if he wasn't caught now, he was sure to cause more trouble in the future.

"Did they see which way he went?"

The Afghan shook his head. "They were busy storming the open gate."

"James and I saw it, too," Grimaldi stated. "But just as he was going out."

"Keep looking for the Stingers," Bolan said.

Fortunately the search for the Stingers was more successful.

"I think I hit the jackpot, Striker," Manning transmitted over his com link. "There are over a dozen Stingers up here on the second floor."

"I'll be right up."

The large room was set up with heavy wooden tables along one wall and bundled electrical cables taped to the well-worn floorboards. A Stinger missile was lying in the middle of one of the tables surrounded by electronic test equipment and tools. The fiberglass housing for the missile's tracking unit was open, and a Century Microdyne-marked foam battery package was lying next to it. More of the missiles were stacked on the floor next to the table.

"Get Noor up here," Bolan called down to Kader.

When the Afghan leader arrived with the gunrunner, Noor looked around the lab as if he were seeing it for the first time.

"Are any of the missiles missing?" Katz asked him.

"Like I said before, sir, I have no way of knowing. Fuad kept me well away from this part of his operation, and I have not been in this room since he took over my home."

"But your men were involved with buying the Stingers for him, right?"

"That is correct, but after they brought them back here, Fuad took them over completely. I never saw them."

"Is there any way that you can find out how many of them were bought?"

"I can try," he said.

"You do that."

ENCIZO WALKED INTO the lab with a man in tow who wore a white lab coat instead of desert-camouflage fatigues, and wore glasses. The Cuban grinned as he shoved the man forward. "I think this is the guy who goes with this room full of test equipment. At least he's dressed like he's a lab tech of some kind."

"Where did you find him?" Bolan asked.

"He was down in the mess hall hiding under the cook's table, pretending to be a sack of flour."

"Are you the one who was working on these missiles?" Katz asked in Arabic when he saw the man's eyes sweep over the instruments on the table.

The technician nodded slightly. "Yes," he answered in accented English.

"Why were you working on them when you knew what they were going to be used for?"

The technician shrugged. "I was just following my orders to repair the missiles."

"That's what the Nazis said," Katz snapped. "But it didn't work for them and it's not going to work for you, either."

"That is easy enough for you to say," the technician shot back. "You are not living under the ayatollahs. I was ordered to come here and work on those missiles. I had no other choice if I wanted to live."

"I'm going to give you another choice right now," Katz said. "You can either cooperate with us completely and tell us everything you know, or you can be taken to India, turned over to the authorities there for prosecution and spend the rest of your life in a prison cell as a terrorist. Which way do you want it?"

"I will do what I can to help," the man promised. "But I know very little about Fuad's operational plans. All I know is that six of the missiles were sent to India yesterday and two more of them were loaded into one of the trucks in the courtyard."

"Six missiles went out yesterday?" Katz repeated as he looked over at Noor.

"I did not know that," the gunrunner said quickly before he could be asked why he hadn't mentioned this before. "Like I told you, Fuad did not tell me his plans."

"Noor tells the truth," the technician said. "He knows even less about Fuad's operation than I do."

Bolan nodded toward the technician. "Kader, put a couple of your men on this guy and make sure that he doesn't get out of their sight. Not even when he goes to the latrine. We're going to need to talk to him later."

"He will not escape us," the Afghan vowed. "You can be sure of that."

"Now what do we do?" Katz asked, his eyes sweeping over the Stinger missiles stacked in the lab.

"The first thing we do," Bolan replied, "is to get through to Brognola and let them know that we took this place. Then I get to tell him that there are eight missiles still out there somewhere."

Katzenelenbogen's face was tight. "If we can't find those missiles ASAP, we're back to square one."

"I know."

The Land Rovers carrying the Phoenix Force's commo gear had just arrived, so the two men went down to the courtyard to make their report to Stony Man. Brognola wasn't going to be happy, but the gods of war didn't always favor the Stony Man warriors. Sometimes the good guys lost, too. The important thing, though, was to stay in the game. Sometimes the tide turned.

THE FOUR TROOPERS of the Indian border-security force moved through the rocks like lizards, their khaki uniforms blending in perfectly with the barren terrain and brush. They had been boiling water for their morning tea when they had caught the sound of a motor vehicle echoing from the hills in the exclusion zone.

After checking with their base to ensure that there were no motorized patrols in their sector, they left the fifth man of their patrol back with the camels and moved out. Now they were closing in on the unauthorized intruder, their weapons at the ready.

When the border-security force was on parade with their camels, their colorful turbans and bright guidons flying from their steel-tipped bamboo lances, they looked as if they were a throwback to the Victorian Era of the British raj. In the field, however, they were as good a light-infantry force as any in the region, and better than most.

Wriggling the last few yards on their bellies, the Indians reached the top of the ridge and saw a Toyota truck slowly making its way through the heavily rutted wadi. The three men in the Toyota were dressed in civilian clothing, but the AK-47s in their hands meant that they were Muslim terrorists trying to infiltrate from Pakistan.

On the signal from their sergeant, the camel troopers unleashed a hail of automatic fire into the wadi. Taken completely by surprise, the Iranians weren't able to bring their weapons into play before they were riddled.

While his patrol emptied their magazines into the occupants, the sergeant pitched a grenade at the front of the truck. The grenade detonated under the right-front suspension of the Toyota, shredding the tire and lifting the truck off the ground. With the driver dead at the wheel, his foot stuck on the accelerator, the truck tried to run up onto the rocks and flipped onto its side.

"Cease-fire!" the sergeant commanded.

The front wheels of the Toyota were still rotating when the sergeant slid down the side of the gulch and walked up to the truck. The three men were lying motionless where they had been thrown, their blood seeping into the sand. All three looked dead, but he checked them anyway.

"Over here, Sergeant," one of the troopers on the other side of the Toyota called out. "They have something tied up under their truck."

The sergeant tore the plastic sheeting away from one of the long shapes secured up under the frame and saw the olive drab fiberglass housing. Yellow block letters proclaimed it to be a FIM-92A Stinger antiaircraft missile launcher.

"It is an American Stinger missile," the sergeant who read English said. "These dogs are terrorists. Get our radio. I must report this immediately."

"It is too bad that these dogs are dead," the trooper said. "I would have enjoyed talking to them."

His officers would have, too, the sergeant realized. They wouldn't be pleased to learn that they couldn't interrogate them. He shrugged. These things happened. At least they hadn't escaped.

DAVID MCCARTER WAS in no mood to have to mess around with anyone. Spending the night by the side of the road with Peter Browning and his CNN comrades in a broken-down Toyota had done little to sweeten his mood. The newsmen had spent half the night hammering away at him about how and why he had turned up in a remote Indian village flat broke and looking as if he had been in a train wreck. They had gotten nothing out of him, though, not even a hint. He had been interrogated by experts, and these guys were rank amateurs.

Early that morning they had flagged down a truck and had been able to buy a ride to Jammu. Now that they had finally arrived at their destination, Peter Browning was having second thoughts about his hasty promise to his old comrade-in-arms. But it was too late for him to change his mind, since McCarter wasn't having any of it. To him, a promise was a promise, and Browning was committed.

"I'll have to explain this to the home office, you know," the newsman said. "It's not exactly company procedure to let outsiders use our equipment."

McCarter bristled. "Listen, Peter. You gave me your word and I expect you to keep it. Last night you called me a secretive bastard and you're right about that. But you forgot the other part that goes with it. I'm also a nasty bastard. You don't want me to think that you're trying to put one over on me, do you?"

Browning did remember the nasty part of the McCarter equation, as well, and he didn't want to have the Briton seriously on his case.

"All right. But I'll have to be in the van with you. I'm going to have enough to explain as it is, but if I let you into that commo van all by yourself, I'll get canned for sure."

"You can come," McCarter said. "But only you. I don't need any of your pals listening in."

Browning nodded. Inside the van, the CNN man quickly powered up the transmitter and made sure that the antenna was locked on to the satellite orbiting over the Indian subcontinent.

"Where do you need to go with it?" he asked McCarter.

"Just feed it into the satellite that you use to contact the Atlanta head office. That will work nicely."

"There you are." Browning handed him the microphone. "It's ready to go."

McCarter took the microphone. "Stony Base, this is Phoenix Three calling on an unsecured commercial channel. Stony Base, this is Phoenix Three, come in, please."

"Phoenix Three, this is Stony Base." The voice came over the loudspeaker. "Please hold for Stony Control."

A thin smile broke over McCarter's face when he heard the reply. After being away for a while, it was always nice to hear from the folks at home.

MAJOR FUAD DROVE into the small village at midmorning and stopped the Toyota in front of a small building that was doubling as a combination shop and lunch counter. It was a little early for lunch, but he had driven all night and needed to eat and refill his fuel tank before he continued on his way.

As he ate his meal he listened with half an ear to the music on the radio the shopkeeper had behind the counter. When the program ended a news reporter came on with an important news announcement. He said that there was no truth to the Indian claim that the Pakistani government had in any way been responsible for the vehicle that had been intercepted trying to cross the border into India with three hidden American-made Stinger missiles. An official spokesman in Islamabad said that the claim was typical Indian propaganda designed to smear Pakistan in the eyes of the world by branding it a terrorist nation.

Fuad was so stunned at this news that he pushed his plate away from him and stood. This changed his plans completely, but he could still fulfill his mission. Rather than fire his missiles at planes landing at a Pakistani airport, as he had intended to do, he would take them into India.

While it really didn't matter who started the war, his masters in Tehran wanted India to fire the opening shots if it was at all possible. That way, in the eyes of the world, smaller Pakistan would be seen as the victim and would be justified in using its nuclear arsenal to defend itself. For the plan to work the way it was supposed to, a Muslim nation couldn't be seen as a nuclear aggressor.

Back out in his Toyota, Fuad checked his map and saw that he wasn't far from one of Noor's secret smuggler's paths through the heavily guarded border between Pakistan and India. Usually the smugglers used camels or mules to make the trip, but anywhere the animals could go, he could take the Toyota four-wheel-drive truck.

The Americans had attacked the fortress and had forced him to run, but they hadn't won yet. Even the

Indian border patrols having ambushed one of his launch teams didn't mean that the plan was defeated. He still had two Stingers in his truck, and all he had to do was to bring down an Indian airliner with each one of them, and the war would begin.

He still had a chance to become the most famous Islamic warrior of his time. With the help of God, the name of Inman Fuad could still ring down through the ages.

CHAPTER TWENTY-NINE

Stony Man Farm

As soon as Bolan ended his report, Hal Brognola went into the War Room to digest everything he had been told. The big Fed was of several minds about the report on the capture of Noor's fortress. He was glad that the Stony Man team had recovered so many of the Stingers. Every one of the missiles that was destroyed was a terrorist incident that would never take place. But the eight that had gotten away meant that the solution to the crisis was not yet at hand and the danger was far from being over.

That was particularly true since Bolan had reported that the missiles that were missing had been refurbished and were now fully functional.

Brognola was also glad to hear that Grimaldi and McCarter had survived the chopper crash, and that Grimaldi was safe, even if a bit battered. The mysterious disappearance of David McCarter, however, was ominous. He didn't like the idea that one of the Phoenix Force commandos was unaccounted for. Were he to turn up in the wrong place and with his cover broken, it could be trouble.

Rather than the anti-American sentiment lessening with time, as it usually did, the feelings of rage against the United States in both Pakistan and India had increased over the past several days. The fact that the President was working as hard as he could to prevent a nuclear war wasn't appreciated in either nation. Brognola was afraid that the situation that many Western strategic thinkers had feared for a long time had finally come to pass.

For decades the threat of nuclear war had hung over the world like a pall of inescapable doom. Hysterical, overblown stories of nuclear devastation had been common fare in books, newspapers, movies and particularly on television. The antiwar movement was fueled by the hysterical fear of nuclear weapons, and it quickly became an anti-anything-nuclear mind-set, even nuclear medicine. The howling, however, had done nothing to make the world a safer place.

It was rather like crying wolf too many times. Most of the people of the world had learned to ignore the oft-repeated dire pronouncements of doom that never took place. Not that nuclear weapons needed to be ignored, but they weren't the worst thing on the planet. The evil that men did always had that dubious honor.

Back in the days of the Old American West, it had been said that "God created all men, but Sam Colt made them equal." In the post-cold-war era, it was readily apparent that nuclear weapons, not Colt .45 revolvers, were the weapons that made nations equal. More and more small nations had come to see nuclear bombs as their salvation. The antinuclear movement had painted the weapons as being the ultimate horror, but at the same time, they were clearly the thing that made a nation powerful.

The United States was the only remaining superpower in the world, but that had become a meaningless distinction. After the demise of the Soviet Union, the Americans had gone out of their way to show the world that they had no intention of acting like a superpower. And after the Bosnian, Haitian and Somalian foreign-policy debacles, too many people saw the United States as being the only tiger in a jungle full of mice. The tiger could roar and flash his teeth, but if enough of the mice ganged up on him, they could either kill him or ignore him as they chose.

The thing that the Western strategists feared most was the first detonation of a nuclear device by a small nation at war. Whoever did that would instantly gain great prestige. And when the fallout blew away, the world would see that a nuclear weapon wasn't that much more dangerous than the detonation of the equivalent amount of high explosive.

The antinuclear activists made a serious mistake when they exaggerated the effects of nuclear weapons. None of them ever mentioned that the world's first two nuclear targets, Hiroshima and Nagasaki, were now prosperous modern cities, not poisoned, uninhabitable, glassy craters in the ground. To anyone who took a nonprejudiced look at the actual effects of nuclear weapons, both cities were monuments to the fact that a limited nuclear war was survivable.

While this lesson hadn't been picked up by the antiwar crowd, it hadn't been lost on nations like India and Pakistan. They both knew that they could survive a limited nuclear war, and prosper when it was all over and the bodies had been buried. They also knew that the United States would sit by and do nothing about it, no matter what the current President might say. Those two facts had created an explosive mix, and the Stingers were the fuse.

The Stony Man team had done what it had been asked to do, but it hadn't been enough. There were still eight Stinger missiles on the loose, and even one of them would be enough to unleash the demon.

Brognola had no choice but to order Bolan and his team to continue the hunt for the Stingers. The questions was, where should they hunt for them? They had so little time and the Indian subcontinent was so large that it seemed hopeless. Nonetheless, he knew that they had to keep trying as long as they possibly could.

He decided to take the question of *where* to Aaron Kurtzman. If there had ever been a time when he needed a miracle, this was it. And at Stony Man Farm, miracles were Kurtzman's department.

KURTZMAN WAS ALREADY working on the problem. A large-scale map of the Northern Indian provinces filled the big-screen monitor in front of him.

"We just got a piece of good news," the computer genius stated when the big Fed joined him at his desk. "The Indian border-security force came across a four-wheel-drive rig trying to sneak across the border. The three men in it died in the firefight, but three Stinger missiles were recovered intact."

Brognola was happy to hear that, but it wasn't the end of the problem. "That's three more of them," he said. "But Mack said that eight got away from him. We'll have to concentrate on them now, and that's what I need to talk to you about."

"It's going to be a crapshoot, all right," Kurtzman admitted. "But since we have nothing to go on, we might as well roll the dice and see if they turn up snake eyes."

"What's your plan?"

Kurtzman wheeled his chair around to face Brognola. "The way I figure it is this. Our mysterious Major Fuad is a complete fanatic, right?"

Brognola nodded. Only a complete madman would want to bring the devastation of a nuclear war to one of the world's most populous nations. As far as that went, only a madman would want a nuclear war anywhere.

"And he has no doubt that he's doing God's will no matter what he does, right?"

"I can't argue with you there."

"That mind-set means," Kurtzman continued, "that he absolutely has to do everything he possibly can to complete his mission. He won't quit now that he's had a setback. And to try to do that, he has to fire the two missiles we think he has with him."

Again Brognola had to agree, like it or not.

"But," Kurtzman pointed out, "since this guy ran from the fort, I'd say that he isn't dedicated enough to be a suicide commando. I think that he wants to survive the war he's trying to start so he can claim the credit and the glory. In that respect, I'd say that he's more like Carlos the Jackal than like the *jihad* suicide car bombers of Beirut. Carlos killed for the glory of being the greatest assassin of his time. Even when making his most difficult hits, he was always careful not to expose himself to danger."

"So what's the bottom line? What do you think he's going to do next?"

"I think that he's going to take his act on the road to India. Once he crosses the border, he'll find an airport that's still operating and wait for a passenger liner to show up. He'll fire one of his missiles and then go on to his next target. If we're going to find him, we need to look in India."

"Not Pakistan?"

"Nope. That's too easy. Plus he needs India to start the war. As a Muslim nation, Pakistan has to be seen as the victim in this. That way he'll be able to gather support from the bleeding hearts all over the world and they can defend themselves in the Western press and the halls of the United Nations."

"If that's the case," Brognola said, "the only real question is which airport in India he'll choose to hit."

"That's where the dice come in." Kurtzman's smile was grim. "I'm going to get Hunt to help me work up a program to run some probability equations on every airport in Northern India. We'll weigh them by the factors of distance, size, amount of traffic, population density around the airfield and everything else I can think of, including the political tension in that particular area. When we're done, I'll put all the names into the hopper, stir it all up and see what comes out on top. And that airport will be where he'll hit."

Brognola couldn't believe what he was hearing. The world was headed for nuclear war and Kurtzman wanted to play war games on his computer. "You want to leave this decision completely up to your computer?"

Kurtzman nodded.

"I've got to be out of my mind to even consider this." Brognola shook his head. "The President is going to kill me if this doesn't work."

"At least you'll have someone to blame."

"You?"

"No," Kurtzman said with a grin. "The programming."

"That's not exactly what I wanted to hear."

"Do you have a better plan?"

"No."

"I guess that's a go-ahead?"

"God help us."

BARBARA PRICE WAS in her office when the intercom on her desk buzzed. "Yes?"

"We're getting a strange sat-com call on a commercial channel," the radio operator on duty in the communications center said. "But he has the right access-code word and claims to be McCarter."

"Route it to the computer center and I'll be right down there."

Kurtzman handed her the microphone when she walked in. "This is Stony Base," Price said.

"This is Phoenix Three calling on an unsecured commercial channel. How do you read me?"

"You're coming in loud and clear," Price answered. "Where are you?"

"I am in Jammu, India, and am calling from a CNN van. Be advised that a CNN rep is listening to this call."

"I understand."

Kurtzman's fingers flew over his keyboard as he enlarged the map of India on the big-screen monitor. A few more keystrokes brought the map to focus on the area around Jammu, and a window appeared in the lower-left corner showing the street plan of the small town, as well.

"I am completely undocumented," McCarter continued, "and entered the country without clearing with any authority. I need support and extraction ASAP."

While Kurtzman was zeroing in on McCarter's location, Brognola was on the phone to Washington, arranging to have a new set of documents made up for the Briton, including a passport with an entry-visa stamp for India. With the anti-American feelings running high, the last thing he needed right now was a problem trying to get him out of the country.

While Brognola was taking care of that problem, Hunt Wethers took a feed off of Kurtzman's map and plugged it into a travel-agency program covering Northern India. Within seconds he located a suitable hotel in Jammu and copied the address and phone number on his notepad. He handed the hard copy to Price, who glanced at it and smiled.

"Just stay right where you are," she reassured McCarter. "We have you located and we'll get a team to get you ASAP. Call the American Express office at Jammu and let them know where you are. They'll get a new card to you immediately. Once you have it, check into the Three Palms Hotel. It's the only place in town there that takes American Express without adding a surcharge. And wait there to be contacted. If you haven't been picked up in twenty-four hours, call me on a commercial land line. Do you have any questions?"

"That should cover it, Barb. Thanks."

"This channel is terminated," Price said, signing off, "and will not respond again."

She shook her head as she handed the microphone back to Kurtzman. "I can't wait to hear how he got into India."

"I'm sure that will be interesting," Kurtzman replied. "That boy really knows how to have a good time."

"At least he's back under our control," Brognola said.

"And," Kurtzman added, "since he's already in India, he can get started on the new operation."

"What operation?" Price asked, turning to Brognola.

"Let him tell you," the big Fed said, jerking a thumb at Kurtzman. "I don't have the heart."

"WHO IN THE HELL are you working for?" Browning asked when McCarter put down the radio microphone. "Not even the CIA can put something like that together that quickly."

"Do you remember the Official Secrets Act, Peter?"

"I know. If I talk about what I just heard, I'll go to jail and all that rot. Is that what this is all about, mate?"

"No. If you talk about this, mate, you don't get to talk about anything ever again."

Browning's eyes widened. "I do believe that you're serious, old boy."

"As the Yanks would say, 'You bet your sweet ass I am.' I'd hate to think that you were stupid enough to let your news-flack curiosity overload your common sense. I'd miss you on the six-o'clock news."

McCarter grinned. "Now, how about letting me call American Express so I can get my new card and get checked into my hotel. I need to get cleaned up for lunch, you know. I'll pay you for the call."

Browning just shook his head and pointed to the land-line phone. "It's on the house."

CHAPTER THIRTY

Stony Man Farm

Brognola had a grin on his face when he walked into the dining room, where the men of Able Team had gathered for a bite to eat. "Do you boys want to break up this coffee klatch and get back to work now?"

"What do you have?" Carl Lyons couldn't keep the eagerness from his voice. He'd had about all the idleness he could handle and felt the walls closing in on him.

"We've located McCarter, and he needs to be rescued from CNN's clutches in India."

"Do you think we're good enough to handle a mission like that?" Schwarz asked, grinning.

"You'd better be able to handle it," the big Fed said. "The last thing the President needs right now is for CNN to start asking pointed questions about why an ex-SAS British commando with strong American connections is running loose in Northern India without documentation. We have to get him out of there before he gets grabbed up by the locals as a vagrant and tossed into a cell."

"When do we leave?" Lyons asked. If there was anything he hated, it was sitting around jacking his jaws when there was work to be done.

"Charlie Mott will take you to Andrews, where you'll pick up a B-1 bomber with a passenger pack in the bomb bay. It'll take you to Saudi Arabia, where you will board a nonstop commercial fight to New Delhi. From there you'll take a commuter run to a place called Jammu and pick up McCarter. I figure that it'll be about twenty-one, twenty-two hours' travel time all told."

Schwarz groaned and shook his head. "You're talking about the pressurized passenger pack with the Porta Potti in it, right?" he asked.

Brognola grinned. "That's right. Fourteen hours in the air sitting right next to a chemical toilet, Gadgets. You'll love it."

THE STONY MAN TEAM WAS loading its gear into the Land Rovers for the return trip to Peshawar when Manning told Bolan that the Farm was on the line for him.

"The first thing," Brognola said, "is that McCarter has been located in India and Able Team is on the way over to bring him back into the fold. They'll remain there as a backup if you need them."

Bolan was glad to hear that McCarter was being rescued. He hadn't given the veteran warrior up for dead. David had survived much worse many times before. But it was good to know that his luck hadn't run out this time. It was also good to have Able Team on hand if they had to move into India. There was no way they could take Kader's men across the border with them.

"Next I want you to prepare to continue the mission. I have Aaron working some kind of electronic-voodoo program to try to locate Fuad. We are also getting input from every agency we can tie in to. As soon as we can get a handle on him, you'll get the word."

Bolan wasn't surprised that Brognola wanted them to regroup and be ready to move on Fuad and the missing Stingers as soon as Kurtzman developed a lead. With the fate of two nations and millions of people hanging in the balance, as long as they were able to continue the mission, they would drive on. And they would drive on until the last possible second before the mushroom cloud sprang from the ground.

"We'll be pulling out of here as soon as the Stingers have been disposed of," Bolan said. "Call it an hour or so."

"Good. Check in as soon as you get back to Peshawar and I should have more information for you then."

NOW THAT ALI NOOR WAS back in command of his fortress, he decided that the least he could do to repay his saviors was to do everything he could to help them find Major Fuad. To be sure, there was also the element of enlightened self-interest in his search. As long as the Iranian major was on the loose, Noor's life wasn't secure. As soon as the Americans left, Fuad could come back and take his frustrations out on him.

There was also the fact that the Americans had said nothing about their holding him responsible for his part in procuring the Stingers. And as long as they were going to be reasonable about this affair, he would do everything he could to ensure that they stayed that way.

The first thing Noor did to try to find Fuad was to get on the radio to all of his contacts in India and tell them to be on the lookout for the Iranian and his Stinger missiles. He also issued a reward of five thousand American dollars for the man's head. Now that he was back in command of all of his wealth, he could afford to be generous.

Once he put the wheels in motion, Noor turned his attention to his second concern, his new Afghan houseguests. Hassen Kader was still giving Noor looks that said he wouldn't mind slitting the little Pakistani's throat with his razor-sharp dagger. But the bag of jewels and gold he had given the Afghan for Jamillur's daughter had helped smooth things over. With that kind of wealth as a dowry, she could overcome the stigma of having been kidnapped by the Iranians. Even though she hadn't been molested, doubt would always hang over her and the money would do a lot to help her find a good husband when the time came.

To further cement his new relationship with the Afghans, he offered to pay indemnities for the Afghans who had been killed and wounded in retaking his fortress from the Iranians. Then he asked Kader if any of his people wanted to hire on as his new bodyguards. Too many of his old guards had gone over to the enemy for him to ever feel safe around them again. The Afghans had proved themselves to be outstanding fighters, and he wanted to make sure he could sleep at night without having to keep one eye open for treachery. A man in his business always had enemies, but a man also deserved a good night's sleep.

Along with the new guard force of Afghan warriors, Noor was planning to go completely legitimate. His brush with terrorism had given him a fresh outlook on life. From now on he was going to be very careful about what he sold and to whom. He would still deal in weapons—the business was simply too good to let go—but he wouldn't cross the line again.

WHILE NOOR WAS reestablishing his contacts and restoring his empire, the Phoenix Force warriors were busy disposing of the Stinger missiles Fuad had collected. Now that they were back in American hands, Stony Man wanted to make sure that they were completely destroyed.

With the help of the Iranian technician, the missiles were being dismantled and the tracking and guidance systems smashed. The missiles themselves were being taken out of the launchers and set aside for demolition. Even without the tracking and guidance systems, a terrorist could still find a use for the missiles and their warheads, and it was too dangerous to leave them behind.

Calvin James and Gary Manning were in charge of the demolition. They had the missiles taken a half mile way from the fort to a depression in the ground, then placed in a tight circle with the warheads facing inward. Noor's stock had provided them with enough blocks of C-4 plastic explosive and detonation cord to hook everything together. After all the missiles were laid out, they spent the better part of an hour setting up the demolition charges so that all the warheads would detonate at the same time.

When the last of the charges had been connected, the two men backed off two hundred yards and touched it off. The explosion had the sharp crack of C-4, and a cloud of black smoke and red dust rose into the air.

"That takes care of them," Manning said as he watched the cloud of smoke drift away.

"How many millions of dollars do you think we just blew up?" James asked.

"I don't know," the Canadian replied with a shake of his head. "But it was enough to keep us all in beer for a long time."

"Speaking of beer," James said, "I've just about had it with this place. I could sure use a cool one."

"I hear that," Manning replied. "Even though they don't drink in this country, maybe we can scrounge one up when we get back to Peshawar."

"God willing," James said, grinning.

THE DRIVE BACK to Peshawar was uneventful, but the Phoenix Force warriors still kept their eyes open. They had no way of knowing where Fuad had gone or if he had more of his Islamic commandos in the vicinity.

When they arrived at the warehouse, they saw that the lock was still on the door. "I'll be damned." Manning looked around at the crates and boxes in the warehouse. "We still have our survey gear. I expected that the locals would have stripped this place right down to the floorboards by now."

"Too bad they didn't," James commented. "Now we have to load all that junk back into that Herky."

"You better be glad that stuff's still here," Katz said. "Otherwise we'd be flying into India without our hardware. We need those crates to stash our weapons in."

"Is Aaron smoothing things with the customs people for us again?"

"If he doesn't," Katz said, "we'll be screwed for sure. We're already short one of our official survey team, and we still can't stand to go though a complete inspection."

Grimaldi grinned. "While you gentlemen are getting our gear ready to be loaded up, you can find me out on the tarmac preflighting our ride out of here."

"You're not going to give us a hand with the gear?" Manning asked.

"Sorry, pal. You know, division of labor and all that. I have to see to the technical end of things around here instead of the grunt labor."

"You just wait till the next time you need help refueling one of your birds from fifty-five-gallon drums. Since that's 'technical' work, old buddy, I'm going to remember this and you'll be all on your own."

"But then you'd have to walk," the pilot answered.

WHEN HAL BROGNOLA WALKED into the computer lab, Aaron Kurtzman and Hunt Wethers were staring intently at a line of numbers sliding down the monitor screen. It didn't mean anything to him, but it had their undivided attention. Kurtzman clicked a final key and turned in his wheelchair.

"Hal! You're just in time to see the results of the lottery."

"About time."

"Here it is." Kurtzman ripped the hard copy from the printer. "Srinagar."

"Where in the hell is that?"

"More important than where it is, is what it is," Kurtzman said as his fingers flashed over the keyboard and brought up a large map of Jammu and Kashmir State in Northern India. The map showed Srinagar to be a sprawling city on the edge of Dal Lake in a lush Himalayan valley.

"This idyllic setting," Kurtzman said, "is one of the hottest hotbeds of the Kashmiri Muslim independence movement. In kinder, gentler days, it was a popular retreat for the upper classes seeking to escape the heat. With the lake to provide irrigation water, it was a productive agricultural area before the trouble started. Since 1990, though, it's been an armed camp with the Indian police fighting gun battles on the streets with Islamic guerrillas and terrorists."

"But why there and not somewhere else?" Brognola asked. "Like somewhere with a bigger airport?"

"That's where all the variables we put in factored out to. Personally I'd have probably picked New Delhi or Bombay, but that's not what the computer said."

"If you'd pick someplace else as your first choice, why won't Fuad?"

"For the same reason that I would," Kurtzman explained. "You've got to remember that this guy knows his fight and his people much better than I do. He knows the things about this place that Hunt had to research to learn. He knows that this is the place were he can get the most bang for his buck."

"The situation in Srinagar is tense," Wethers broke in to explain, "and it has been since the Muslim separatists rekindled their insurrection in 1990. Blood flowed in the streets until the army moved in. Then the fighting became more of an urban guerrilla war. Pakistan was secretly arming the insurrectionists, and while claiming to have backed off, they are still seen as being behind the uprising.

"If he pops a planeload of Hindus in this particular town, the population will explode. The Muslim half will take to the streets rejoicing, and that will cause the Hindu half to follow them out to take vengeance on what they'll see as another act of Islamic terrorism. The entire state of Jammu and Kashmir will go into rebellion, and the Indian government will rightfully think that the missiles were imported from Pakistan. They won't have any other option but to go to war."

"I can't argue with you on this," Brognola said, shaking his head wearily. "All I can say is that if your prediction isn't right on, I think I'm going to send you over there with the cleanup crew."

"If I'm not right," Kurtzman replied, "there won't be anything left to clean up. It'll all have been blown away."

"Okay," Brognola said. "I'll talk to the Man and get his clearance on this. I just hope that he has more faith in computers than I have."

"He'd better have faith," Kurtzman warned. "Time's running out and this is the best chance we have."

CHAPTER THIRTY-ONE

On the Indian-Pakistani Border

Late that afternoon Major Fuad parked his Toyota four-wheel-drive in a wadi a few miles back from the border and patiently waited until night before attempting to cross into India. Regardless of their antiquated appearance, he knew that the camel troops of the Indian border-security force were not to be taken lightly. More than likely they had been the ones who had intercepted his launch team and killed them. He still had hopes that the second team would be able to make it through, but he couldn't count on that happening.

The success of the plan had been given into his hands, and his alone, to carry out. But with God's help, he would prove worthy of the task.

Once the sun was down, he backed the truck out of its hiding place and set out for the smuggler's track that would take him across the border into India. The Toyota was fairly new and had a good muffler, but he knew how easily sound carried at night, particularly in the cool air of the mountains. He would only use the engine to pull the vehicle up the hills. On the down side, he would turn the engine off and coast, using the brakes to control his descent.

To keep the brake lights from giving him away, he had unscrewed the taillight lenses while he had been waiting and had removed the light bulbs from their sockets. He put the bulbs in the breast pocket of his fatigue jacket and made a mental note to put them back in the light units once he was safely on the other side. He didn't need a nosy Indian cop at a highway checkpoint to ask him why his brake lights weren't working.

The smuggler's track went along the side of a gorge next to a raging mountain stream. Even though the start of the rainy season was still a few weeks off, a recent squall in the hills had put water in the normally dry streambed. The sound of the water rushing past the rocks would work well to muffle the sound of his engine.

Leaving the engine at an idle, he started slowly up the trail. Even at low speed, the Toyota picked its way along the rocks and gullies like a mountain goat. At the top of each rise in the ground, he stopped the truck and went ahead on foot to make sure that the way was clear. It would take all night to make the passage that way, but he had the time to spend if it ensured that he would make it.

He had crested another of the hills and walked ahead a few yards to scout the way when he caught the clink of metal on a rock. Slipping silently back to the truck, he turned the engine off and waited, the AK switched to full automatic and ready in his hands.

As if the hand of God himself was shielding him, the Indian patrol passed below without even a glance at the hillside above. It was only when the faint sounds of their footsteps faded that Fuad relaxed.

After giving the Indians a full half hour to get clear, he got back in the Toyota and continued on his way.

Stony Man Farm

THE WAR ROOM at Stony Man Farm was tense as Brognola waited for confirmation from the President to put Kurtzman's plan into action. It hadn't been easy to explain what the computer genius had come up with, much less make a decision on it himself. To stake the fate of the world on the roll of electronic dice didn't seem like a good idea to him. But he had to admit that he didn't have a better one.

Under more normal circumstances, the CIA would have given the information about Fuad and his Stingers to their counterparts in the Indian government and they would have taken care of it themselves. As it was, though, with the anti-America paranoia so strong right now, the Man had nixed that idea. He feared that the Indians would think that it was some kind of a CIA plot.

Plus, to fully explain the situation would require revealing the presence of Phoenix Force and Able Team in India and Pakistan. That would put them at risk of at least being taken into custody, if not being gunned down as foreign terrorists.

Brognola snatched the phone in midring. "Brognola."

It was difficult for Price or Kurtzman to read Brognola's face as he talked to the President. As well as they knew him, he had the ability to keep his emotions well masked, and Kurtzman thought that if he ever had to play poker with the big Fed, he would remember to cheat.

Brognola's face didn't change when he put the phone back down. "It's a go," he stated, locking eyes with Kurtzman. "I hope you're right about this wild-assed scheme of yours." He turned to Price.

"Barb, you'd better let Able and Striker know what's going down."

Northern India

ONCE FUAD WAS WELL CLEAR of the border-security zone, he set out for the nearest Indian village. The first thing he needed was civilian clothing. He knew better than to try to pass for a Hindu, but with the proper clothing he could easily pass for a Kashmiri Muslim. While the Arabic dialect was different from the one he had learned as a boy, it was similar to the Pakistani dialect and he had been able to pass without notice there.

After raiding a clothesline behind a house on the outskirts of town, he pulled the truck off of the road into a stand of trees and shut off the engine. After making sure that he hadn't been followed, he changed out of his desert-camouflage fatigues and into the civilian clothing. He walked out into the nearby field with the discarded military uniform, dug a hole in the soft earth and buried it.

Back in the truck, he made himself comfortable in the driver's seat and laid his AK across his lap. Once dawn broke and the highway was crowded with normal traffic, he would join the flow and continue on to his target.

WHEN ABLE TEAM DROVE UP to David McCarter's hotel in Jammu the next morning, they found him sitting on the veranda of his hotel sipping an early beer. For a man who had been shot down, imprisoned and then lost in the desert, he looked pretty good. The American Express card had done more than just secure him a comfortable hotel bed and a bath. He was sporting a new set of clothing, complete with chukka boots and a tan safari jacket with a dark silk ascot at the throat.

"Nice to see you boys," McCarter called when he saw the travel-worn trio step out of their cab. "How did you get Hal to let you out of your rooms?"

Schwarz grinned back. "He said something about our needing to rescue an errant Brit before the locals put a rope around his neck and strung him up."

"You made good time," McCarter said. "Pull up a chair and wet your thirst. I can recommend the Tiger beer. Stay away from the Elephant Brew. It tastes like the beast has kidney stones."

"That's the best offer I've had in the last twenty-four hours." Schwarz flopped into the chair across the table from him. "Crossing the Atlantic with a Porta Potti in your face is not my idea of a fun vacation."

Two Tiger beers later, Lyons laid a thick packet on the table in front of McCarter. "Here's another copy of your Canadian passport, and it has an Indian entry stamp so you can get out of here if you want. Also, there's a little walking-around money."

"I hope you brought me a weapon in your carry-ons," McCarter said as he pocketed the packet. "I've got a feeling that this mission isn't over yet."

"You mean an Iranian terrorist named Fuad and a fort full of Stingers?"

"Something like that."

"Mack cleared out the fort last night and Grimaldi is okay. But you're right about this thing not being over. Fuad made a getaway, and earlier yesterday he put at least two loads of bad guys with Stinger missiles on the road."

"Does anyone have a lead on them?"

"The Bear's working on it," Lyons replied.

"He'd better work fast," McCarter said. "The CNN guys who let me use their phone were saying that the entire Indian military is on full alert for the next war. That's why they're here. They want to be on hand for the opening round."

"A little bloodthirsty, aren't they?"

"They just want to get a head start on their nuclear tan. If they start glowing in the dark, they can save on lighting when they do their night shots.

"What do we do now?" McCarter asked.

Lyons finished his beer and set the glass down. "We brought a portable sat-com link, and Barbara wanted us to check in as soon as we made contact with you. She thinks that we might have to work the Indian end of this if it looks like Fuad headed this way."

"How in the hell are we going to get a handle on this guy if he doesn't want to be found? This is a bloody big country, you know. There's a lot of airports he can hit."

"Like I said, Kurtzman's working up something. He was mumbling about probability theory and the terrorist mind-set when we left."

"Leave that," McCarter said when Schwarz reached for his bag. "You're in India and they have porters to take care of your bags. You carry that yourself and some poor old boy will have to go without his rice and curry tonight."

"When in Rome," Lyons said.

Up in McCarter's room, Lyons plugged the sat-com link's transformer pack into the wall socket while Schwarz held the antenna out the window.

"Stony Base, Stony Base," he called. "This is Able One, over."

"This is Stony Base, hold for Stony Control."

A moment later Barbara Price's voice came over the loudspeaker. "This is Stony Control, go."

"We have Phoenix Three in hand and he's intact. Where do you want us to go from here?"

"I want all four of you to take the train to Srinagar this afternoon. Striker and the others are flying in, and I want you to meet them there. You'll need to arrange for transportation and rent a building somewhere close to the airport to set up a command post."

"I think we can handle that," Lyons said. "Is there anything else?"

"Not now, but check in as soon as you reach Srinagar."

"Got it."

Srinagar, India

JACK GRIMALDI BANKED the C-130 over the placid waters of Dal Lake as he turned into the downwind leg of the approach to the Srinagar airport. With the majestic, snowcapped mountains in the background, the lush valley with its rows of crops and fruit trees didn't look like a place where people were dying almost every day because they worshiped different gods.

But the reality of Srinagar belied its peaceful surroundings. As the pilot flew over the city, he could see the burned-out buildings in the center of town and the police sandbag bunkers below. This ancient city was the front line in the battle for the Kashmiri Muslim insurrection against Hindu India. And so far the Muslims were winning. More than a quarter-million Hindus had fled the violent region since the uprising had broken out. Those who had stayed were prepared to fight to the death.

In the copilot's seat, Gary Manning got ready to drop the landing gear on Grimaldi's command. In the back, Bolan, Katz, Encizo and James were making sure that their weapons and ammunition were well hidden in the crates of oil-survey equipment. With tensions still high between India and the United States, a slipup could see all of them slapped into a cell.

Grimaldi's landing was smoother this time and he taxied the four-engine transport to the customs area of the tarmac. David McCarter and Able Team were on hand to greet their comrades-in-arms with the three rented Land Rovers McCarter had personally inspected for their mechanical fitness.

Again the customs inspection was cursory. The Indians might have been paranoid about Americans, but since their cover was that of a Canadian firm, there was no problem. McCarter had also rented a truck and porters to carry their cargo to the building that would serve as their command post during their stay in Srinagar.

As soon as the porters had unloaded the crates, McCarter sought out Bolan. "What's this about our staking out an airport when we don't even know that it's been targeted?"

"It's Aaron's idea," Bolan replied. "He thinks that since we don't have a clue where this guy's gone, we have to leave it in the hands of the gods of probability that live in the microchips."

"He'd better be right about this," McCarter said. "If we're sitting around here and Fuad shows up somewhere else and pops an airliner or two, we're all going to be in a world of hurt. We're looking at being at ground zero of a nuclear war."

"I know," Bolan said, "but we're going to have to trust him on this one."

McCarter shook his head. He was certainly not a technophobe by any definition of the word. As he was well aware, Stony Man's continued success was largely a result of the best high-tech gear American technology could provide. But staking their lives, and the lives of millions, on the roll of the electronic dice wasn't exactly his idea of having the odds on their side.

"I guess we'd better get this command post set up so we can get out there and start looking for this guy."

"That's the program."

CHAPTER THIRTY-TWO

Srinagar, India

The airport at Srinagar was a typical Indian commuter-short-haul airfield. Because land was so precious in a country that was always on the verge of starving to death because it couldn't control its population, all small Indian airports looked more or less alike. The Srinagar version had been built right up against the town, so as not to take up any more valuable farmland than was absolutely necessary, and the town itself was spread out along the western shore of Dal Lake.

Major Fuad carefully surveyed the terrain around the town from his vantage point on top of the tallest barren hill a mile and a half away. Situated in a valley the way it was, there was little in the way of high ground anywhere around the town from where to launch the Stinger. He would have to go down onto the flat along the lakeshore to make his kill, but make it he would.

Twice a week an Air India Airbus flew into Srinagar from Delhi, and the next flight was due the next day. According to his intelligence sources, the plane should be packed to better than its maximum-rated capacity. And on Air India, children, goats and chickens didn't count on the manifest. Best of all, the vast majority of the passengers would be Hindus trying to escape the heat of the plains by visiting a popular shrine to Vishnu built on the shore at the end of the lake.

He would wait until the airliner was committed to its final approach, then make the hit while it was still six or eight hundred feet in the air. Since small houses crowded both sides of the runway, if the plane exploded within a half mile of the passenger terminal, the flaming debris would shower on the rats' warren of twisting alleys and hovels and kill hundreds more. If he had any luck, he could easily kill five hundred people with only one of the missiles.

And since he intended to leave the empty Stinger launcher behind as a calling card, the Indian government would have to act. Since the border-security force had already intercepted one Toyota load of Stingers trying to infiltrate from Pakistan, they would rightly assume that he had come from Pakistan, as well. The Bhutto government of Pakistan would deny any connection with the incident, but the Hindus wouldn't believe their claims of innocence. Pakistan had stirred the boiling pot that was called Kashmir far too many times.

If that didn't do it, though, he knew the aftermath of the flaming crash would. Thousands of Muslims would be urged on by the Muslim separatists to take to the streets in rejoicing. Grieving Hindus would respond to the riots with demonstrations of their own. Clashes would occur, and people would die on both sides. Indian troops and police would move in and try to control the situation with guns, which would only make matters worse, and the end would be the same.

Fuad climbed back in his Toyota and started the engine. There was an Islamic Party cell in Srinagar, and it would be safe for him to spend the night there. He wouldn't invite the other Iranians to take part in his mission, though. He and he alone would carry out this sacred task.

"WE JUST RECEIVED a DIA radio intercept," Kurtzman announced. "Another Toyota full of terrorists was caught trying to cross the border from Pakistan into India."

An indication of the emphasis the President was putting on the mission could be seen by the fact that they had received this from the DIA without their having to ask. Normally the agencies guarded their own turf much better than that.

"Were they carrying Stingers?" Brognola asked. He had awakened early that morning and was staying close to Kurtzman because there was nothing else for him to do at that point in the game. He would remain there until Bolan called to report success, or until that part of the world went up in a nuclear fireball. There were times when he really hated this job.

"We've got confirmation, three of them."

That was the second of the two teams that Bolan had reported had been sent out the afternoon before they assaulted Noor's fortress. "That cuts the odds again," Brognola said hopefully.

"That still leaves Fuad, though," Kurtzman reminded him. "He's always been the dangerous one, and he supposedly has two of the missiles with him."

The big Fed reached into his pocket for a roll of antacid tablets. It was going to be a long day.

AS SOON AS their communications gear was set up in the small building next to the airport, Bolan and Katzenelenbogen bent over a series of satellite photos Kurtzman had faxed them of their target area. Kurtzman had sent the biggest computer-enhanced blowups he could make of the airport and the five-mile radius surrounding it. All it took was one look at the photos for them to see that it wasn't going to be easy to cover that much ground.

"Even if he's here," Katz said, "how do we figure out where he's going to position himself? The Stinger's got a range of three miles and can reach up to five thousand feet. He could be damned near anywhere along the flight path once the plane starts its approach."

"But Aaron said that this guy wants to create the maximum amount of destruction, right?"

Katzenelenbogen nodded. "That's the profile, yes."

"Then I'd say that he wants to hit it close in to the airfield itself so the wreckage will fall in the populated area. He'll get more casualties that way."

The Israeli's eyes swept over the photos again. "That still leaves us a lot of ground to cover."

"Yeah, but there are ten of us now and we'll lease two more vehicles so we can field five teams. Since

Able Team's here, we might as well put them to work."

"I heard that," Lyons said. "And you'd *better* put us to work. Gadgets didn't fly all this way with his nose jammed up against a chemical toilet just to sit around sunning himself and taking it easy."

"There's also the matter of when he's going to strike," McCarter added. "We can be sitting out there for a long time if we don't know when he's going to make his move."

"I'd say he's planning to do it tomorrow," Katzenelenbogen replied. "Kurtzman sent us an Air India schedule, and it shows a flight coming in from Delhi at 2:35. Every seat on the plane is sold. That's over three hundred people."

"When's the next one due in after that?"

"The next flight from a large city isn't until Friday."

"That's it, then," McCarter stated with certainty. "He won't want to wait that long. The longer he's here, there's a greater chance of something going wrong."

"So we're back to figuring out where he's going to hit." James's eyes flicked over the photos. "Anybody bring their crystal ball?"

Stony Man Farm

IT WAS THE DEAD OF NIGHT, but Barbara Price found Aaron Kurtzman still sitting at his computer console.

His hair was rumpled, and he looked as if he could use a shower.

"You need to get some sleep," she said gently as she walked into the room. "You'll eventually crash if you're tired."

"I'll sleep when this is over," he replied without turning to face her.

"You're worried, aren't you?"

Kurtzman ran a hand over the back of his neck and took a deep breath. "Yeah," he said, sighing, "I guess I am."

"About what? The program that sent Mack and the teams to Srinagar?"

He shook his head. "No. That program's as tight as I could make it. Right now I'm trying to figure out how I can tell a late-model Toyota four-wheel-drive from everything else at a range of almost four hundred miles."

"What in the world are you talking about?"

Kurtzman spun his chair to face her. "Even though I'm sure about the computer prediction that Fuad will strike at the Srinagar airfield, I still think that we've sent Mack on a fool's errand."

"How's that?" she asked.

"Guarding an airliner in flight while you're on the ground isn't easy even if you know where the terrorists are going to strike. That Stinger's got a three-mile range, so Fuad can be anywhere along the approach to the airport, still make his hit and get away."

He shook his head in frustration. "I've sent them into a classical needle-in-a-haystack situation. How in the hell are they going to find that guy unless they bump into him by sheer accident? And the Stinger's the biggest part of the problem. There's no way that it can be detected prior to the launch because it's a self-active system. If the damned thing was radar guided or had a laser designator, we'd have a better chance of spotting it before it was launched."

"You've got a good point," she said carefully. "But what does that have to do with your being able to spot a Toyota truck from space?"

"It's simple. Both of the launch teams that the Indians picked off on their way across the border were in Toyotas. I don't know if Toyota has the four-wheel-drive concession in Tehran or what, but they seem to be real popular with Iranian terrorists."

Price could see where the train of thought was leading and wanted to put her two cents' worth in before he let it run away with him. "They also sell Toyota four-wheel-drives in India, Aaron. Lots of them."

"I know," he replied. "But if I can spot all the Toyota four-wheel-drive rigs in the area, maybe I can figure out which one of them has an Iranian with a Stinger driving it."

"How are you going to do that?"

"That's what I don't know yet." He spun back to his keyboard. "But I just had an idea."

Price poured herself a cup of Kurtzman's killer coffee from the pot and took a seat at a vacated work space while he developed his brainstorm. Now that he was on a roll, she wanted to be there in case he needed something.

Kurtzman first called up all the Toyota articles from the past five years of *Car and Driver, Road and Track* and *Four Wheel Drive* magazines and scanned them. His hands flew as he entered the dimensions and characteristics of all the different Toyota light-truck models built during that period of time. He then added data from the other makes of light trucks and set the computer to sorting, comparing and contrasting the data.

"I think I've got it," Kurtzman finally said as he turned to look at her. "I know how I'll be able to tell the Toyotas from all the other light trucks and four-wheel-drive rigs."

"How's that?"

"Their windshields."

"Windshields?"

Kurtzman's grin showed that he was very pleased with himself. "I was looking for something I can see from a vertical angle, and that doesn't leave very much. Every light truck looks pretty much like another one from the top. One's longer or wider and the hoods may be different, but that's about it. There are too many similarities between the makes. The Toyotas, however, have one distinguishing characteristic. They have a greater curve to their windshields, and that shows up best from above.

"I can program in the parameters of a Toyota four-wheel-drive rig and scan the satellite feed to locate and mark them. Since I'll be getting the pictures in real time, even with the transmission lag, I'll be less than sixty seconds behind what Mack is seeing. Once I spot this guy, I can lock on to him and send the teams directly into him."

Price shook her head. "You're talking about guiding them into the target from half the world away using pictures you're getting from four hundred miles up in space."

"What's wrong with that?"

"Only you could ask a question like that, Aaron. Go ahead with your plan, but I don't think you should mention this to Hal. He's high-teched out and is jumpy enough about the program as it is."

"That's what's wrong with the Beltway crowd. They're Luddites."

Price's face went blank. "They're what?"

"Technophobes." Kurtzman grinned. "We could handle most of our problems far better if we'd simply do what the machines tell us to do."

Srinagar, India

EARLY THE NEXT MORNING Srinagar time, Bolan got a call from Kurtzman. "Striker," he said, "Hunt and I have worked out a way for you to spot your man when he shows up."

"You've been reading my mind. Katz and I went over that last night for hours and couldn't come up with anything that sounded foolproof."

"I'm going to use the Keyhole satellites to spot him for you. I've worked out a way to spot Toyotas from above."

Bolan immediately saw the genius of Kurtzman's plan, but didn't bother to ask how he was going to do it. If it worked, that was good enough for him and he had no problem with leaving the search for the target up to the computer. Being on the ground, he could see how impossible it was going to be to find a lone terrorist in a city like Srinagar.

"To help me out," Kurtzman said, "get some paint from somewhere and paint numbers on the hoods of your vehicles so I can see them from the air. Make them at least a foot tall so the computer can pick them up."

"I'll get them ready," Bolan said.

"Let me know as soon as you move out so I can start tracking you."

Bolan called Manning over. "Go downtown and find some paint. Any kind, any color. Spray paint would probably work best."

Never one to ask unnecessary questions, the Canadian hopped into one of their vehicles and soon found an open-front hardware store that sold cans of Japanese spray paint. He bought three cans of flat black and took them back to the command post. It took Bolan only a few minutes to paint the numbers one through five in broad strokes on the hoods of their five vehicles.

CHAPTER THIRTY-THREE

Srinagar, India

Kurtzman's plan was simple. The five vehicles would spread out along the flight path of the incoming airliner and be ready to move when Kurtzman located their target. Bolan and Katz had picked their initial stakeout locations from the photos, and each vehicle drove directly to it. Manning had the sat-com link with Bolan in the number-one vehicle, which would act as their mobile command center. When Kurtzman called him, Manning would relay the information to the other vehicles through their individual com links.

"We're in position," the Executioner told him. "Call the Farm and give them a go-ahead."

"Stony Base, this is Phoenix One. We're in position."

"Stony Base, roger."

FOUR HUNDRED AND thirty-nine miles above the earth's surface, the Keyhole 11 series satellite, code-named Sierra Three, responded to Kurtzman's instructions. Spinning on her gyros, she reoriented her video camera to look down on the city of Srinagar, India. Another coded message made the video lens extend on teflon bearings designed to withstand the cold of space until it reached its maximum magnification. The last command aligned the antenna and sent the picture to Stony Man Farm, Virginia.

"I've got the picture," Wethers said, "and it's clear, just as the weather service said it would be."

The only flaw in Kurtzman's plan was that if the area was under cloud cover, the satellite's video camera would be useless.

"Shift it over here," Kurtzman commanded.

When the aerial view of Srinagar showed on the big-screen monitor above Kurtzman's workstation, it looked like the view from a low-flying helicopter rather than a shot from over four hundred miles in space. People could be clearly seen going about their daily lives, and there were trucks everywhere.

"I've got all your vehicles spotted," Kurtzman told Manning. "They've been plugged into the program so the computer will track them automatically. I'm starting the program to try to locate the Toyotas now."

"Good luck."

Kurtzman soon found that his program to detect Toyotas from space was working well, maybe too well. As Price had predicted, there were hundreds of Toyota trucks in Srinagar. Making a command decision, he quickly instructed the program to eliminate all of the Toyotas with cargo in their beds. Since Fuad would need speed to make his escape after the attack, he wouldn't want to have the truck weighed down.

Then he programmed out all of the trucks with more than one person in them. Even though Srinagar had no shortage of Muslim extremists eager to commit a terrorist act, he didn't see the Iranian being willing to share the glory that would be his when he made the hit.

Those two changes cut the number of trucks he was trying to keep track of down to something a little more manageable. He only hoped that he hadn't factored the killer's vehicle out of the parameters with those changes.

JAMES WAS TEAMED with McCarter in the number-three vehicle. He had fitted the sniper's scope to his H&K, but he hadn't had a chance to rezero the scope. Even though the assault rifle was fitted with a no-zero mount, as he well knew, the knocking around it had taken over the past couple of days could have thrown off the alignment. With all the Indian police and army security in Srinagar, he hadn't dared to fire the three rounds he needed to check his zero, so he would have to go with what he had.

"I've got a target for number three," Kurtzman radioed to Manning. "There's a Toyota at four-seven-three, two-zero-six, with a single man in it and he's taking a long object out of the cab that could be a Stinger."

"Roger," Manning acknowledged, glancing at the GPS readout. "I've got the location."

"Phoenix Three," he said, switching over to the team's com link frequency. "This is One. Your target is nine hundred yards to your southeast. The truck is parked by an irrigation ditch off the main road."

"This is Three," McCarter said. "We're on it."

Slamming the gearshift into first, he dropped the clutch and hammered the throttle. The Toyota truck jumped forward under the acceleration and almost dumped James out of the back. "Watch it!" he yelled. "You almost lost me!"

"Hang on, dammit!" McCarter roared.

"Phoenix One," Kurtzman said. "I have number three in sight and he is closing in. Tell them to take the next right and cut up the hill behind the field."

"Roger."

Manning relayed the instructions in time for McCarter to make the turn. So far, this long-distance recon was working better than he had expected.

"Stop here!" James shouted to McCarter when he saw that he had a direct line of sight down to the target.

The Briton slammed the truck to a stop and bailed out with his field glasses to act as the sniper's spotter. James threw the rifle up to his shoulder and focused his scope on the driver. Instead of the terrorist with a missile, he saw that the man was an old Indian with a length of plastic irrigation pipe over his shoulder.

"Damn!" he said as he snapped the rifle off target. "That's not him! Call Manning!"

"Phoenix One, this is Three," McCarter transmitted. "Calvin says that it's not our man."

"Roger," Manning replied. "Stay where you are for the moment. You might have a better view from there."

Carl Lyons and Hermann Schwarz were teamed in the number-five vehicle and were monitoring the com link. "Damn!" Lyons said. "I knew this bullshit wasn't going to work. There's no way they can spot that guy from space." He shook his head. "This isn't going to work."

"Patience," Schwarz told him. "I've got a lot of faith in the Bear."

"I've got a lot more faith in Stinger missiles, and we're going to see one hit its target here today. Unless, of course, that guy happens to be in Bombay or Calcutta. We don't know if he's even here or not."

"He's here, all right," Schwarz stated flatly. "Aaron said he would be here, so he'll be here. That's the way it works."

Lyons snorted. "Get a life, Gadgets."

MAJOR FUAD PARKED the Toyota behind a bamboo brake and checked his watch. He was right on time. This position just back from the lakeshore was perfect. The plane would pass right in front of him a little more than a mile from the airport. He would have a good deflection shot as soon as it passed, and the missile would make its intercept less than a quarter mile from the end of the runway.

It would be a killing to go down in history.

Taking the Stinger launcher from behind the seat, he laid it on the vehicle's hood and checked his watch again.

"ALL VEHICLES, HEADS UP," Manning called out over the com link. "The plane's inbound. You should be able to see it right about now."

Looking to the east, Bolan picked up a glint of metal high in the sky. The Airbus 330 was banking for its run across the lake before lining up for the airport runway. As it dropped lower over the water, he could see the brightly colored markings of Air India, and still there was no call from Kurtzman.

"Three and Five, this is One," Manning suddenly shouted. "Aaron has a Toyota truck with one man in it behind a clump of trees to your northeast a couple of hundred yards back from the lakeshore. Get moving and I'll vector you in!"

Bolan glanced at the GPS readout and saw that the reported location was right along the flight path of the Airbus, but off to one side. It was a perfect place to launch a Stinger and the Airbus was almost within range.

"Go! Go! Go!" he shouted over the com link.

This time James was ready for McCarter's race-car-driver ride and held on. "There he is!" he shouted to McCarter. "Left front six hundred yards!"

As Fuad raised the launcher to his shoulder, he saw a truck racing down the lakeshore toward him, but it was too far away to reach him in time. Ignoring it, he centered the approaching Airbus in the optic sight and activated the tracking system. Inside the missile, the gyros spun up to speed, the nitrogen dumped to cool the IR head and the UV receiver started looking for blank spots in the sky.

McCarter saw the launcher go up on the man's shoulder and knew that he had only a few seconds before the airliner passed and exposed its hot jet exhausts to the Stinger's IR guidance system. He couldn't get there before the missile was launched, but a bullet could.

Locking the brakes, he slammed to a stop. "Take the shot!" he yelled to James.

Bracing himself against the back of the cab, James centered the scope on the man with the Stinger on his shoulder and slowly tightened his finger on the H&K's trigger. The rifle's report sent the butt slamming back comfortably into his shoulder.

Through the scope, James saw the 7.62 mm round take Fuad high in the left chest. The man staggered back a step, but stayed upright. A second snap shot staggered him again, and he saw the launcher drop.

The Stinger's launch lock-on tone was beeping, but Fuad didn't hear it as the Stinger launcher suddenly turned very heavy and slipped from his shoulder. As it fell, his right hand tightened on the trigger, but the weapon's safety interlock had come on when the sight was pulled off target, and the missile didn't launch.

Overhead, the Air India Airbus had her flaps and gear down as she headed for the end of the runway. Inside were three hundred men, women and children who had no idea of the drama that had just played itself out below them. They had no idea that they owed their lives to an American spy satellite and ten men who placed their lives on the line so that others could live.

WHEN MACK BOLAN REACHED Inman Fuad's Toyota, the Iranian was dead, the Stinger lying by his side.

He knew only too well, though, that the Iranian's death wouldn't end the tension along the Indian-Pakistani border. That was something that not even the Stony Man teams could accomplish. The hatred between the Muslim and Hindu peoples of the subcontinent was so ancient that it was ingrained as deeply into the culture as were the languages the two peoples spoke.

The Hindu Indians and Muslim Pakistanis would continue to hate one another as they had done for centuries. But for the moment, the threat of a nuclear war breaking out between the two nations had diminished. Under pressure from the United States and the rest of the Western world, the two governments would back down from their hot-trigger alert status and agree to continue to talk at the nuclear-arms-reduction table.

He also knew that Fuad's death didn't mean that Stinger missiles in the hands of terrorists wouldn't appear in the headlines again. As surely as it was an uncertain world, sometime, somewhere, one of the American-made weapons would be fired by a terrorist. As with the nuclear threat, the Stony Man team had only bought the world a little breathing space from the Stinger threat. In that precious time, other agencies could go back to trying to remove the rest of the deadly missiles from the world's arms markets.

GOLD
EAGLE